China Doll

by

Joe Cosentino

A Jana Lane Mystery

China Doll

Cover Art by *Debbie Taylor*

The Wild Rose Press, Inc.
PO Box 708
Adams Basin, NY 14410-0708
Visit us at www.thewildrosepress.com

Publishing History
First Vintage Rose Edition, 2016
Print ISBN 978-1-5092-0751-0
Digital ISBN 978-1-5092-0752-7

A Jana Lane Mystery
Published in the United States of America

Jana came face to face with Stanley.

"If Tate and Gary go, so do I."

"Don't do it for me, Jana," Tate and Gary said in unison.

Stanley grinned. "Listen to your deviant friends, Jana."

Tate held Jana's arm to stifle her from replying to Stanley.

Stanley glared at Sally Chen. "And if anyone doesn't like the size of her role, I'll accept your resignation." Then staring at Savannah and Jana, he said, "And if any of you regrets signing a contract with me for this show, let this be a business lesson for you. Lawyers enforce contracts." Stanley clapped his hands again. "Tony, Tate, and Gary, you are released. Kat, please take a seat in the house. Jose, back to your stage manager's console. Everyone else, please make a circle around me, and I will lead you in some warm up exercises."

As everyone moved around Stanley on stage in a state of shocked pandemonium, the bookcase set piece teetered back and forth then crashed down on top of the producer.

Praise for Joe Cosentino

"A superbly crafted mystery with an eclectic cast of characters that will engage you and elicit some very emotional responses as you are completely caught up in the events that unfold in these pages."

~Fresh Fiction

~*~

"If you like novels that are filled with new and old Hollywood, and a range of sub-plots, you are going to love this!"

~Saguaro Moon Reviews

~*~

"I liked that there was enough evidence for each of the suspects to keep me guessing until the very end."

~Molly Lolly Reviews

~*~

"Joe Cosentino knows how to keep his readers' interest with every page."

~Universal Creativity Digital Magazine

Dedication

To Fred for everything over all these years,
to Melanie and the staff at The Wild Rose Press,
to everyone who loved *Paper Doll*, *Porcelain Doll*,
and *Satin Doll* and begged for
another Jana Lane mystery,
and to the child star in each of us.

Chapter 1

1984

Jana Lane, America's most famous ex-child star, stood in terror in a dark theatre. Hearing footsteps from backstage, Jana attempted to exit the stage, but instead bumped into a sofa. As the footsteps grew louder, Jana's pulse quickened. With her heart pounding in her chest, Jana gasped at the silhouette of her attacker. Backing away from the menacing gray shadow, she screamed and fell.

Gasping for air, Jana Lane Otley sat up in her ruby satin-covered canopy bed and rested her back against the gold circular headboard. *It's only a dream.*

Her husband joined her, reaching out his muscular arms. "I'm here, babe."

She squeezed Brian's thick hand. *You're my rock.*

He squeezed back. "Another theatre dream?"

Jana noticed her silver satin nightgown was soaking wet. Rising and walking past the gold settee, floor-length oval mirror, and island fireplace, Jana headed into her large walk-in closet to change. She called out, "The nightmares started after Simon called to tell me about *China Doll.*"

"Babe—"

"Don't say it."

"Don't say what?"

In a new nightgown, Jana sat at her pink crushed velvet-trimmed vanity, looked in the mirror, and ran a brush through her famous strawberry-blonde hair. "You're going to tell me not to do the play."

"I didn't say that."

"You didn't have to."

"Jan, you were the biggest child star in America. You made a successful comeback film…two of them—and you won an Academy Award. What's left for you to prove?"

She looked over at him. Wearing boxers and a sleeveless T-shirt, Brian's biceps swelled like melons as he sat up in bed and rested his elbows on his knees. "I'm not trying to prove anything, Brian. I want to go back to where I started—on Broadway."

Brian ran thick fingers through his chestnut hair. "You were five years old when you did *Sweet Nothings* on Broadway and Simon discovered you."

"And as Simon said, it's time I go back. You're not considered a real actor unless you do theatre. It's time for me to see if I can pull my weight on stage—as an adult." She looked in the mirror at her tired crystal-blue eyes. "Besides, you'll be away making your malls in Las Vegas, thinking about budgets and materials. Devon and Ed will be at summer camp with visions of races, basketball, swimming, and hamburgers."

Brian slid to the edge of the bed. "All right, but I'm not sure about B.J. being in the play. He's only three years old."

Jana walked back to the bed, kneeled behind her husband, and wrapped her porcelain arms around his V-shaped back. "B.J. will be with *me*. He's excited about the trip to New York City. And I hired a nanny. His name is Gary Royale. He has great references, and he's even taking a pay cut from his last job to work for us. He's very mature. My age. Actually, a year younger."

"That old?"

Jana threw a pillow at him.

After a playful wrestle, Brian cradled her in his arms. His hazel eyes softened. "Is this what you really want, babe?"

She looked up at his handsome face. "It's what I *need*, Brian." Jana rose from the bed and stood on the balcony. A ribbon of gold magically turned the gray sky into a canvas of violet, crimson, and vermillion reigning over the majestic mountains in the distance. *What are my dreams telling me this time?*

Brian towered over her, enveloping Jana in a bear hug. "Promise me you'll be careful, babe?"

Turning around to face the man she loved for so many years, Jana replied, "Of course."

He tweaked her nose. "I've heard *that* before."

"And Simon will be with me."

"He always is."

"Simon talked them into casting my nephew in one of the roles, so I'll get to see him again. And most importantly, I'll get to work with our son." She felt like a little girl again. "And it will be so much fun to see the old crew from *Sweet Nothings* again! It's been thirty-seven years since we did that play." She paced on the Persian rug. "There was Stanley Rothman, the producer. Katrina Wright, the playwright. And Savannah Stevens who was the play's leading lady. And they're all involved in *China Doll*!"

Brian raised his hands up in the air like a bank teller in an old cops and robbers movie. "Okay, you

win. Do your play. Have a great time being Jana Lane."
He brought her into his powerful chest. "But don't
forget Jana Otley."

"Never." *You're my everything.*

"I'll miss you so much, babe."

I love you more each day. "You'll always be in my
thoughts—and in my heart."

They shared a long, sensuous kiss, which led them
back to bed.

Their lovemaking session was cut short when Brian
Jr. screamed, "Mommy!" from his bedroom, and
Devon, twelve, and Ed, eight, ran out of their bedrooms
and burst into the master bedroom screaming, "Ghosts
beware! Ghostbusters are here!"

*Thanks for taking them to see that movie, Brian—
three times!*

Brian went into the master bathroom to take a
shower in their huge glass-enclosed shower with gold
falcon-shaped faucets. Jana put on her peach silk robe
and sat with the boys on her bed.

Ed said, "I hope you have as much fun in your play
as we're going to have at camp."

"That's not possible!" Devon added. "How could
being in a play be as much fun as playing paint ball
attack at the lake?"

You'd be surprised. Jana hugged her boys. "I'll
miss you both like crazy! But it's time to get ready."

Jana felt as if caught in the eye of a hurricane as
she got Brian packed and off in his car to his job in Las
Vegas, Devon and Ed packed and on their bus to
summer camp, and B.J. fed, washed, and dressed. Then
she packed her and B.J.'s things while her youngest son
sang an impromptu packing song, "Mommy packs. B.J.

on a train. Mommy needs clothes!"

Already missing the three men in her life, Jana shed more than a few tears as she worked out in her home gym to Bruce Springstein's "Cover Me" as B.J. jumped up and down next to her.

While B.J. played with his stuffed animals in his room, Jana hurried to her bedroom, took off her lemon-colored leotard, leggings, and scrunchie, and changed into cranberry slacks and a beige peasant blouse. After teasing her hair into layers that framed her beautiful face, Jana applied cranberry eye shadow, blush, and lipstick. Slipping on cranberry shoes as she raced down the spiral staircase holding B.J.'s hand, Jana called out last-minute instructions about the house to her maid, Theresa. The elderly woman jotted them down on her pad in the two-island kitchen while she watched her afternoon soap opera.

When the doorbell rang, Jana checked her diamond wristwatch, amazed she was ready on time. She passed through her cathedral ceilinged entryway, and opened her double doors to Gary Royale. Standing under the prism chandelier, the tall, thin, blond, forty-one-year-old man said, "I'm ready for duty."

"Welcome, Gary," Jana said. "Let's sit on the window seat and go over your duties."

"No need." Wearing a white shirt buttoned to his Adam's apple and black pants that ended at his ankles, Gary pushed his large black glasses up the bridge of his long nose. "As you know, I've been a nanny for many years. After working for a Hollywood producer with three children"—he smiled at B.J.—"taking care of B.J. will be like going on a vacation."

We'll talk in a week.

B.J. stood under the skylights and jumped up and down on the saffron marble floor. "We go to New York Sippy!"

On cue, Cornelius Chamberlain drove his motorcycle through the stone columns at the entrance of Jana's mansion with Simon Huckby clutching for dear life at his partner's rail-thin back. At nearly seven feet tall, Cornelius wore turquoise parachute pants, a tangerine T-shirt, and lime suspenders. Simon Huckby, short, bald, and emaciated, was dressed in a chartreuse jumpsuit, tangerine waist pouch, and apple-green scarf. The musician helped his partner off the motorcycle, then Cornelius loaded Jana's car with Jana's and Gary's luggage. Jana waved goodbye to her five-acre Hyde Park estate, as Cornelius drove Jana, Simon, Gary, and B.J. to the Metro North train station in Poughkeepsie amidst B.J.'s impromptu car song. Following hugs and kisses to Cornelius at the train platform, Jana and her crew were off to the start of a new adventure.

As Jana sat at the window seat on the train, she marveled at the view of towering mountains surrounding sunlit waters. Gazing out at the twinkling Hudson River, Jana said to Simon, "No matter how many times I ride on this train, it still takes my breath away."

Sitting opposite her, wearing boys' slacks and a polo shirt, B.J. agreed. "Take my bread away."

Gary smiled at B.J. sitting next to him. "That's *breath*, B.J."

"Breath!" B.J. mimed pulling a train whistle. "Tooooot Tooooot."

Sitting next to Jana as usual, Simon watched over his client like a guard dog at Fort Knox. Jana's agent was somewhere between his sixties and the undertaker. Wiping a mascara-stained tear from his eye, Simon said, "I love you in cranberry, baby doll. It brings out your pink cheeks. I made the wardrobe woman put you in cranberry in *The Adorable Orphan, Young Mermaid, Hawaiian Holiday, Surfer Girl, The Sweet Candy Striper,* and *The Little Shop Girl.*"

Jana smiled and took Simon's tiny hand. *You were more of a father to me than my real father.*

Gary said to Jana, "I watched your movies in secret as a kid, so the other boys wouldn't make fun of me. They made fun of me anyway."

Simon's claws emerged. "Why would they make fun of you? Jana Lane was the top child star from 1948 through 1966!"

With his voice breaking like a teenager at Sunday morning choir practice, Gary replied, "I think it was because I'm...I was...different than most other boys."

Simon's brown eyes turned to slits. "Boys, girls, men, women, *everyone* loved Jana Lane movies until..." He looked away.

"I retired at eighteen after shooting *Sugar and Spice,*" Jana explained to Gary.

"I think I missed that one," Gary answered.

"Then you missed perfection!" Simon replied as if scolding a juvenile delinquent.

Jana laughed. "I am far from perfect—then and now."

"Mommy's perfect!" B.J. shouted.

"Right you are, B.J." Simon grinned like a shark meeting a guppy. "And I am going to make *you* a star, just like I did for your mommy."

Down, Mama Rose.

Not terribly impressed with stardom, B.J. asked, "Are we there yet?"

"Not yet, honey," Jana answered, followed by a big kiss on B.J.'s chubby cheek.

Simon asked Jana, "I don't know why you wouldn't let me hire a limo. The production company had agreed to pay for it."

"B.J. likes the train," Jana explained. "So do I."

"You're a celebrity. It's not safe."

"I have you to protect me," Jana said, followed by a kiss on Simon's sunken cheek.

Simon pointed to Jana's sunhat and sunglasses, as if a lawyer acknowledging Exhibit A to a jury. "Gary, do you see these?"

Gary nodded.

"Jana Lane wears these because after *His Obsession* and *Madam Senator*, my baby girl is back on top where she belongs, and the fans know it."

"Actually, it has more to do with the sunny day and my aging eyes," Jana explained.

Simon's makeup cracked. "It has *everything* to do with you being the brightest star in the galaxy!"

Gary took a toy train from one of the luggage pieces on the overhead rack and gave it to B.J. "When I read in the newspaper that Jana Lane was coming to Broadway in Katrina Wright's new play *China Doll*, it piqued my interest."

Simon adjusted his scarf like the Queen of England adjusting a diamond necklace. "I discovered my baby girl at five years old playing opposite her father and Savannah Stevens in *Sweet Nothings* by Katrina Wright. A year later my doll face made her first film, *Daddy's Girl*, and the rest is Hollywood history."

Jana smiled at Gary. "You didn't mention being a Broadway buff when I interviewed you for the job."

"But I am!" Gary pushed his glasses up the bridge of his nose. "That's why I applied for the job. My parents were out working most of the time when I was a kid. Since we lived near New York City, I'd take the bus in and see show after show. Sitting in those theatres was like a religious experience for me. The actors on stage were my friends, and their lives were my life. I'd even wait at the stage doors and get their autographs." He looked away. "I don't know how I would have gotten through my younger years without them."

Simon asked like a detective interrogating a terrorist, "Who was the first Mame on Broadway?"

Gary replied, "Mary Martin?"

"Wrong." Simon adjusted the diaper under his jumpsuit, always a sign that he meant business. "Who starred in the original production of *Gypsy*?"

Gary blushed. "Carol Channing?"

"Wrong again!"

B.J. saved the day. "I have to go bathroom!"

"Follow me, B.J. Excuse us." Gary took B.J. by the hand, and they walked to the next car with B.J. chattering about trains and bathrooms.

Jana called out, "Listen to Gary, B.J."

Simon glared at Jana.

"What?"

"Why did you hire *him*?"

Jana sighed. "The agency gave Gary top recommendations. I was lucky to get him. He just left his position as the nanny for a Hollywood producer."

Simon chortled. "Hollywood producers can certainly use nannies."

"For his children." She playfully hit Simon's thin arm.

"Why did Gary leave his position? Was he *asked* to leave?"

"Gary didn't say." Jana shifted in her seat. "What is it about Gary that bothers you?"

The wrinkles on Simon's face deepened. "Though he claims to be one, he isn't a thespian."

"Neither is Brian."

"I rest my case."

"Not again."

"You should have married someone in the business, baby doll. I've always said that."

That you did.

Simon scratched at the dyed carrot-red hair surrounding his bald head. "And don't you think Gary Royale is a bit long in the tooth to be a nanny?"

"He's forty-one, not eighty-one. Besides, there isn't an age restriction to be a nanny." Jana crinkled her nose and giggled. "Mary Poppins was ageless."

Simon said softly, "*And* Gary is in the closet."

Jana raised her eyes to the blurs of treetops outside her window. "How do you know?"

"Do you have to ask?"

Jana paused to think. "I hope Gary isn't afraid to tell me, because he is taking care of B.J."

"I said he's gay not a pedophile. Most pedophiles are straight, baby girl."

"I know that, Simon. I just don't want him to be uncomfortable. If Gary is good with B.J., that's all that matters to me. His sexual orientation, and if and when he tells me about it, is his own business."

Simon folded his small hands over his tiny lap. "I

don't like him."

"I'm sure Cornelius will be relieved he doesn't have competition."

Simon smirked. "I didn't say that."

They shared a laugh.

"Simon, the truth is I need help with B.J., and Gary fits the bill."

Jana's agent bounced on the seat like a ball on a trampoline. "Speaking of billing, I negotiated your name over the title on the marquee." He passed his hand through the air as if he were a magician. "Stanley Rothman presents Jana Lane in *China Doll*, a new thriller by Katrina Wright, co-starring Savannah Stevens." Simon purred like the Cheshire Cat. "We also get the star dressing room."

We?

"I'm staying with Cornelius in our house in Rhinebeck."

Jana exhaled.

"But I'll be popping in from time to time to make sure all is well."

I don't doubt it. "Thank you for negotiating the package deal."

Simon pulled back his narrow shoulders. "I told Rothman it was you, Buddy, and B.J., or no deal."

"My nephew now calls himself Brad. Something about numerology, luck, and making a lot of money."

"Which he hasn't done in Hollywood as a waiter."

"Maybe his luck will change in New York."

"Rothman and Katrina liked his audition. Your nephew will be staying in the second bedroom in your hotel suite. It's a gorgeous three-bedroom suite on the top floor of the hotel with panoramic views of the city."

"It sounds lovely." *But I'll be sleeping without Brian.*

Simon said like a society woman at a luncheon, "I hear Savannah Stevens insisted on a package deal for her and her son, Peter, and a suite at the same hotel. With his amazing good looks and the notoriety from this play, my guess is Peter Stevens will soon be headed for Hollywood on a gold carpet."

"How old is Savannah's son?"

"In his thirties I guess."

Jana smiled. "I remember Savannah at twenty-three years old when we did *Sweet Nothings*. It's hard to believe she has a grown son. She must be close to sixty by now."

"We all age, girly"—he giggled—"except me." His eyes narrowed. "Savannah's lucky Rothman and Katrina are her old friends, and they agreed to her deal. Savannah Stevens, as we delicately say in the business, is 'a total has-been.'"

"Hey, I was a total has-been once."

Simon looked as if he had been stabbed in the heart. "You were not!"

"I didn't work for twenty years."

"Savannah Stevens is very different from Jana Lane. After Savannah's Tony Award for Best Featured Actress in *Sweet Nothings*—which you should have won, she starred in Katrina's next Broadway play, then she went to Hollywood. After three hit movies, Katrina did a bomb then another bomb then another. As they say in Hollywood, 'three bombs and the war is over.' After years of not working, Savannah did that silly sitcom as the nosey neighbor for five seasons. When that went off the air, so did Savannah. She hasn't worked since."

"Did she marry?"

"Three times. All dead now. The second one was Peter's father. None of them were in show business. See what happens when you marry outside the faith?"

I'll ignore that. "Simon, isn't it odd that none of us get to read the play until the first cast read-through at the theatre?"

Simon shrugged and Jana heard a crack. "Until her last two flops, Katrina Wright was the most successful playwright on Broadway with seventeen hit plays! She has a right to her idiosyncrasies."

Jana scrunched her eyebrows. "Katrina rewrote *Sweet Nothings* all through rehearsals, but we had the script prior to the first read-through. I've never heard of an author not giving the actors at least a draft of the script in advance."

Simon said like a gossip columnist facing a sea of microphones, "The play is top secret. Katrina and Rothman won't breathe a word about the plot or ending to anyone." He looked insulted. "Including to me!" He slid to the edge of his seat. "But I *do* know your character is an amateur sleuth who solves the crime—like in real life—*and* you embark on a romance with the handsome Peter Stevens."

"Don't tell Brian."

"My lips are sealed. But *yours* won't be in the love scenes. Rothman said it's Katrina's best play yet. The first read-through is tomorrow morning at nine o'clock in the theatre."

"I can't wait to read it. And I'm looking forward to seeing Stanley, Savannah, and Katrina again."

"Stanley is in his seventies. Widowed. Katrina's

nearly eighty. She married young to a man who died in a plane crash before they could have children."

"I'm sorry to hear that."

Simon chuckled. "But Katrina made up for it lately by marrying Tony Cuccioli, a muscular, handsome stage manager half her age who, wouldn't you know, is directing his first play—*China Doll*."

Good for Katrina. "Who else is cast in the play?"

Simon's brown eyes glistened like marbles. "Bella Talloway."

"Who's Bella Talloway?"

"A pretty young blonde making her Broadway debut. She just *happens* to be Stanley Rothman's granddaughter. And there's Tate Moonglow, a young gorgeous Native American actor from Off-Broadway, and Sally Chen."

"Didn't she just win a Tony Award?"

"Yes."

"Impressive cast."

"With *you* as the star."

Jana sighed.

"What is it, baby doll?"

There's no point trying to keep anything from you. "I've been having nightmares where I'm attacked on stage."

"I've heard of the actor's nightmare where an actor forgets lines in a dream, but being attacked?" Simon placed a small hand over his thick lips. "You know what happens each time you have a nightmare about being attacked?"

Jana nodded.

Simon sat back in his seat. "I have the feeling this is going to be a bumpy ride."

When they arrived at Grand Central Station, a car was waiting to take them to their hotel. Simon bid them farewell for a meeting with Stanley Rothman, and Jana promised Simon she would take care of herself and her little group.

The lobby of their hotel was spacious and luxurious. Jana and crew checked in, then B.J. screamed with delight as they took the elevator to the top floor. As they entered the living room of their suite, they marveled at the panoramic views of the city, and the Hudson River in the distance. They gazed joyously at the large sitting room with floor-to-ceiling windows and all white furniture, including a piano, bookshelf, a sofa, loveseat, wingback chairs, table and chairs, and a white marble fireplace. Jana followed B.J. and Gary across the hall to their mahogany bedroom and bathroom with two double beds, a window seat, and a toy chest. B.J. jumped up and down on his bed as Gary unpacked.

Jana walked down the chandelier-laden hallway and looked into the colonial style bedroom with accompanying bathroom for Brad. Coming to the peach-colored French provincial bedroom with a brass bed, wardrobe, chaise, easy chair, and desk, Jana unpacked her things. She was happy to see the adjoining bathroom sported a sauna bathtub, circular glass shower, and vanity.

When they were finished unpacking, they walked to a Jewish delicatessen nearby for lunch, then took a taxi to the Empire State Building. Jana was never as happy about the invention of the elevator as they rode the long way to the top, where they enjoyed the amazing view.

Since B.J. had the energy of a squirrel in a field of chestnuts, they continued on by taxi to a car show, children's museum, and finally dinner at the hotel dining room.

When they returned with sore feet and tired bodies to their hotel suite, they found Jana's nephew hanging up the phone in the living room. Upon seeing him, Jana's eyes welled up with tears. She threw her arms around the muscular, young man. "Buddy!"

He returned the hug. "It's Brad Lane now, Aunt Jana."

As if looking in the mirror, Jana stared at the twenty-three-year old's strawberry blond hair and small features. "It's so good to see you again—whatever your name is."

Wearing light slacks and a sea-green rugby shirt that matched his eyes, Brad replied, "How are Brian, Devon, and Ed?"

"Fine. They miss you."

B.J. ran into Brad's arms. "Who are you?"

Brad gave B.J. a big hug then playfully mussed the boy's chestnut hair. "I'm your cousin Brad."

"My cousin Brad?"

"That's right."

"Yeah!"

Jana wiped her eyes with a tissue then motioned to Gary. "This is Gary Royale, my new nanny. I mean B.J.'s new nanny."

"I figured that out," Brad said as the two men shook hands.

It was clear that Gary was taken in by Brad's striking good looks. "Hi. Hello. N-nice to meet you."

"You, too, Gary. I used to be Aunt Jana's nanny,"

16

Brad said.

"That was a long time ago," Jana added.

Brad asked, "Are you in show business, Gary?"

"Just as an audience member. I—"

Brad quickly lost interest. He looked around the living room. "This is some suite, huh?"

"B.J. is tired!" B.J. announced like a sportscaster.

Gary picked up his cue. "I'll get B.J. ready for bed, and let you know when you can tuck him in, Jana."

"I want my cousin Brad," B.J. demanded.

"Can I tuck him in?" Brad asked Jana.

Jana blinked back tears. "Of course."

"Come, my cousin Brad!"

"I will soon."

Gary ran off after B.J. who was already exploring his new bedroom.

Brad said to Jana, "B.J.'s amazing. He's quite a little actor."

"It runs in the family." Jana rested a hand on Brad's shoulder. "Did you eat dinner? Can I order something for you?"

"I called room service before you got back. They have terrific lobster. I charged it to the room. I hope you don't mind."

My nephew has expensive tastes for a young waiter. "Of course not. I'm glad you ate." Jana sat on the loveseat and patted the space next to her. "Did you unpack?"

"Yup." Brad sat beside her. "Nice bedroom."

"I'm glad you like it." Jana took his strong hand. "What have you been doing in LA?"

Brad groaned. "Busting my hump at the restaurant nights while I go on auditions during the day."

"Have you gotten any acting jobs?"

"I did a local commercial, and a play in a fifty-seat theatre." He leaned back on the loveseat. "After four years at college and nearly another four years in LA, it's a pretty pathetic résumé."

Jana smiled. "And now you're in a new Broadway play by Katrina Wright."

As if she had given him a stick of gum, Brad said, "Thanks for that, Aunt Jana. And I really *should* be starring in plays and films. I'm a good-looking guy. I'm straight. I know I can act. I just don't get why it hasn't happened for me yet."

Jana put her arm around him. "Bu—Brad, I remember us having this conversation in the past."

"I know. I know. I should be patient."

"Well, you should."

"Says the woman who was a movie star at six years old."

Jana took off her shoes and rubbed her tired feet. "Brad, we've been through this before. What happened to me was a gift. A once in a million chance. My father got Stanley Rothman and Katrina Wright to put me in their play with him; Simon saw me, and Cavoto Films was looking for a new child actress. I listened to my teachers, obeyed my directors, and I worked very hard."

"*I'm* willing to work hard."

You remind me of your grandfather. "And the timing was right."

Brad looked like B.J. when the cookie jar was empty. "But why isn't the timing ever right for *me*?"

"It will be one day. And if it isn't, there's more to life than show business."

He replied with a serious look on his handsome

face, "Like what?"

Jana dug her feet into the white shag carpet. "Don't you have friends in LA? Are you in love with anyone?"

"My friends are all actors. So, they're in love—with themselves." Brad stretched his legs out in front of him. "I can relate to the guy in that old movie, *Rosemary's Baby*."

"You mean the man who sold his wife to Satan for a leading role in a movie?"

Brad nodded. "Aunt Jana, I'd do *anything* to get ahead."

"Brad, being an actor is an amazing thing, but being a good person is much more important."

"You've won an Academy Award, Aunt Jana. I don't think you'd say the same thing if you were a nobody like me."

"No one is any better than anyone else."

"Unless he's a movie star." He looked older than his years. "There's nothing I want more than to become a star. It's what gets me out of bed each morning, and keeps my heart beating throughout the day. I fantasize about it every minute of each day, then dream about it at night. Aunt Jana, I don't think I'll be able to go on if my break doesn't come soon." Brad slumped off to B.J.'s room.

Jana massaged her neck, and picked up the phone to call Devon and Ed at camp. Once her maternal senses were appeased by hearing about their delight in playing basketball, soccer, water polo, and making individualized pizzas, Jana called Brian. Though the travel day had taken its toll on her, Jana delighted in whispering sweet nothings into the phone with Brian, then staggering to her bedroom for a restless sleep.

****

Standing between the marquees for *Hurlyburly* and *The Rink*, Jana Lane looked up at the Broadway marquee for *China Doll* with her name on it and smiled. Having tossed and turned most of the night, she had risen early, exercised in the hotel gym, ordered breakfast, fed her three charges, and led them by taxi to the theatre. Following them inside past the box office through the outer lobby, Jana breathed in the candy sweet smell of the inner lobby. Then she walked by the bar, a sandwich board sign with her picture on it, and photographs on the wall from past productions.

As the others went into the theatre, Jana noticed a heavyset man, wearing a blue suit with a pink handkerchief popping out of his jacket pocket. He hovered over her like a vulture during a garbage strike. "Congratulations on the play, Miss Lane."

"Thank you."

"I'm Rollo R. Rorror. Roll for short. May I ask you some questions?"

A microphone appeared. *A reporter.* "I only have a few minutes before the start of my rehearsal."

"That's all I need." He licked his lips like a cat at a fishing hole. "Why is Katrina Wright mum about the mystery's plot? Is she afraid someone will leak the ending?"

Probably someone like you. "You'll have to ask Katrina."

"After sitting around a movie set in La La Land, how does it feel to be starring on the *legitimate* stage?"

Take a breath. You've done this many times before. "I began on the stage when I was five years old, Mr. Rorror."

He scratched his chins. "Please, call me Roll." Pushing the microphone closer to her face, he said, "You played on stage as a child, but now you're back at past middle age."

Count to ten. "Mr....Roll, whatever the age of an actor, and in whichever medium he or she is acting, an actor acts." She walked to the wide door leading into the theatre.

He followed. "Why is an Academy Award winner starring in a Broadway thriller? Wouldn't it be easier to simply rest on your laurels in Hollywood?"

Jana dug her heels into the carpet. "I don't live in Hollywood. And I certainly don't have a great deal of time to rest on anything."

Running his hand through his crewcut, Roll asked, "Since you've been working in films with boom microphones and cameras, do you think you will be able to project your voice to the last row of the balcony?"

"How's this for projection?" Jana shouted. "Goodbye, Roll!"

She opened the wide door and entered the theatre. Jana Lane was home. Savoring every moment, the star of *China Doll* stood in the orchestra seating area and gasped at the gorgeous historic theatre's crimson velvet proscenium curtain, carpeting, and seats. She marveled at the intricate gold molding, and faded but still glorious tapestries of cavorting Greek gods and goddesses on the walls and ceilings. Then Jana looked up and admired the spacious box seats, gigantic crystal chandelier, and endless balcony.

"Thirty-seven years. What took you so long?"

Jana turned to a familiar, yet older, face. "Stanley

Rothman!" She hugged the tall, thin, elderly producer, careful not to crack any of his bones. "It's so good to see you."

The house lights lit up Stanley's white hair, gray eyes, cherry-red bowtie and jacket, and puckish smile. "It's about time you came back to your roots."

"I was just thinking the same thing."

"Good. Because now that we have you back, we're not letting you leave us again."

"Sounds good to me."

Stanley took her hands. It was as if being held by a lobster. "You look older, Jana."

So do you. "I should hope so. I'm a mother of three now."

"But you still have the same spunk you did as a child," he whispered in her ear. "I saw your latest films, *His Obsession* and *Madam Senator*. This play is better." Stanley giggled. "But don't tell the author. We don't want her to get a big head."

Jana had a flashback to watching Stanley and Katrina during rehearsals for *Sweet Nothings*. "I remember how well you and Katrina worked together." She smiled. "Back then, I thought you two were married."

A tear appeared in his aging eye. "I'll be honest, Jana. One of the reasons I agreed to produce *Sweet Nothings* was I fell in love with Katrina the first moment I saw her in the old neighborhood. She was the sweetest, warmest, most considerate woman I had ever met." He winked. "And she had a great script—and the money to put it on stage."

"I don't mean to pry, but after working on twenty shows together, and both being widowed, I can't help but wonder why you and Katrina never got together."

"I often ask myself the same thing. It's not for lack of trying. Right, Katrina?"

Katrina Wright, eighty, thin, with soft white hair, shook Jana's hand. In her apricot business suit, shoulder pads, and gold rope jewelry, the famous author looked like the epitome of wealth and success. "Don't believe a word this man says, Jana Lane. He could have had any woman he wanted."

"Except you, Kat," Stanley said.

Jana smiled. "It's wonderful to see you again, Katrina. I'm honored to be in another one of your plays."

Katrina's aqua eyes sparkled. "How fitting it is that Jana Lane appears in my first play—and in my last."

"This isn't your last play, Kat," Stanley said, waving his hands at her like an airport flagger.

"Yes it is, Stan."

He replied, "Why? Why is this your last play?"

The famous playwright rubbed her liver-spotted hands. "I'm out of ideas. I'm old. And I'm tired."

"You'll never be old to me, Kat," Stanley said with adoring eyes.

"Hey? Who's old and tired?" Tony Cuccioli, wearing black chinos and a black T-shirt that showed off his impressive muscles, put his arm around Katrina. "Not my wife. No way. No how." He grabbed Jana's hand. "Tony Cuccioli. How you doin'?"

Jana shook his strong, calloused hand. "It's a pleasure to meet you." *Can I have my hand back while it still works?*

"Hey, I'm your director," Tony said with a white-capped smile.

Stanley's spine stiffened. "Tony started as a set builder for us then he moved up to stage manager. When our director got called to Hollywood, Kat suggested Tony."

I'm sure.

"And like they says, the rest is historical," Tony added, rolling his gold rings around his fingers. *No doubt bought by Katrina.* "You'll like working with me, Jana. I'm a street fighter from the Bronx. I take the punches, and never give up until I win. Like I won my terrific wife, hah? Kat and I make a great team. Personally and professionally." He kissed Katrina's sagging cheek. "We're gonna have a great show."

Stanley's jaw tightened. He gestured to the stage. "Let's join everyone on stage for the first read-through. Follow me."

The moment Jana got on stage, B.J. flung himself into her arms. "B.J. likes the stage!"

You're definitely a Lane.

Gary took B.J.'s hand. "Come on, B.J., there's a sign with your name on it at this chair."

"I have a sign, Mommy!"

She kissed B.J.'s cheek. "Welcome to the theatre, honey."

After Gary and B.J. took their seats at the table, Jana noticed a strikingly beautiful older woman with jet-black hair, violet eyes, and a still gorgeous figure. Savannah Stevens filled out every inch of her antique-white, low-cut dress. "Jana, I used to read fairytales to you in my dressing room during rehearsal breaks."

Jana embraced the older woman, careful not to mess Savannah's thick makeup, or cut herself on Savannah's large diamond ring. "Savannah, it's so good to see you again."

The aging actress smelled of violets. "It seems like only yesterday we did *Sweet Nothings*—in this same theatre! How is your father?"

Jana felt her face tighten. "He's no longer with us."

"I'm sorry. We're losing more and more actors of my generation." Savannah motioned to her son standing next to her. "It's up to you youngsters to carry the torch."

"I'm hardly a youngster, Mom."

Savannah pinched his cheek. "Jana, this is my son, Peter. Peter, this is Jana Lane."

Jana looked up at the most gorgeous man she had ever seen in her life. *I hope you didn't notice my knees dip.*

"Look at those green eyes. Just like his father's," Savannah said to Jana. "My second husband."

Tall, muscular, aristocratic-looking with dark hair and blushed cheeks, Peter shook Jana's hand. "It's a pleasure to meet you, Miss Lane."

Feeling the warmth and smoothness of his strong hand, Jana felt like a shut-in at a blind date with Mr. America. "It's Miss Otley...rather Mrs. Lane...Mrs. Otley, but please call me Peter." Jana felt herself turn the color of her avocado dress.

He seemed to enjoy her attraction to him. Amazing dimples emerged as Peter said, "I thought *I* was Peter."

Jana giggled in spite of herself. "You *are*. I'm Nana. I mean...I'm Jana."

Peter's peaches and cream complexion complimented his white pants, coral T-shirt, and marigold blazer. He whispered in her ear, and she smelled fresh mint. "I'm nervous, too. Everyone's thinking I got this role because I'm Savannah Stevens' son. They're probably right."

I have to stop gawking at him. "I'm sure you'll be fine."

Peter seemed genuinely touched. "That means a lot to me, coming from such a fine actress. I hope you'll give me a few tips in rehearsals."

Savannah said, "Peter, don't bother Jana. She has an adorable child of her own to take care of."

Before Jana could object, Savannah added, "I'll run lines with you and work out your motivations like usual."

Stanley clapped his hands like a Kindergarten teacher. "Everyone, please take your seats around the table."

Katrina replied, "I see you're sitting at the head of the table, Stan."

Savannah added, "That's so he can keep an eye on the two of us, Kat."

"I always need to keep an eye on the two of you," Stan said with a laugh.

Jana noticed the easy comradery between Stanley, Katrina, and Savannah, recalling they were all friends and neighbors during *Sweet Nothings*. She was happy to see they had maintained their friendship over the years, and she respected Stanley and Katrina for giving Savannah a job when she needed one.

As Stanley took his seat, the producer said, "Welcome everyone. Now that the casting, negotiations, theatre booking, contracting, and publicity layouts are complete, it is my great pleasure to welcome you to the first read-through of Katrina Wright's—"

Tony Cuccioli cleared his throat. "That's Katrina

Wright *Cuccioli*."

Stanley grimaced. "To the esteemed playwright's twentieth play, *China Doll*." After the applause died down, the producer continued. "This production is like old home week. It's the twentieth collaboration between Katrina and me, our third collaboration with Savannah Stevens, and our second with Jana Lane." He rode the end of the applause. "But that's not all. Katrina's new husband, Tony Cuccioli, is directing." Tony and Sally Chen applauded loudly. "Savannah's son, Peter, is playing the leading man." Savannah beamed and Peter looked down at his European shoes. "Jana's son, B.J., is making his stage debut."

B.J. shouted, "That's me!"

Stanley smiled. "And Jana's nephew, Brad, is making his Broadway debut."

Brad bowed his head, clearly enjoying the attention.

"And my lovely granddaughter, Zelda Goldberger—"

The young bleached blonde petite beauty raised her contact lens blue eyes to the Fresnel lights and crinkled her tiny fake-looking nose. "It's Bella Talloway now, Grandpop."

Stanley glowed like a spotlight. "Remember that name, everyone."

She'll no doubt remind us if we forget.

Dressed all in pink, wearing leggings, a lace skirt, an off-the-shoulder midriff blouse that read *Girls Just Want To Have Fun*, and fingerless gloves, Bella giggled. "Ah, Grandpop."

Stanley winked at Bella. "Before I turn things over to our director, I would like to go around the table and have each of you introduce yourself."

Sitting to Stanley's right, Savannah adjusted her diamond necklace. "I'm Savannah Stevens. Stan told my agent I'm playing Bella's mother. I always wanted a daughter. But watching over my son takes up most of my time."

Everyone laughed except Gary who grimaced.

Perhaps Gary didn't like Savannah's sitcom.

Following the polite laughter, sitting next to Savannah, Peter said, "I'm Peter Stevens. I'm not Savannah's daughter."

He has a sense of humor, too!

"I heard I play the police detective." Peter added with a wink at Jana, "And Jana Lane's love interest."

Looking at her wedding ring, Jana reminded herself, *Acting is make believe.* "I'm Jana Lane, and I understand I play an amateur sleuth."

Bella gasped. "I've read about you. Didn't you solve a murder case in Washington, DC during *Madam Senator*, and also during *His Obsession* in your Hyde Park estate?"

B.J. cackled. "B.J. lives in Hyde Park!"

"I'm sure what you read was exaggerated, Bella," Jana said, anxious to get the attention off her sleuthing skills.

"I hope none of *us* gets murdered," Bella said.

Gary was next. "I'm B.J.'s nanny." He pushed his glasses up the bridge of his nose and coughed. "Not in the play. In real life."

Next around the table, Tony said, "Hey, how yiz doin'. I'm Tony. You'll hear more from me later, hah? Next?"

Sitting beside Tony, and gazing at him, Sally Chen

batted her long eyelashes and flicked back her lengthy black hair. The gorgeous young woman leaned forward, revealing ample cleavage in her amber midriff blouse. "Hi, everyone. I'm Sally Chen." She licked her blood-red lips. "I hope we all get rich and famous from this play."

"Not likely with Stanley producing."

Stanley hit Savannah's shoulder playfully.

Sitting between Sally and Bella, Brad Lane looked happier than a puppy with a bag of treats. Handsome in a Kelly-green polo shirt with a white sweater tied around his neck, Brad said, "I'm Brad Lane." He smiled at Bella. "I hope I play Bella's lover."

Clearly enjoying the focus on her, and Brad's masculine good looks, Bella crinkled her new nose. "I think I'm going to like working with you, Brad."

Stanley didn't seem too happy with his granddaughter's flirtation. "Tate! You're next."

A tall, thin, young Native American man with a square jaw, dark eyes, and a haunting look said, "I'm Tate Moonglow."

Taking her eyes off Tony for a moment, Sally said, "I bet you play my love interest, Tate."

"If Tate isn't interested, there's enough of me to go around for both of you ladies."

Jana sighed at Brad's comment, and Tate squirmed in his chair. However, Bella seemed to find Brad's sexism adorable.

The playwright spoke. "I'm Katrina Wright Cuccioli." When the applause ceased, she said, "Thank you all for bearing with me on not getting the script to you until today. I have been working on it practically around the clock. Since this is a mystery, after you read it today, I ask you not to divulge the plot to anyone."

Everyone murmured his and her solemn oath of secrecy.

Katrina said, "I am honored to have an Academy Award winner, a Tony Award winner, and a legend in my play."

Jana felt herself blush. Sally beamed. Savannah took it in stride.

Katrina continued. "And I am equally excited about the up-and-coming young stars in our cast."

Bella and Brad looked at one another and grinned. Savannah took her son's hand. Tate looked down at his script on the table. B.J. shouted, "We do a play!"

"You got that right, B.J., hah?" Tony Cuccioli rested his elbows on the table. "As most of youse know, this is my first time at the bat directing a show. But nobody should have no worries." He rubbed his Roman nose. "You guys are in good hands. I met with everybody and took care of everything."

Stanley interjected, "Tony means he met with our set designer, lighting designer, costume designer, prop master, and set décor designer; and the technical aspects of our show will be top notch."

Tony replied, "That's what I just says, ain't it?"

Katrina broke the tension between her husband and her friend. "There is a model of the set offstage in the wings. Everyone is welcome to see it during the break between the reading of Act I and Act II. The set will rotate, transporting our audience to three different living rooms."

Bella, who had obviously seen the model, added, "Mine, Sally's, and Jana's."

Brad looked like a dog under a buffet table. He put

his arm around the back of Bella's chair. "I can't wait to see your apartment, Bella."

Heel, nephew!

Katrina continued. "Chrissy, our wardrobe mistress, is also backstage waiting to measure all of you for your costumes during the break."

"I don't want anyone to know my dress size," Savannah said, garnering laughs from her co-stars.

Stanley added, "And a photographer will be back there ready to take a picture of each of you for the display cases in front of the theatre and in the lobby.

The stage manager, a balding, heavyset, older man, entered from backstage wearing jeans and a sweatshirt. "It's time to elect the Equity Deputy."

Peter raised his hand. "Jose, I nominate Jana."

Jana looked at Peter in shock. "What does the Equity Deputy do?"

"Represent an actor if he gets into any trouble with the management," Jose explained.

Peter whispered to her, "I'm hoping you'll help me if I get into any trouble."

Jana looked at Peter's gorgeous face. *Who's going to help me?*

Savannah said, "Peter, Jana is a big star. She doesn't have time to be the Equity Deputy."

Before Jana could reply, Jose said, "Are there any other nominations?"

As Jana tried to think of a way to decline gracefully, Jose shouted, "With no other nominations, Jana Lane is the company Equity Deputy."

"Congratulations, Jana." Peter winked at her.

"But I—"

Before Jana could decline, Tony opened his script.

"Okay, everybody take a look at the script in front of yiz, and read your lines loud like and with feeling and all, hah?"

Stanley spoke up again. "I know this is your first time reading the script, people. Katrina has been polishing it up until late last night. So please do the best you can."

"Yeah, no worries about motivation and crap like that," Tony said. Before Stanley could interject again, Tony said, "Let's get started, hah?"

The actors read through Act I. Jana thought how each cast member fit his or her role well. She was proud to be in a company with such fine actors. She noticed that during the reading Gary took notes, Savannah looked pale, Tate wiped sweat off his forehead and drank water continuously, Sally glared at Tony, and Bella and Brad played footsie under the table.

When Jose called for an Actors Equity Association mandatory break, the cast members headed to the wings. Gary held B.J.'s hands, and steered him away from the set model. During Jana's wardrobe fitting backstage, she heard the other cast members crying, "ohhhhh" and "ahhhhhh" at the model set. Once her fitting was finished, Jana complimented Chrissy on the sketches of Jana's eight different costumes—and costume changes—took a quick peek at the set model, posed for her picture to be placed under the theatre marquee, then cornered Brad next to a sandbag.

"Looks like you're taken with Bella," Jana said softly.

Brad combed his hair. "Bella seems pretty taken with me, too."

"So I see."

Brad did a double-take. "What's the problem? We're both single and over twenty-one."

Jana put her arm around Brad's broad shoulders. "Want some advice from your old aunt?"

"Sure."

"Take things slowly. If things don't work out on a personal level with you and Bella, it will be uncomfortable for you two during the run of the show."

"Don't worry, Aunt Jana. Bella's grandfather is Stanley Rothman." Brad smiled. "I'll make sure everything works out just fine."

Brad left Jana to join Bella, so Jana checked to make sure B.J. was behaving himself during his fitting. Then she walked backstage. On route to the ladies' room, she passed the star dressing room and saw her name on it. Jana Lane felt like a little girl again standing in front of her father's dressing room during *Sweet Nothings*. Coming back to the present, she continued down the hallway and noticed Savannah's name on the next dressing room door—the same dressing room Savannah, then an ingénue, had in *Sweet Nothings*. Jana's old dressing room was assigned to Peter. The remaining dressing rooms were for Bella, Tate, Brad, and B.J. When Jana passed by the last dressing room—assigned to Sally Chen, she spotted Sally in the arms of Tony Cuccioli.

Jana walked quickly to the ladies' room door, where she heard two women shouting.

"You and Stanley promised me, Kat," Savannah Stevens projected as if to the balcony.

There was a sigh, then Katrina said, "Save your drama for the stage, Savvie. You're finally back on Broadway. Isn't that what you wanted?"

"But at what cost to me?"

"Well, it's done, and there's nothing you can do about it."

"We'll see about that."

As Savannah stormed out, Jana entered and met Katrina at the sink. "It sounds like Savannah isn't happy."

Katrina repaired her lipstick. "Savvie is never happy."

"Doesn't she enjoy playing her role?"

"Savvie always enjoys playing her role." Her face hardened. "But I won't let her ruin this production."

"What do you mean, if you don't mind me asking?"

The playwright seated Jana next to her on an upholstered bench. "Jana, I know we haven't seen each other in a long time, but for some reason I feel I can trust you."

Probably because I was everyone's best friend in my old movies. "You can, Katrina."

Katrina smiled. "At five years old, you were such a sweet and obedient child. Smart as a whip. Adult beyond your years. And what a terrific actress. As your character in *Sweet Nothings* found a second wife for your widowed father, you understood and felt every emotion." Katrina sighed. "I never had any children. Since I couldn't create human life, I did something even better. I created *many* lives—in my plays. And my plays are my family." Her eyes glistened. "I had seventeen happy, healthy, loved, successful children, then two that died far too prematurely." She sat back on the bench. "It's funny how you don't remember the successes, as much as you wallow in the failures."

Katrina reached for Jana's hand. "Thank you for agreeing to star in my play, Jana. Your name over the title will attract audiences far more than mine at this point. And I need this play to be a hit. I need it more than I've ever needed anything in my life."

"Why is that?"

Katrina spoke softly. "Please keep this confidential. Only Tony, Savvie, and of course Stan know. I've been diagnosed with breast cancer."

"I'm so sorry, Katrina. What treatment are you—"

"It's too late."

"But there are many treatments—"

"Not when the cancer has spread throughout the lymphatic system."

Jana blinked back tears. "Katrina."

"I'm eighty years old. I don't want pity, tears, or condolences."

"What can I do for you?"

"Get me a hit play—this one. Can you do that for me?"

"I'll work as hard as I can, Katrina."

"That's all I ask."

Jana rose then sat down again. "I know this isn't any of my business, but why did you...especially now...how come you've never—"

"Married Stan?"

Jana nodded.

Katrina seemed miles away. "Stan and I have been lovers for thirty-seven years. That is lovers of the brain, heart, and soul. Stan and I fit together like a puzzle. I'm flattered by his interest in me, but marrying Stan would be like marrying my brother—if I had one." She hung her head. "Marrying Tony was a desperate attempt by an old woman to try to feel young again. Sadly, it didn't work. I feel older every day."

"I'll keep your secrets, Katrina. And I'll do everything in my power to make *China Doll* the hit play you want it to be."

Jana finished in the ladies' room, then walked back to her seat at the table on stage and pondered *China Doll's* plot in Act I. *So Bella Tarnowsky plays a poor young woman who falls in love with Tate Moonglow's character who impregnates her. I play Bella's friend and neighbor, and Brad's friend and neighbor. Savannah Stevens is Bella's mother. Sally Chen plays a recent beneficiary of a large family fortune from China. To Bella's dismay, Tate's character seduces Sally into marrying him, then talks Bella into getting an abortion. Bella cries to her mother, and the two women come up with a plan for revenge, whereby Bella becomes Sally's fast friend. However, their friendship is short lived as Sally dies from a heart attack with Bella hiding Sally's digitalis.*

Jana heard angry voices. Looking over her shoulder, she saw Stanley and Katrina standing on the apron of the stage with their backs to her.

"Don't push me on this, Stan," said Katrina.

"He's an embarrassment, Kat. He's a moron."

"He's my husband."

"He doesn't deserve you."

"I don't deserve him."

"You can say that again."

"Stan, Tony is a fine man who has stood by me through...everything."

Stanley lowered his voice. "Which is the only reason I agreed to this abomination."

"*You* hired Tony years ago."

"To build sets and later to stage manage! He doesn't know a thing about blocking, pacing, working with actors, collaborating with designers. He doesn't know much about *anything* for that matter. Let's stop this insanity before Tony destroys your play."

"No."

"Paul Coleman is available."

"No."

"Coleman's one of the best directors in New York."

"I said no. Tony will be fine. The actors are strong and won't need much directing. Jose is an experienced stage manager. We can help Tony along the way. Everybody has to start somewhere."

"You're making a huge mistake, Kat."

"Tony is important to me, Stan."

"I thought your play was important to you, too. And I thought *I* was important to you."

"Let's not start that again, Stan."

"You've had two husbands, Kat. The third one could be the charm."

At Jose's call, the group resumed their places at the table to read Act II. Again Jana marveled at how well each role was cast. Since Jana wasn't in the third scene of the second act, she read ahead to the end of the play and thought about the play's conclusion. *In Act II, according to plan, Bella comforts widower Tate in his "time of loss," and the two past lovers are happily married—until Bella throws Tate off their apartment balcony, pretending it was an accident. This leaves Bella, a wealthy woman, to turn her charms on her delighted friend and neighbor, Brad. My character is a widow who, after embarking on a romance with the local police detective played by the handsome Peter Stevens, solves the crime, thanks to something B.J., my babysitting charge, overhears in the hallway when Bella and her mother discuss their plan in Bella's apartment. It all leads to a white-knuckle climax in my apartment, where I confront Bella with the truth, escape her attack, save my babysitting charge, and expose Bella and her mother, Savannah, for killing Sally and Tate for revenge and wealth. Though a bit hard to believe, Katrina's latest play is a well-written thriller that should keep the audience in heart-pounding delight through its nerve-tingling conclusion.*

The cast applauded and praised Katrina's play. Bella blew a kiss at Rothman. "Thank you, Grandpop. I can't wait until my parents see the play."

The widower waved his hand as if swatting flies. "Your parents never appreciated show business." He beamed like a lighthouse. "Unlike their daughter."

Bella held her hand to her heart, and said to Katrina, "I love my role!"

Katrina replied, "And even in the first read you played her with ambition, prowess, and vulnerability."

Like in real life.

Brad winked at Bella. "I like my part, too, especially when I ask Bella to marry me."

Bella giggled and cooed.

Jana noticed Tate Moonglow's eyes were dilated, and he continued to mop the sweat from his face with his handkerchief. She said to him, "Is there anything you need?"

Tate looked down at his script. "I'll be okay. Thank you."

Watching Peter take Savannah's hand, Jana whispered to Peter. "Is your mother all right?"

Peter whispered back, "It's been a long time since Mom has acted. I think she's a bit choked up."

I think it's more likely she finds her role too small. Had it been during the time of Sweet Nothings, Savannah would have played Bella's role.

B.J. cried out. "B.J. is in a play!"

"And you said your lines beautifully, B.J.," Katrina added.

Thanks to Gary whispering them in B.J.'s ear.

"It's quite a play," Gary said, adjusting the fastened top button of his white shirt. "However, if I may, there is one thing I'm concerned about with B.J.'s role."

Was drama critic in your job description? "Gary, I don't think Katrina—"

"No, let him speak." Stanley Rothman waved his hand at Gary like a king permitting an audience to his servant.

Gary pressed his eyeglasses back up the bridge of his nose. "When B.J. overhears Bella and Savannah plotting to kill Tate, shouldn't B.J. be traumatized? He didn't know Tate all that well, except to pass by Tate's character in the hallway, but B.J.'s a little kid hearing about murder in his own apartment building."

Katrina wrote a note on her script. "I'll think about it."

Gary cleared his throat. "And I have another suggestion."

"Shouldn't we—"

Katrina hushed Jana. "Go on, please."

Gary nodded. "At the end of the play, instead of

Jana turning Bella over to the police, I think it would be more realistic if Jana and Bella split the inherited money."

"Yo, we already got a playwright, Gary, hah?" Tony said, looking down his Roman nose at the nanny. "Thanks anyways. But no thanks."

"I was just trying to help."

Before Gary could run off to Sardis with the theatre critics, he had to run off after B.J. who was trying to close the stage curtain.

"Excuse me." Sally Chen raised a blood red nail. "Though it's a wonderful play, Katrina, since it's a first draft, will there be rewrites before opening?" She leaned toward Katrina. "That's the way it was in my last play—when I won a Tony Award."

"I think the play is terrific," Brad said, sharing a smile with Bella.

Sally smiled at Katrina. "Yes, it's a beautifully written play, Katrina, but between the acts Tony and I discussed a few possible ideas…for tweaking."

Tony scratched his mountainous pectoral muscles and didn't look Katrina in the eyes. "Sally and I was just kicking around a few ideas is all. We can talk about it some other time, Kat, hah?"

Katrina unleashed a forced smile. "I would like to hear the ideas now."

"Terrific!" Sally stood like an advertising executive making a pitch to a top client. "Tony and I were thinking, though the play is amazing, how it could be even better if *my* character came back in Act II."

Bella groaned. "How can your character come back, Sally? She's dead."

Sally replied like a district attorney with secret

evidence in a hushed courtroom, "But what if my character isn't really dead? What if I figured out Tate married me for my family's money, and that Bella is out for revenge against Tate? So I faked my heart attack to spy on them!"

"And the coroner wouldn't know this?" Stanley asked.

"He would know, but he wouldn't say anything, because I paid him off," Sally replied as if it was obvious.

Tony put down his script. "Let's all go get some lunch, hah, then come back and—"

"Tell them your idea, Tony," Sally said with piercing eyes.

"It can wait—"

"I'd like to hear it," Katrina said with a no-nonsense look.

Sally answered, "What if I come out of hiding in Act II. And instead of Bella killing Tate, *I* kill Tate, then I go after Bella and Savannah to take back my inheritance!"

Brad smiled at Katrina. "I think the play is fine as written."

Sally moaned. "Of course you do. You don't die at the end of Act I."

Bella said, "You have to die, Sally, otherwise the play isn't a murder mystery."

Sally glared at Bella. "The mystery is why an Asian actress who just won a Tony Award is starring in a play called *China Doll*, but she isn't in Act II!"

"Sally may be on to something. I think Bella's and my role as her mother should be rewritten," said Savannah.

Stanley sighed. "And why is that, Savvie?"

"They're not likeable." Savannah repaired her lipstick. "After Tate's character dumps Bella for Sally, what if Sally tries to kill Bella, and *I* save my daughter?"

Thank goodness I'm an actress and not a playwright.

Savannah looked into her compact mirror. "There's no subtlety in the play, Kat. Bella's character and her mother kill Sally and Tate for revenge and money. I think it would be a far more interesting play if Sally is the secret mastermind behind Tate leaving Bella, and Sally kills all of us when she finds out Tate only wants her for her family's money. My character should be the last to go—as I confront Sally with the truth right before she kills me."

"I like it!" Sally said.

Katrina looked as if she was going to explode. Noticing, Tony said, "Hey, all a yiz listen up now. Kat is the writer. She decides what words all of youse say. Got it?"

Sally glared at Tony. "So much for collaboration!"

"Yiz can cohabitate all youse like, but it's Kat's play. Nothing changes unless Kat says so."

"What about my career?" Sally asked in a rage.

Stanley said, "You didn't have to take the role when it was offered to you, Sally."

Sally replied, "My agent told me I was playing the title role. I couldn't read the play until today like everyone else. Except for your granddaughter, I assume."

Brad stood up. "Hey, that's not fair!"

"And it's also not true," Bella said.

As everyone argued, Jana noticed Tate's face grow pale. His head swayed from side to side. Before she could reach him, Tate Moonglow fell backward off his chair and landed still on the stage floor.

Chapter 2

Jana watched in fear as Gary Royale kneeled at Tate Moonglow's side. "I've had some first aid training as a nanny," Gary said. "Everyone stand back, please." He checked Tate's pulse and breathing. "He's alive."

"Should I call for an ambulance?" Jose the stage manager asked.

Tate ran a hand through his dark locks. "I'm all right." He tried to sit up, but when his head swayed, he stayed down.

"Take things slowly." Gary cautiously helped Tate to his feet.

"Why did the man go down boom?" B.J. asked Jana.

Jana held B.J.'s hand, keeping him away from Tate. "Tate needed a nap."

"Like me sometimes," B.J. said.

"Right."

Stanley Rothman stood next to Tate Moonglow. The producer asked, "Are you ill?"

Gary helped Tate to his chair, then sat next to him. "I saw the whole thing," Gary said as if he were Tate's lawyer. "Tate leaned back in his chair and it tipped over, sending poor Tate flying."

"Did you hit your head?" Stanley asked Tate.

Tate took a drink of water. "I don't think so."

Gary said, "I'm sure he will be fine."

"You don't look fine," the producer said. "Are you well enough to continue, Tate?"

Jana asked, "Jose, is it time to break for lunch?"

Jose checked his watch. "In two minutes."

"Tate will no doubt feel better after eating something," Jana said. "The first day of rehearsal is always stressful."

"I loved it!" B.J. proclaimed, which eased the tension a bit on stage.

Jose counted down the last few seconds on his watch. "One hour break for lunch everybody."

Everyone else dispersed in small clusters, as Gary took charge of B.J., and Jana sat next to Tate. "How are you feeling, Tate?"

"Better, thank you. I just feel a little lightheaded," Tate replied with a quivering smile.

"Let's have something to eat." Jana looked around the empty stage. "Sorry, I've grown accustomed to film sets where meals are catered." She laughed. "I guess I'll have to do my own hair and makeup, too. Doing theatre is really roughing it."

Tate laughed then steadied himself.

Jana said, "I'll get you something from the deli across the street."

"Thank you, but that won't be necessary, Miss Lane." Tate blushed.

"It's Jana. And we all have to eat."

Gary stood near the table with B.J. "We'll go. What would you like at the deli?"

Jana and Tate gave Gary their orders, then the nanny left with B.J.

Once they were alone, Jana took Tate's hand and looked up at his thin, handsome face. "I hope you know you can trust me."

He smiled. "I've read about your lobbying for AIDS funding and research, and your fundraisers."

"Unfortunately our elected officials aren't listening."

"But people with AIDS are."

"Are you one of them?"

He sighed. "What gave me away? My oversized clothes, dehydration, sweating, dizziness, labored breathing?"

She squeezed his hand. "It doesn't matter. What matters is how you are feeling, and if you are getting the proper care."

Tate let out a sad laugh. "How do you get proper care for a disease with no cure?"

"In April, Dr. Gallo of the National Cancer Institute isolated the virus that causes AIDS. HTLV-III. New treatments will be coming forth any day now."

He nodded, clearly not believing it. "I hope they come soon."

"What is your T cell count?"

He swallowed hard. "One hundred and twenty."

She tried not to show her disappointment. "Are you getting enough rest? Eating well?"

"Yes, and I'm doing what I love to do—act."

"Will you be able to do the play?"

"I sure hope so." Tears welled up in his dark eyes. "Because without acting, I have nothing to live for."

Jana slid to the edge of her seat. "Do you have any family nearby?"

Tate looked like a child with coal in his Christmas stocking. "My parents live on a reservation. They understand about what Native Americans call the *two-*

spirited people, but they don't understand about AIDS. I guess I don't either."

"Do you have a partner?"

"Not anymore."

"Friends?"

His handsome face hardened. "Only fair weather friends."

"I'm sorry, Tate. I hope you will consider me your friend."

"Didn't you say that to little Timmy in *The Cowgirl and the Bandit*?"

"And in most of my other childhood movies."

They shared a laugh.

Tate wiped his eyes with his handkerchief. "Thank you for saying it to me now. It means a lot, Jana."

"It's my pleasure, Tate."

"And it is generally *my* pleasure to know what's going on in one of my productions." Stanley Rothman towered over them. "When were you planning to tell me you have AIDS, Tate? When you collapse on stage during opening night?"

Tate opened his mouth, but nothing came out.

Jana stood next to Stanley. Though she was only five two, she felt ten feet tall. "Stanley, an actor's personal medical information is not part of his résumé."

"It is if he has AIDS." Stanley glared at Tate. "You could give this thing to my entire cast!"

Jana stood between them. "AIDS is not contracted from acting in a play with someone."

"He has to kiss Bella, my granddaughter!"

"Or from a stage kiss," Jana explained.

Stanley replied, "We won't have to test that theory, because Tate is fired."

Jana followed Stanley to the wings. "You can't do that."

"I have to protect my company."

"Your company is fine."

Stanley stopped at the model of the set. "I also have to honor my religious beliefs as an Orthodox Jew."

What hypocrisy! "I remember rehearsing *Sweet Nothings* on Saturdays as you worked in your office, turning lights on and off. And what's that I smell on your breath, Stanley? A BLT for lunch?"

"The Torah is very clear about homosexuality being an abomination."

"And it is equally clear about stoning to death your unbelieving neighbor, women who marry as non-virgins, and people who eat shellfish. Tell me, Stanley, have you sold your daughter into slavery yet?"

Stanley's eyes bulged out of his head like golf balls. "Don't you *dare* defame my religion!"

"I have the utmost respect for your religion, Stanley. But right now, contrary to my childhood impressions of you, I have very little respect for *you*."

"Don't you throw your atheist propaganda at me."

Jana followed Stanley down the stairs to his office, where Katrina and Tony sat at a table eating their lunch. "I'm not an atheist, Stanley. But I believe the Torah, like all holy books, is the inspired word of God, written during a certain time for a specific reason. And translated and rewritten by fallible *men* over the ages. And it should *never* be used to persecute others."

"Your friend Tate is the one trying to persecute my cast. And I won't let him do it."

Katrina and Tony did a double-take.

"What in the world is going on?" Katrina asked.

Stanley plopped into his desk chair. "Tate Moonglow has AIDS. I just fired him. Our bleeding heart liberal star isn't happy about it."

Katrina put down her tuna salad sandwich. "The poor man."

"The poor man?" Stanley pounded his fist on the desk. "He's a homosexual who got what's coming to him."

"Nobody deserves AIDS, or any other illness," Jana said. "Most of the people who contracted this disease in Africa are heterosexual. Do *they* deserve it, too?"

"Don't try to bully me." Stanley pointed his finger at Jana. "The Jews have been persecuted for years."

"That is very true," Jana said. "As have African Americans, Native Americas, and now gays. Let's all be big enough to stop the cycle of persecution."

"Jana, please sit down."

Jana obeyed Katrina, and sat on a chair between Stanley's desk and the table.

Katrina ran a hand through her white hair. "My concern is for Tate."

"Thank you, Katrina," Jana replied, resting back in her chair.

Katrina continued. "I don't think working is good for his...condition."

Not around people like Stanley. "Tate said acting helps him feel better. And, like all of us, he has an understudy. Should Tate become ill—"

Katrina raised a finger to silence Jana. "I don't think we can risk this."

"Risk what?" Jana raised her hands to the ancient

light fixture. "Tate isn't a bomb. He's a human being."

"A human being who can infect other human beings," Stanley said with a sneer.

Jana stood over his desk. "I'm sure Tate has no intentions of having sex with anyone in the company, or giving any of us a blood transfusion."

"That's not what I mean." Katrina selected her words carefully. "I am a Christian. Tate is…what Tate is goes against everything I've been taught by my religion."

But marrying twice follows your teachings? Jana made her way to Katrina. "I don't recall Jesus condemning gay people in the Bible stories. But I *do* remember him ministering to everyone, including the downtrodden and abhorred, even the lepers. I also recall where he cautioned his followers not to judge, and he asked everyone to love your neighbor as yourself."

Tony looked up from his hamburger. "Hey, don't look at me. I'm Catholic. We don't read the Bible."

Jana stood in the center of the room. "We are supposed to be a company, a unit, a family, a group of theatre people putting on a play for an audience. Shouldn't we take care of our own?"

"I'm the producer. Kat is the playwright. Tate Moonglow is fired!"

Jana came in for the kill. "Stanley, if you fire Tate Moonglow, I quit."

"So do I." Peter Stevens stood at the doorway next to his mother. "Tate isn't bothering anyone. He's good in his role."

Savannah looked at Katrina and Stanley. "You two can't fool me with your holier than thou act. We go back too far."

Stanley and Katrina locked gazes. After a few moments, Stanley said, "All right. But I don't want Tate anywhere near me or my granddaughter."

Jana looked at Katrina. "I'm sure Katrina can cut their kiss."

Katrina nodded.

"Do it, Kat." Stanley stood next to Jana. "If Tate Moonglow has any more episodes like he did this morning, he is out on his perverted ass. Do I make myself clear?"

Savannah said, "As clear and as synthetic as cellophane, Stan."

"Excuse me?" Sally Chen made her way past Peter. "I don't mean to interrupt, but I really need to talk to Stanley and Katrina about my role."

Jana said to Stanley, "I believe we're finished."

Sally held Jana's arm. "Please, everyone stay. I think we all agree my role in the play isn't...fleshed out."

"Your role is fine," Stanley said, sitting back behind his desk.

Sally glared at Tony. He stood and put his arm around Sally. "Hear her out, Stan, hah? She's got some good ideas."

Did Sally explain them to you when you two were kissing during the break?

Stanley looked at his watch. "It's nearly time to get back upstairs."

Sally looked at Katrina. "Please, will you think about filling out my role, Katrina?"

"She will do nothing of the kind," Stanley said. "If Kat tries to make your role larger, it will be a different play."

Savannah replied, "That's not a bad idea."

Katrina looked like a mother bear protecting her cub. "The plot of *China Doll* will remain unaltered."

Sally stood her ground. "But the size of my role is an insult. I wonder if any other Tony Award winning actress would do it."

Stanley replied in a rage, "Then quit and we'll find out."

Tony said, "Yo, Stan, Kat, think about it? Sally's a terrific actress, hah?"

Katrina looked at her husband with pain in her eyes. "That's very clear, but I'm not rewriting the role."

"Case closed." Stanley ushered the four actors out of the room. "We will see you all upstairs in a few minutes to start rehearsing."

As Jana, Peter, and his mother climbed the steps, Sally raced past them in tears, and headed for the pay phone backstage.

Making their way to the wings, Jana said, "Thank you both."

"For what?" Peter asked.

"For standing up for Tate. I don't know how much of Stanley's insanity you heard."

"I heard enough to know Jana Lane is an amazing woman." Peter's eyes sparkled.

Savannah stood between them. "We did what any decent person would do. Unfortunately, Kat and Stan have forgotten how to be decent."

Peter smiled at Jana. "But Jana Lane hasn't. You are our star in more ways than one."

Jana laughed. "My name may be over the title, but this is an ensemble show."

"Yeah, we're one big happy family," Savannah

said sarcastically.

Peter said to Jana, "I wasn't talking about the show, though you're the star of that, too." His pectoral muscles nearly burst out of his T-shirt as he reached past his mother and took Jana's arm. "What you did down there makes you a star in my book. You're an amazing woman, Jana Lane."

"Thank you." Jana felt incredibly drawn to Peter Stevens. It wasn't just his handsome face, muscular physique, and warm manner. There was something comfortable, familiar, and engaging about him. Perhaps they were married in another life. *But not this one.*

Reminding Jana of her family, B.J. threw himself into her arms. "Mommy! I missed you!"

Savannah said to Peter, "B.J. is Jana's and...what's your husband's name?"

"Brian."

"Jana's and Brian's son," Savannah said to Peter.

Peter said, "B.J. definitely has the Lane family acting gene."

"I'm not in jeans!" Then B.J. said to Peter, "I like your jacket. For me?"

Peter playfully messed B.J.'s hair. "Just as soon as you're my size."

"Oh boy!"

Jana and Peter laughed.

Do his biceps always bulge out of his jacket when he laughs? If so, I better find some new jokes.

"B.J. ate pastranami," B.J. announced. "Mommy didn't."

Jana said to Peter, "That's my cobb salad on the table on stage."

"Peter and I had the same thing at a restaurant

down the block," Savannah said, clutching onto her son's arm.

We even have the same taste in food.

Peter put his hand on her back and led Jana to the table on stage. "Eat your lunch. You'll need the energy for our love scenes."

I hope you're referring to the scenes in the play.

B.J. sat next to his mother and nibbled on her chicken, while she ate her salad. Savannah asked Peter if she could speak with him in the wings.

Coming from the men's room backstage, Tate sat next to Gary at the other end of the table from Jana.

"Didn't your lunch agree with you?" Gary asked Tate.

"Nothing agrees with me lately, including our producer," Tate replied. "Thank you."

"For what?"

"For telling Rothman I fell down."

"It popped into my head."

"That's because you're a nice guy." Tate smiled. "And thank you for the chicken soup."

"As my mother used to say, it cures what ails you. I hope you're feeling better."

Tate smiled. "I am now."

Gary pushed his glasses up the bridge of his nose. "I think you read your part very well—until you blacked out."

Tate laughed. "Thanks."

"You don't feel like you have to black out again, do you?"

"No. I'm okay."

"Good." Gary's gaze traversed Tate's square jaw and broad shoulders. "You're a very good looking man.

It's hard to believe you have AIDS."

"Good looking people get AIDS, too."

Gary wiped the sweat off his forehead. "I know. I meant…you don't look sick." He grinned like a lovesick teenager. "You look really good."

"Thanks. I'll go home and rest after rehearsal."

Gary slid to the edge of his seat. "After I get B.J. off to bed, I could bring you more soup from the deli."

Tate squirmed in his seat. "Gary, thank you, but—"

"Don't thank me. Just say yes, and give me your address."

Tate cleared his throat. "I don't think that's a good idea."

"Eating dinner?"

"You coming over to my place."

"Why not? You have a mad dog?"

"No." Tate sighed. "Gary, you're a nice guy. And I think you're adorable. Under different circumstances I would…but I don't want to be anyone's charity case." Tate leaned in closer to Gary. "And I don't want to burden anybody with this."

Gary's voice cracked like an aging choir boy's. "It's not a burden. I'd like to help you."

"I appreciate your support. But I need to be upfront with people—especially now." Tate looked into Gary's adoring eyes. "I hope you understand. I'm not dating anybody."

"Neither am I."

"I mean, even though you're a terrific guy, given my…situation, I don't want to start anything with you…or anyone."

"What do you mean?"

"I mean, I'm attracted to you, but I don't want to

date you."

Gary sucked in air as if he had been hit in the stomach. "*Date* me? Did you think I was talking about you dating me?"

"You just said you wanted to—"

Gary's face turned pale. "You thought….You think….I'm not….Why would you…?"

Tate leaned back in his chair. "I didn't mean to upset you."

"Who's upset? Why would I be upset?" Gary waved his arms like a cheerleader. "I'm not upset at all. I was just trying to make a new friend. I don't know anyone in the cast, and I'll be staying here for a while. What I said to you was in no way a pick-up—of any kind. How old are you?"

"Twenty-five."

"See? I am a *lot* older than you. And more importantly, I am definitely not gay! I mean it's fine with me if somebody is gay, but I am absolutely not!"

"Not a problem, Gary."

"Yes, it's a *big* problem. I wasn't asking you out on a date. I was just trying to make a new friend and help a guy."

"Okay. I get it."

"I hope so, because I've never done anything with another guy. I don't even have any male friends." Gary's Adam's apple bobbed up and down over his collar button. "I am definitely not a homosexual."

"I understand."

"Good. Because I wouldn't want any confusion."

"There's no confusion…on *my* part," Tate said.

"What's that supposed to mean?"

"It means, are you trying to convince yourself or

56

me?"

"Lunch is over," Jose proclaimed. "Everyone please take a seat in the front of the house." As the company members made their way to seats in the audience, Jose set up chairs on stage to represent the sofa, easy chairs, coffee table, bar, and doorway of Bella and Savannah's living room set.

Katrina, Stanley, and Tony sat in the center of the front row. Jose sat further down the row with a pad and pen in hand, ready to write down the actor's blocking and cues. Jana, B.J., Peter, Savannah, Tate, and Sally were in the second row. Last to arrive in their seats next to one another in the third row were Brad and Bella, giggling like children with a secret. Gary stood under a box seat.

Tony posed in front of the orchestra pit and addressed the cast. "Tate, Bella, and Savannah. Can youse three get up on stage?" As they followed their director's orders, Tony shouted, "The rest of yiz can relax while I block the first scene. But nobody go nowheres, hah, since I may need yiz for the next scene after that."

Stanley rose and whispered to Tony, "Don't you want to start off with warm-up exercises with the full cast?"

"No." Tony walked up the steps to the stage and stood far stage left. "Now just like Kat wrote in the script, Bella and Tate, yiz start out on the sofa stage right, hah? Savannah you're offstage left."

As the three actors complied, Stanley followed Tony up on stage and tapped the director on his broad shoulder. "How about starting with an improvisation to help the cast get into their characters?"

"No," Tony replied with a tight jaw.

"Or ask each cast member to write a character biography?"

"No."

"What about discussing their character's actions, objectives, motivations?"

Tony said quickly, "Yo, Bella and Tate, youse are hot for each other. Savannah, you approve. Now you three got your motivations."

Stanley replied, "Don't you think that is simplifying things a bit?"

"No." Tony addressed the three onstage actors who looked like children watching their parents argue. "Let's get started. Bella, your first line, hah?"

Stanley interrupted again. "Tony, actors need more direction than, 'start with your first line.' As their director you need to speak with them about using emotional recall and sense memory to relive memories from their own lives in order for them to share the same feelings as their characters. How else will their performances be realistic?"

"How's this for reality, Stan? You're driving me nuts. A play can have only one director, and it ain't you."

"But I'm the producer."

"Then produce, and let me direct."

"Since you are a novice director, I am trying to help."

"You want to help me, Stan?"

Stanley nodded.

"Then sit down in the house, and shut the hell up."

The producer bristled as he took the stairs back to his seat.

While Stanley and Katrina argued sotto voce from their seats in the audience, Tony gave the actors their stage movements. When they finished the scene, Stanley walked up the steps and stood next to his granddaughter down center stage. "Bella, you were marvelous, honey."

Bella beamed like a lighthouse. Brad whistled from his seat in the audience.

"Tate, don't sit so close to Bella on the sofa," Stanley said with a sneer.

"But I'm telling Bella that I love her," Tate replied.

"Tell her from farther away," Stanley shouted. "And Savvie, the mother is happy about her daughter's engagement to Tate. You looked upset about it."

Tony motioned to Katrina.

Noticing, Katrina said, "Stan, may I speak with you, please?"

As Stanley took his seat and resumed his argument with Katrina, Tony called out, "Yo, Jana, come up on stage, hah?"

Jana gave B.J. to Gary then headed for the stage. As Tony blocked the scene where Jana pays a neighborly visit to Bella and Bella's fiancé Tate, it took every ounce of concentration she had as an actress to get through it, since Savannah had come down from the stage and was speaking with Katrina and Stanley. Jana couldn't hear what they were talking about, but it didn't seem like a reunion of old friends. Savannah's violet eyes displayed anger. Katrina shook her head back and forth like a chicken. Stanley's face was red.

Jana started to exit in the scene, and she was nearly knocked over by two large bookcases.

"Yo! Aye!" Tony hurried center stage. "What

gives?"

Two tall men in overalls placed the bookcase set piece against the upstage wall. The heavyset man said, "This is the first set piece from the shop, Tony."

The thin man added, "We'll be bringing over more pieces as they're built and painted."

Tony replied, "Thanks, guys. Just don't kill none of my cast members, hah? We need them for opening night."

Tony called up Brad then led the actors through the next scene, where Tate leaves, and Jana introduces Bella to their new, young, single neighbor, Brad. The chemistry between the two young actors was palpable. When Bella and Brad looked as if they were going to jump into each other's arms, Jana adlibbed a tug on Brad's arm to separate them.

Jose called for a break, and Jana returned to her seat next to Peter in the house. Her goosebumps had goosebumps as her handsome leading man leaned over and whispered in her ear, "You were terrific."

I've received compliments before on my acting. Why am I short of breath? "It was just a blocking rehearsal."

"But you brought out the character's warm maternal instincts and intelligence." He smiled. "As a matter of fact, the character seems very much like Jana Lane."

Their shoulders touched and Jana shivered. "I am so very much looking forward to our scenes together, Peter." *When did I turn sixty and become British?*

"Me too. It's an honor to be working with a legend."

Now I feel eighty. "Speaking of legends, how is

your mother doing?"

Peter's handsome face saddened. "Not too well."

"I saw her arguing with Stanley and Katrina. I thought they were old friends."

"They are. But Mom's not too happy with them right now."

"Is *anybody* happy in the company?"

"Certainly not Tate or Sally."

"Or Tony," Jana added.

Peter's luscious dimples emerged. "Well, what are you going to do about it, Equity Deputy?"

Jana laughed. "I am going to ask you to be more careful about who you nominate in the future, and I plan to advise my nephew and my son to never become producers—or at least not to become a producer like Stanley Rothman."

Peter looked back at Brad who was whispering and giggling with Bella in the third row. "It looks like Brad has other things on his mind than becoming a producer."

Jana pointed to B.J. in the far right aisle, who was parroting his upcoming lines in the play to Gary. "B.J. appears content in the life of an actor."

He wrapped his muscular arm around the back of her chair. "B.J. is amazing. Just like his mother."

"Peter." Finished with her argument, Savannah stood in the aisle next to them. "I'm going to my dressing room to rest."

Her son rose. "I'll come with you."

The actress unleashed a weak smile. "Thank you, dear."

"Please excuse us, Jana," Peter said.

Jana rose. "My dressing room, the corner one, has

a sofa in it. Please use it to lie down."

"Thank you. That sounds like a good idea," Savannah replied.

Jose approached. "Savannah, Chrissy didn't get your measurements."

Savannah smirked. "I thought I was being cagey."

"She's waiting for you offstage right," the stage manager said.

Savannah took Peter's hand. "I'll meet you in Jana's dressing room in five minutes." She turned to Jana. "No need to come, Jana. I'm sure you'll be needed at rehearsal." The aging actress said behind tight lips, "Your role is so much larger than mine."

When Savannah and Jose were gone, Peter said, "I'm worried about her."

"You're a devoted son." *Another irresistible trait!* "I hope my son is half as concerned about me when he's your age. *And I'm in the old actor's home trying to remember his name.*

They sat back down in their seats, and Peter said, "My dad wasn't around much when I was a kid. He worked long hours, went away a lot on business, and he died at forty-one of cancer."

"I'm sorry, Peter."

"My mother was the biggest female box office star in Hollywood, and she turned down films to be home with me. Even though I was all grown, she took the sitcom to have time to help me with my career." He looked like a puppy begging for affection. "Though the series was a hit and ran for five years, playing that dotty neighbor ended Mom's career. She went from playing a vamp to a leading lady to camp. I know she seems overbearing and protective of me, but I'm all she has."

Jana slid to the edge of her seat. "Peter, what's wrong with Savannah? You can trust me."

Peter looked into her eyes. "I knew that. From the first moment I met you."

"Then please tell me."

After a deep breath, he replied, "When Stanley called Mom to offer her the show, he gave her a stipulation. Mom had to invest in the show."

"Savannah is an angel?"

"Well, I wouldn't go that far." He smiled. "Yes, Mom is a show angel, a silent investor in *China Doll* to the tune of half a million dollars."

Jana felt as if her eyes doubled in size. "With all of Katrina's hit shows, why does Stanley need Savannah's money for *China Doll*?"

Peter spoke in a hushed tone. "Katrina's last two plays lost money. The critics...and the audiences felt Katrina had run out of ideas, and her last two plays were pale carbon copies of two of her earlier successes."

"And Savannah put up all that money for *China Doll* without reading the script?"

Peter nodded. "Mom wanted desperately to get back on Broadway. When Katrina and Stanley asked, Mom saw *China Doll* as her last chance, and she grabbed it."

"How did Savannah get that much money?"

"Mom sold some of her jewelry and furs. She also cashed in some of her savings."

"Then what were Savannah, Stanley, and Katrina arguing about?"

Peter scratched his thick locks. "Mom feels her status as a show angel should entitle her to script approval."

And to expand her role. "And Stanley and Katrina don't see it that way?"

He nodded.

"B.J. knows his lines." B.J. plopped himself onto his mother's lap.

"I'm impressed," Peter said.

"You learned your lines before your mother learned hers." Jana kissed her son's cheeks.

Since B.J. was with Jana, Gary made his way to the front row. "Excuse me, Mrs. Cuccioli, may I speak with you about B.J.'s role in the play?"

Katrina looked at Gary skeptically. "What is your concern?"

Gary sat in the theatre seat next to hers. "I have no background in the theatre."

"I sensed that."

Pushing his glasses up the bridge of his nose, Gary said, "But I know little boys. I was one."

"I assumed."

"And I've taken care of many of them as a professional nanny."

"What is your point?"

"As I mentioned at the read-through, a little boy wouldn't be so easily silenced by Bella's character toward the end of the play. Bella and her mother would have to do something to get the boy to keep silent about overhearing their plan to murder Sally and Tate."

"Such as?"

Gary shrugged. "Maybe Bella could threaten to tell his parents he was a bad boy for listening at their door. Or perhaps Bella's mother could bribe B.J. with ice cream."

Jana approached Gary to try to stop him from continuing. She noticed Katrina's face had turned pale. Jana followed Katrina's gaze to Tony and Sally in the wings, clearly in the throes of a passionate embrace.

"Why are you bothering the playwright?" Stanley Rothman stood over Gary.

The nanny replied meekly, "Since B.J.'s under my charge, I was sharing my ideas about B.J.'s character."

Stanley replied in a rage, "Mr., whatever your name is, you are B.J.'s nanny, not his script consultant. Please keep your opinions to yourself—unless they are about wiping B.J.'s bottom."

Gary gasped. "B.J. is potty trained!"

"Stanley, I think Gary was just trying to help," Jana said like a U.N. mediator.

"It doesn't help"—Stanley screamed—"when your homosexual nanny believes he is the playwright!"

Gary cringed. "I am not a homosexual!"

Stanley laughed. "Maybe I was wrong. Perhaps you *are* a playwright. After all, you just created quite a piece of fiction."

"How dare you!"

Calm down, Gary.

Stanley looked at Gary like a lion cornering a rabbit. "I am the producer. This is *my* show. I can do anything I like! Observe." Stanley clapped his hands. "May I have everyone's attention?" He looked into the wings at Tony and Sally. "While your director is *otherwise engaged*, I am calling the break over."

Jose shouted from his stage manager console on stage. "We have five more minutes, Stanley."

"We need to stick to Equity rules, Stanley," Jana as Equity Deputy stated with authority.

"Fine," Stanley replied. "Everyone can use the remaining time to come up on stage. I have some important announcements."

Jana asked Gary to watch B.J., and stop talking to Katrina. Then she made a detour to her dressing room, where she found Savannah sitting on the sofa, staring out the window at the theatre across the street.

Savannah offered Jana a sad smile. "Remember when your father, you, and I sat on this sofa and went over our lines?"

Jana nodded. "I was in such awe of the both of you. Your acting skills, dedication to the theatre, and professionalism were amazing." Jana laughed. "I remember when you fixed my hair like yours, and you let me put on your makeup. I felt like such a grown up." She sighed. "You were so beautiful. And you still are."

Savannah patted the seat on the sofa next to her. "I loved *Sweet Nothings*. It was my first show. I cherished my time on Broadway, and all the years later in Hollywood. But since you're on the actress train, Jana, let me tell you what's in store for your future. When you start out, every ounce of your energy is spent trying to get someone to notice you. Then somebody does and you get your big break. It's all so exciting, because you're the new girl in town. Your name is on everyone's lips like a new brand of soft drink. Everyone wants you. And everyone loves you. You're the toast of the town. After a few hits, you own the town. You call the shots, and you love it." Her eyes filled with tears. "But then you get older, and new actresses hit town and get noticed. You find the offers get less. Your phone calls aren't returned. People shun you in public. And before you know it, you're thrown out of the town on your ear."

"But there's more to life than acting."

"Is there?"

"Of course."

"Being a wife and mother? You'll find out it's not all it's cracked up to be."

Peter leaned into the dressing room. "We're needed on stage, ladies."

Jana and Savannah walked with Peter to the stage. Tony and Sally followed from the wings. Already on stage, Gary, shooting dagger eyes at Stanley, held B.J.'s hand. Bella and Brad didn't take their eyes off one another. Since Jana noticed Tate holding onto a chair from the makeshift set, she joined him and held his elbow for added support.

Pulling focus, Stanley stood upstage center, while the company members gathered around him. "As producer of this show, it is my prerogative to make decisions that I believe are in the best interest of this production. So before we continue rehearsing, I would like to inform you of the following changes."

The stage was as silent as a morgue.

Stanley looked at Tony. "First, as of this moment, I am taking over as director of this production."

"Hey, you can't do that!" Tony shouted.

"I can, and I have," Stanley replied, clearly enjoying his triumph.

Tony turned to Katrina. "Kat!"

Katrina looked at Stanley as if for the first time. "Stan, don't do this."

"I'm sorry, Kat. My mind is made up." Stanley pointed to Tate. "I have also decided that Tate Moonglow will be replaced by his understudy."

Tate held his head in his hands.

Jana spoke up. "As Equity Deputy, I will fight this. You have no just cause for firing Tate."

Stanley replied, "I do, and you know it." The producer glared at Gary. "And your son's nanny is barred from all future rehearsals."

B.J. asked Gary, "What does *barred* mean?"

"It means I'm canned," Gary replied.

"It means nothing of the kind." Jana came face to face with Stanley. "If Tate and Gary go, so do I."

"Don't do it for me, Jana," Tate and Gary said in unison.

Stanley grinned. "Listen to your deviant friends, Jana."

Tate held Jana's arm to stifle her from replying to Stanley.

Stanley glared at Sally Chen. "And if anyone doesn't like the size of her role, I'll accept your resignation." Then staring at Savannah and Jana, he said, "And if any of you regrets signing a contract with me for this show, let this be a business lesson for you. Lawyers enforce contracts." Stanley clapped his hands again. "Tony, Tate, and Gary, you are released. Kat, please take a seat in the house. Jose, back to your stage manager's console. Everyone else, please make a circle around me, and I will lead you in some warm up exercises."

As everyone moved around Stanley on stage in a state of shocked pandemonium, the bookcase set piece teetered back and forth then crashed down on top of the producer.

Chapter 3

The star of Broadway's *China Doll* sat in front of her dressing room mirror. *Think this through, girl. What was each cast member doing when the set piece fell on Stanley? What motive does each of them have for wanting to murder him?*

A tall, bald, muscular African American man interrupted Jana's thoughts. "Jana Lane. What do you know?" He smiled and showed his badge. "Detective Dwayne Douglas."

She rose and shook his large hand. "Hello, Detective."

"Call me, Dwayne."

"I will if you call me, Jana."

"Please take a seat, Jana."

Jana sat on the sofa.

Dwayne joined her, careful not to wrinkle his suit. "I'm a fan by the way."

"Thank you, but I'd rather not talk about my movies right now."

"I'm not talking about your movies. I can't stand movies." He looked at her more closely. "I'm about your age. I remember my little sister going to your movies. You wouldn't catch me in that movie theatre with all those giggling little girls."

"But you just said you were a fan of mine."

"I am. A fan of your police work. I read in the

newspapers about how you solved those murders at your mansion in Hyde Park, New York, and in Washington, DC. You're a regular Nancy Drew."

But old enough to be her mother. At least he didn't say I'm Miss Marple. "Dwayne, can you please tell me what's going on?"

"Your stage manager called to tell me a wooden piece of scenery, a bookcase, fell on your producer and killed him. He said you insisted it was murder. I asked him to have each of you stay in your dressing rooms until I got here."

"Did you tape off the stage as a crime scene?"

"Done."

"Did you get the specifics on what happened from Jose?"

"Done."

"How about interviewing everyone who was on stage?"

"That's what I'm doing now."

"Am I first?"

"First, second, third, and so on. As the Equity Deputy, you'll be accompanying me on all the interviews—to ensure I treat everyone well." He chuckled. "At least that's what we'll be telling everyone. The truth is you have a great brain, lady. I want your insight." He leaned back on the sofa. "I do wonder though why it is that murder seems to follow you."

"Am I suspect?"

"Let's take this one step at a time." He took a pad and pen from his suit jacket pocket. "Tell me what happened out there."

"You said Jose already explained everything."

"I'd like to hear it from you."

Jana relayed the events of the day to the detective.

"In examining the gash on Rothman's head, I think it was an accident. Why are you so sure it was murder?"

"The bookcase scenery was leaning against the back wall of the stage. It was quite heavy and wouldn't have toppled over unless someone pushed it."

"How do you know?"

"It's just like in my old film."

"Your old film?"

She nodded. "*The Little Shop Girl.*"

He looked at her skeptically. "Okay?"

"With the store full of customers and salespeople, a clerk unobtrusively pushed over a bookcase full of lamps and killed my father for firing him."

"And you think the same thing happened to Mr. Rothman?"

"Yes. Stanley Rothman was not well liked by the company."

"Who do you think did it?"

"That's what I've been trying to figure out."

"Talk it through for me. What did you see?"

Jana closed her eyes. "Stanley stood upstage center—"

"The strongest place to stand on stage to get everyone's attention."

She opened her eyes. "How do you know that?"

He revealed a row of straight white teeth. "I said I hated movies. I didn't say I hated theatre. I like musicals."

The detective is a musical theatre buff. Only in New York City.

"I loved *Chicago, A Chorus Line, Sweeny Todd,*

Pippin, Grease, Annie, Applause. Lately I've been doing community theatre. I played the Tinman in *The Wiz*. But hey, I also liked *La Cage Aux Folles*. I know you like the gays. And I'm cool with that."

"Where were we?" Jana asked.

"Stanley was upstage center."

"Right. Stanley told us to gather for warm up theatre exercises. Everyone moved in various directions all around him."

"Wasn't the bookcase piece fastened to anything?"

Jana shook her head. "The builders had just delivered it from the scene shop. Anyone could have nudged it forward, and set it off balance—without being noticed."

"And everyone was near it?

"I'm afraid so."

He looked around the dressing room. "Who do you play in *China Doll*?"

"Are you coming to see it?"

He shook his head. "I only like musicals. Who do you play?"

"An amateur sleuth."

"That fits."

"By the end of the play, I figure out that my neighbor has murdered two people."

"Why?"

"My neighbor's fiancé left her to marry an heiress with a weak heart. So my neighbor killed the heiress, married him, then killed him."

"For the money?"

Jana nodded. "And for revenge, since he talked her into getting an abortion."

"How does your character figure it out?"

"By talking to a little boy in the building who overheard the murderer and her mother plotting the murders."

Dwayne said, "It sounds pretty lame. Maybe you can add some songs before opening night."

I can see Bella and me singing a duet as she attacks me and I wrestle her to the ground. "Don't tell Katrina Wright."

"The playwright?"

"The *famous* playwright of twenty thrillers."

Dwayne stood. "Let's go."

"Where?"

"To start the interviews. Let's see if there's anything to your murder theory. Follow me, little shop girl."

Jana followed the detective into Savannah Stevens' dressing room next door. The aging legend sat in an easy chair, looking out the window down at the busy city street.

"Miss Stevens, I'm Detective Douglas. Jana Lane is accompanying me as Equity Deputy. I would like to ask you some questions."

"Of course."

As Jana and Dwayne sat on stools at the makeup table, she noticed tears in Savannah's eyes. "Are you all right, Savannah?"

Savannah waved a manicured hand. "I'll be fine. Stan and I had our disagreements, but we went back nearly forty years. As you get older, that means a lot."

"I have only a few questions for you." The detective asked, "Where were you when the bookcase piece fell on Stanley Rothman?"

"I had come from Jana's dressing room, and I was

standing with everyone on stage. When Stan called us to encircle him for theatre exercises, we all moved forward."

"Did you see anyone touch the bookcase scenery?"

"No." Savannah added, "Though we were all so close to it, anybody could have done so."

"You said you've known Mr. Rothman for forty years?" Douglas asked.

Savannah replied, "He, Kat, and I were old friends. He produced my first play in New York, *Sweet Nothings* by Katrina Wright." She smiled at Jana. "Starring Scott Lane and his five-year-old daughter, Jana, making her Broadway debut." She seemed to pull back the pages of time. "I was with my second husband at the time."

"And all these years later Rothman offered you a role in *China Doll*?"

"Not exactly." Savannah sat up straight. "I called *him*. I also phoned Kat. This was about a year ago. My career was at a...pause. I wanted to return to my roots. I asked them if they had a play for me. A month ago, Stan called and said he did. I was thrilled."

Jana said, "And you must have been so disappointed when we did the first read-through and you didn't like your role."

"What's wrong with it?" Dwayne asked.

She doesn't sing a ballad at the end of Act I.

Savannah looked at herself in the dressing room mirror on the wall. "It seems I've been relegated to play the killer's evil mother."

So different from the heroine beauties you played on screen.

Dwayne shook his head from side to side. "How

ironic that you all are doing a play about murder, and the producer of the play may have been murdered."

Savannah unleashed a sad smile. "Life is full of irony, detective."

Dwayne continued. "Your stage manager told me your son is in the cast. Have you and your son worked together before?"

"No." Savannah's forehead wrinkled and her makeup cracked. "But I've been getting him ready for this day for quite a while."

"Getting him ready?"

"When I was a young woman, I was determined to be a success. My star rose quickly. After Broadway, I went to Hollywood at twenty-four. There were a number of hit films, then a few flops. Then a few more. That led to television then to unemployment. I advised Peter to study, learn his craft, do theatre Off-Broadway, take things slowly."

He's thirty-six.

"My son is an amazing talent, and an incredibly good-looking young man."

I think I noticed. "My agent predicted Peter will be offered film roles after *China Doll* opens."

Savannah nodded proudly. "And when that happens I will guide him to the right properties. Otherwise when he's sixty, he'll be playing a role like mine in *China Doll*."

And need to put up the money to produce it. "Savannah, Peter told me you invested a great deal of money into the show."

Savannah said, "Stan told me they lost money on Katrina's last two plays. He said I could either put up the cash or look for another stale sitcom. So I put up the cash."

Jana asked, "While I was rehearsing my scene with Bella and Brad on stage, is that what you, Stanley, and Katrina argued about in the house?"

"Is everything all right, Mom?"

"Come in, Mr. Stevens." Detective Douglas led Peter Stevens to a stool at the makeup table next to Jana's. "We were talking with your mother about the tragic incident on the stage earlier today."

"Peter was standing next to me when the bookcase came crashing down."

"I can speak for myself, Mom," Peter said like a teenager at parents' night.

As Peter ran a thick hand through his shiny hair, Jana noticed his biceps bulge. *My palpitation just had a palpitation.*

"I was focused on my mother since she wasn't feeling well," Peter explained to Douglas.

"Are you all right now, Miss Stevens?"

"I will be…once I'm allowed to go back to my hotel suite and rest."

"That will happen very soon." Dwayne shifted his focus to Savannah's son. "Mr. Stevens, how well did you know Mr. Rothman?"

Peter replied, "I didn't know him at all. Mom talked about *the good old days on the upper West side* constantly, but I was too young to remember. I've lived most of my life in LA."

"But Savannah told us you've been doing theatre rather than films," Jana said.

"Mom and I sublet a place downtown when I'm doing a play in New York," Peter answered.

Dwayne asked, "So you didn't meet Stanley

Rothman until today?"

Before Peter could respond, Savannah said, "Stanley was *my* old friend, not my son's."

The detective asked, "Who do you play in *China Doll*, Mr. Stevens?"

"The police detective."

"So you play *me*," Dwayne chortled.

"And I'm Jana's love interest," Peter added.

Dwayne laughed. "Don't get any ideas about me, Jana. I'm happily married with children."

"As am I." Jana felt weak at the knees from Peter's creamy mint scent.

Dwayne said to Peter, "Do you nab the killer in the play?"

Peter put a strong arm around her. "With Jana's help. And B.J.'s."

"I'm B.J.'s son." Jana tried to pull herself together. "I mean, in real life B.J. is my daughter."

Peter removed his arm and Jana was able to speak sensibly. "B.J. is my son in real life. In the play he is my babysitting charge." *Remember the investigation, girl.* "Peter, do you think Stanley's death was an accident?"

Peter's eyes widened. "Hell, no. Every person on that stage despised him. We were each inches away from that bookcase, and there was a great deal of movement just before it fell. I think somebody purposely tipped it over."

Dwayne replied, "Your co-star has the same theory, Mr. Stevens."

Peter squeezed Jana's shoulder into his strong chest. "Geniuses think alike."

"I think we're through here," Dwayne said.

Thank goodness. This is more than any straight woman with a heartbeat should have to resist.

"Miss Stevens, Mr. Stevens, you are both free to leave." The detective added, "Jose will give me your hotel suite contact information if I need anything else."

Peter was inches away from her. "Would you like to share a taxi back to the hotel, Jana?"

What's a hotel?

"Jana has more important things to do," Savannah said with a pat to Peter's shoulder.

Douglas nodded. "As the Equity Representative, Jana needs to stay for all the interviews."

"Since I nominated Jana, I'll stay, too."

"I'd like to get back to the hotel suite, Peter. It's been a long day," Savannah said.

The detective ushered Savannah and Peter out of the dressing room. "I'll drive Jana back to her hotel myself."

Peter locked eyes with Jana. "Are you sure you'll be all right?"

As soon as I stop gaping at you. "Thank you for your concern, Peter. I'll be fine. Unfortunately, I've had a bit of experience in this arena."

Douglas laughed. "I wouldn't be in a movie or play with her. People drop like flies when this woman's around."

Jana said to Peter, "Your mother's right. It's been a long day."

Peter released his adorable dimples and took Jana's hand. "But it's also been an *amazing* day."

"We will see you tomorrow, Jana." Savannah looked deep into Jana's eyes. "Be careful."

Savannah and Peter left, and Douglas and Jana

walked past Peter's empty dressing room into Bella's definitely not empty dressing room. They stood in the center of the room and watched Bella and Brad kissing on Bella's easy chair.

The grieving granddaughter.

Brad and Bella looked up like children caught playing spin-the-bottle.

"I'm Detective Douglas. My condolences for your loss, Miss Talloway."

Bella seemed to remember her deceased grandfather. "Oh, thank you, detective." A tear filled her eye. "I miss him already."

I may have underrated Bella as an actress. Jana took a seat. "Brad, why don't you sit at the makeup table with me?" She turned to Dwayne. "Brad is my nephew."

"In the play?" Dwayne asked.

"In real life."

"I'm Bella's love interest and neighbor in the play," Brad explained.

The two young people seemed like stretched rubber as they reluctantly took their separate seats.

Dwayne sat on the windowsill. "Miss Talloway, your grandfather has been taken to the hospital."

"A lot of good *that* will do," Bella replied.

"By now he is probably in the morgue. Your parents have been called to identify him and make the arrangements," Dwayne explained.

Bella laughed. "That's rich."

"What do you mean?" Jana asked.

"My parents couldn't stand Grandpop, and he detested them. His funeral will be tomorrow. In his religion, the deceased are buried quickly. My mother will put on a good show by weeping and wailing. It's ironic that she hates theatre so much. She's a pretty good actress."

Jana asked, "Your parents aren't supportive of your career?"

Bella chuckled. "They want me to be a secretary. Grandpop was the only one who ever believed in me…and my talents."

Jana asked, "Do you share your grandfather's religion?"

"No. Neither do my parents. That's the only thing my parents and I have in common."

The detective rubbed his large chin. "Where were you both when Miss Talloway's grandfather was hit by the bookcase?"

Brad answered, "Bella and I were standing around Mr. Rothman, liked he asked us to."

"Did you see anyone touch the bookcase piece?" the detective asked.

Bella leaped out of her chair. "I just remembered. I saw Tony touch it!"

Dwayne asked Jana, "Who's Tony?"

"Tony Cuccioli is our director." Jana added, "And our playwright's husband."

"How did Tony touch the set piece?" Douglas asked.

Bella closed her eyes. "The set piece shook a bit. Tony straightened it against the back wall of the stage."

Dwayne asked, "When was this?"

"It was when Grandpop made his announcements. Before he asked us to surround him."

"So the timing wasn't right for Tony to move the scenery piece to fall on your grandfather," Dwayne replied.

"I guess not." Bella sighed and sat down.

Dwayne said to Jana, "If the set piece was shaking, it could have been an accident."

Jana thought of her rags to riches character in *The Adorable Orphan.* "Bella, have you seen your grandfather's will?"

"No," Bella replied. "But I know what it says."

"How?" the detective asked.

"Grandpop told me."

Jana slid to the edge of her seat. "Who inherits Stanley's money?"

"I do. Well, half of it." Bella added, "I also get his stocks, bonds, his duplex on the east side, the lake house in Connecticut, and Grandpop's car."

Brad salivated like a starving dog at a cookout.

"Who gets the other half of Rothman's money?" the detective asked.

Bella replied, "Katrina."

Brad stood. "Don't you think you've asked Bella enough questions, detective? She's just suffered an incredible loss."

Jana patted the actor on his strong shoulder. "I'm sure you'll comfort Bella."

Dwayne rose. "You are both free to go."

As Dwayne and Jana left Bella's dressing room, the ingénue and juvenile were in the throes of a passionate kiss.

Tate met them at his dressing room entrance. "Am I still fired?"

Jana explained to Dwayne, "Stanley fired Tate this afternoon."

"Why?" Dwayne asked, showing Tate his badge.

"Personal reasons," Jana replied.

Tate said, "I have AIDS, detective."

"Let's come inside." Dwayne led Tate to the easy chair and Jana to a stool at the table. He stood between them. "What did Rothman say when he fired you?"

Tate cringed. "Due to his religion, I can't stay in the cast." He added, "And because he needs to protect his granddaughter."

Dwayne looked at Jana. "Didn't Rothman know people don't get AIDS from sharing a stage?"

"Obviously not," Jana replied.

"How did you feel about being fired, Mr. Moonglow?"

"Obviously, I wasn't happy about it, detective."

Dwayne asked Jana, "Does he have a large role in the play?"

Jana answered, "Yes. Tate plays Bella's first love who leaves her for Sally's money, and talks Bella into getting an abortion. After Bella kills Sally, she marries Tate herself."

"Then she kills me," Tate replied.

"Sounds like a role worth fighting for." The detective moved to the window. "Were you standing with Miss Talloway before the bookcase fell on Mr. Rothman?"

"Tate was next to me," Jana said.

"I had a dizzy spell. Jana offered me support," Tate explained.

"And were you two together when Rothman asked everyone to come around him for the exercise?" Dwayne asked.

"We were separated in all the activity." Tate walked over to Jana. "Am I still in the cast, Jana?"

"Of course you are." Jana rose. "My assumption is Katrina or Tony will take over as producer."

"Katrina doesn't want me in the show either," Tate replied.

"Why not?" Dwayne asked.

"I'm against her religion, too," Tate replied.

Dwayne looked at Jana. "Is this a Broadway show or a church?"

Jana patted Tate's shoulder. "We'll work it out. Go home and get some rest."

"May I?" Tate asked Dwayne.

"You heard the boss," the detective replied.

Jana and Dwayne passed Brad's empty dressing room. Standing in front of B.J.'s dressing room, her son threw himself into Jana's arms. "Mommy!"

"Hello, honey. This is Detective Douglas."

"What's a defective?" B.J. asked.

He laughed. "Let's go inside and I'll explain it to you, B.J." Dwayne led Jana and B.J. into B.J.'s dressing room, where Gary sat on the floor next to a plastic space station.

"Enjoying yourself, Gary?" Jana asked with a smile.

Gary rose and pushed his glasses up the bridge of his nose. "B.J. was beating me in an intergalactic battle."

"B.J. is space captain!" The three-year-old grabbed a toy spaceship and waved it around, making a woooshing sound.

Jana sat on the easy chair with B.J. and the spaceship on her lap. Dwayne and Gary took the stools at the makeup table.

"B.J., Detective Douglas is a police officer," Jana

explained.

"I want to be a policeman!"

Dwayne wants to be on Broadway. So you're even.

"B.J., how would you like to help me?" Dwayne asked.

"Yeah!" B.J. jumped up and down on Jana's lap.

Dwayne asked, "Were you on the stage when the bookcase fell on Mr. Rothman?"

"B.J. with Gary," B.J. answered.

"Did you touch the bookcase, B.J., or did you see anyone else touch it?" Dwayne asked.

"B.J. wanted to play. Gary said no." B.J. giggled. "But Gary played."

Gary scratched his neck.

"When did Gary play with the bookcase, B.J.?" Dwayne asked.

"When B.J. was on stage," B.J. answered.

"How about when Mr. Rothman talked to everyone? Did Gary play with the bookcase then?" Dwayne asked.

"No!" B.J. shouted. "Gary with B.J. Gary is B.J.'s natty!"

"That's nanny, honey." Jana kissed B.J.'s neck.

Dwayne asked, "B.J., where were you before the bookcase fell down?"

"B.J. lost Gary!"

Gary explained, "I was holding B.J.'s hand. When everyone came forward to encircle Stanley for the warm up exercise, B.J. and I lost contact briefly."

"Gary found B.J.!"

"Thank goodness." Jana hugged her son.

Dwayne turned his attention to Gary. "Are you enjoying your position, Gary?"

Gary sneered. "I was—until Stanley Rothman barred me from the theatre."

Jana explained, "Gary offered Katrina his opinions on the play. Not always a safe thing to do to a playwright."

"I assume you don't like the play," Dwayne said to Gary.

Gary raised his eyes to the ceiling molding. "The play isn't believable."

"How so?" Dwayne asked.

"Bella and Savannah ask B.J. not to tell anyone what he overheard," Gary said.

"That Bella and Savannah killed Sally and Tate," Jana explained to Dwayne.

Gary said, "Why would they expect B.J. to do what they say, unless they bribed him or threatened him in some way for eavesdropping?"

Jana replied, "In the play, B.J.'s character tells my character what he overheard." Jana said to Dwayne, "Which leads to a physical confrontation between Bella's character and my character at the climax."

Gary continued. "But Bella's and Savannah's characters aren't stupid. Why would they simply ask B.J. not to tell?" He scratched his long nose. "And since Brad marries Bella at the end, and they're all friends, why wouldn't Bella and Jana just keep the inheritance money?"

Maybe because my character has morals. "Gary, I appreciate your interest in B.J. and the play, but playwrights like to write their own plays. They can get very touchy when other people critique them."

Gary replied like a spoiled child, "But Rothman didn't have to bar me from the theatre just for speaking my mind."

Dwayne rested his hand on Gary's narrow shoulder. "I understand how you feel, Gary. After I saw *Grease*, I wondered why Danny didn't go with Rizzo and forget Sandy. Rizzo was much more fun."

B.J. asked, "Mommy, when do we play on stage?"

Jana replied, "Tomorrow, honey."

"Will Stanley be there?"

"I'm afraid not, honey."

"Where is Stanley?" B.J. asked.

"He's resting, honey."

"Okay. He's really old." B.J. ran to Gary with his toy spaceship. "Play battle!"

Gary looked to Jana, and Jana looked to Dwayne who said, "Thank you for your time, B.J. You, too, Gary."

"Gary, can you please take B.J. back to the hotel and order dinner for both of you?" Jana asked.

"Sure," Gary replied.

"B.J. wants pastranami!" B.J. shouted.

"That's pastrami," Gary said.

B.J.'s a New Yorker in no time.

"I'll take him to the deli," Gary said to Jana.

"I'll have Jana back shortly," Dwayne said.

Jana said softly to Dwayne, "I hope all this doesn't mar B.J."

"I doubt he'll remember much about it as time goes on."

Gary said to Dwayne, "As a nanny, I've taken a number of classes about children's behaviors. Psychologists believe kids store memories beginning at three years old. B.J. may remember more than you think."

I hope B.J. isn't on a psychiatrist's couch by the time the play closes.

Dwayne smiled. "On the positive side, B.J. will remember performing in a Broadway play." He winked at Jana. "If he's anything like his mother, this is only his first production."

Jana and Dwayne found Sally and Tony in whispered conversation in Sally's dressing room. Dwayne showed his badge. "I would like to ask you a couple of questions about Stanley Rothman's accident earlier today."

Accident?

Jana, Sally, and Tony sat opposite the makeup table, and Dwayne stood across from them. "Miss Chen and Mr. Cuccioli, can you please tell me where you were when the set piece fell on Stanley Rothman?"

Sally repaired her blood-red lipstick. "I was swept up in the crowd."

Tony replied, "I was sulking on stage."

"Why is that?" Dwayne asked.

"'Cause Stanley had just given me the ax, hah?"

"Did either of you see anything suspicious before the bookcase fell?"

Sally replied, "I wasn't paying attention."

"Why not?" the detective asked.

"I had a...concern about my role in the play." Sally glared at Tony. "And nobody seemed to care."

Dwayne asked Jana, "Care to fill me in on this?"

Jana explained, "Sally plays the wealthy heiress with a heart condition who Tate marries and Bella murders."

"And the problem is?"

Jana replied, "Sally's character dies at the end of

Act I."

Dwayne said to Sally, "Whatever happened to, 'there are no small roles only small actors'?"

Sally replied, "I had a few ideas to make my role—and thereby the play—more interesting." Sally crossed her shapely legs. "The play is called *China Doll*, after *my* character."

Jana said to Sally, "It was clear that Stanley and Katrina were not interested in hearing your ideas, but Tony spoke to them on your behalf. Yet, you seem angry with Tony now. Why?"

"Because Tony didn't plead my case enough to Katrina."

"Hey, I tried," Tony replied. "But Kat's the playwright, ain't she?"

"And *you're* the director—and her husband," Sally said with a sniff.

Jana slid to the edge of her stool. "I was standing in the house with Gary and Katrina when you two kissed in the wings. Katrina looked in shock."

"Wouldn't you be in shock if your husband loved someone else?" Sally flicked her dark hair behind her ears.

"Eh, Sally, cut it out, hah?"

Sally threw up her thin arms. "Why keep it a secret, Tony? You said you were going to tell Katrina."

"*After* we get up the show, hah?" Tony replied.

Dwayne said, "So you two working together could be a problem if Katrina Wright finds out about your…relationship?"

"It's not a problem, detective." Katrina entered the dressing room. "I've known about their affair for quite some time."

Chapter 4

Since Detective Douglas received an emergency phone call, Jana left the theatre that evening alone.

"Jana, I hear Stanley Rothman is dead." Rollo R. Rorro winked a bloodshot eye at her. "Given your past encounters with murder, are you assisting the police in the investigation?"

Standing in front of the theatre, Jana nearly chipped a tooth on the microphone near her mouth. "Detective Dwayne Douglas is investigating."

Roll blocked her way. "Since Stanley was Bella Talloway's grandfather, will the end of Stanley mean the end of nepotism—resulting in Bella on unemployment?"

"No cast changes have been made." Jana walked down the block.

Roll followed and said to her back, "Are the rumors true that you and Sally Chen are in a *Dynasty*-type cat fight for star status?"

Jana turned to face him. "The play is an ensemble piece."

He scratched at his oily skin and looked up. "Yet, your name is over the title on the marquee."

Maybe it will fall on you. "Speak to Katrina Wright."

His eyes glimmered. "Is it true that you and handsome Peter Stevens are an item—to Savannah

Stevens' chagrin?"

"Of course not. I only have eyes for you, Roll." Jana hailed a taxi and was off.

Jana entered her hotel suite to the sound of Tina Turner's "What's Love Got to Do with It?" blaring from Brad's bedroom. Since his door was open, Jana stood at the doorway and gasped at the sight of her nephew and Bella Talloway in the throes of lovemaking.

I guess she got over her mourning for Grandpop. Jana closed Brad's door and headed to her bedroom, where she sat on the white satin chaise next to the window and looked out at the panoramic view of New York City. The tall buildings and multicolored lights were quite a different view from her upstate New York mansion's scenes of trees, mountains, rivers, gardens, and lawn. She picked up the ornate gold phone and called Devan and Ed at camp. Her boys caught Jana up on all of their activities, including canoeing, paint-balling, playing basketball, swimming, wrestling, and eating at cookouts. Jana told them how much she loved them, and they promised to behave, then Jana reluctantly hung up the phone. Since she had a message from the hotel clerk to call Brian, Jana was about to pick up the phone again when it rang. "Yes?"

"I was hoping you would say that."

"Peter?"

"You *are* a good sleuth."

They shared a laugh.

Jana asked, "How's your mother?"

"Sound asleep, thanks to a tranquilizer. How come I don't hear B.J.?"

"Gary took him to a Jewish delicatessen for

dinner."

"Smart boy. Did Brad go with them?"

"Not exactly." Jana rose and closed her bedroom door. "Brad's in his bedroom—with Bella."

"Brad works fast."

"Bella does, too. After she leaves, I'm calling room service and collapsing onto this enormous brass bed with silk sheets."

"But you just said, yes."

"To what?"

"Letting me take you out to dinner."

She sat on the chaise. "Thank you, Peter, but I'm too tired to go out anywhere." *Even with you.*

"Who said anything about going out? I hear the restaurant at the top floor of the hotel has an amazing view and equally amazing cuisine."

"I don't want to get all dressed up."

"You looked terrific today. Stay in those clothes." He laughed. "I never thought I'd hear myself ask a beautiful woman to stay dressed."

"I don't know." *If I can trust myself alone with you.*

"You have to eat."

Jana let herself admit she wanted to have dinner with Peter. "All right. Thank you."

"My pleasure. I'll meet you there in fifteen minutes."

"It's a date." *No it isn't!*

Jana hung up the phone and heard a knock at her door. "Come in."

Brad looked like a puppy with his tail caught between his legs.

"Is Bella still here?" Jana asked.

"She went back to her apartment."

"And you two didn't go there *because*?"

"Bella said it's not very nice. She's excited about moving into her grandfather's duplex. Besides, I thought you would be staying at the theatre longer. I wanted to show Bella our cool hotel suite."

Jana motioned for Brad to sit next to her on the chaise. "Brad, I don't think anyone would call me a prude."

"Actually, I—"

Jana hit his shoulder playfully. "B.J. is a bright little boy who asks questions about everything, and unfortunately he repeats most things he hears. So, if you are entertaining Bella here, please lower the music, close and lock your bedroom door, and don't open it until both of you are dressed. Okay?"

He nodded. "I'll be more careful."

"Thank you. Now, did you two use birth control?"

"Of course. Bella and I want to be rich and famous before we have kids."

Why am I not surprised?

"Bella's inheritance will help get us on our way."

"Brad, you've only known Bella one day. Take things slowly with her."

Brad raised his eyes to the wall sconces. "If you meet someone who's the right one, why wait? You told me you knew Brian was the guy for you when you two met at a town hall meeting in Hyde Park. It's the same with Bella and me. We really click. I'm nuts about that girl."

Who am I to stand in the way of ten-hour true love? Jana pushed the blond hair off his smooth forehead. "I've missed you. I'm glad we're spending time together."

"Me too." Brad glowed like a light bulb. "And the first day of rehearsal was great."

Except when the producer was murdered.

He revealed his white smile. "I like my role, and I like winding up with Bella at the end of the play."

Though she plays a murderess.

"I bet this leads me to doing movies. Thanks for working this out for me."

"I was happy to help. And Stanley and Katrina liked your audition."

"Stanley, ouch." Brad asked, "What did Detective Douglas say after he talked to everyone at the theatre? Does he think Stanley's death was an accident?"

"Unfortunately, yes."

"But you don't?"

"No."

Brad's bicep bulged as he leaned on the side of the chaise. "Bella's really upset about it."

"She's a good actress."

"I know. We make a great couple on stage." He giggled. "And off."

"You both did very well at rehearsal today, but that's not what I meant." She took his hand. "Bella doesn't seem to be very sad or surprised about her grandfather's death."

"Bella loved her grandfather like crazy, Aunt Jana. But he was really old. She knew he would die someday."

Jana sighed. "We'll all die someday, but hopefully not under suspicious circumstances."

Brad leaned back. "Who do you think killed him?"

"I don't know."

"But I bet you'll find out. Good night, Aunt Jana."

Brad left her bedroom, and Jana thought twice about not dressing up for dinner. She ran into the walk-in closet and changed into a strapless metallic black lycra dress. Then, sitting at the white vanity, she re-teased her hair and re-applied her makeup. Finally, Jana left a note for Gary and said goodbye to Brad—who was on the phone with Bella.

Standing at the doorway to the hotel's restaurant, Jana felt a warm breath on her shoulders, and smelled the scent of fresh mint.

"You look gorgeous."

Jana took in her dinner companion's European dark suit. "I thought we weren't changing for dinner."

Peter smiled. "Looks like we're both liars."

The host sat them at a table overlooking the west side of Manhattan and gave them their menus. Peter ordered white wine. While they waited for their drinks, they sat for a few moments enjoying the gorgeous view. As it was sunset, the tall buildings were surrounded by waves of scarlet, violet, and gold. Lionel Ritchie's "All Night Long" played from the restaurant's sound system.

Once the waiter served their wine, and they perused the menus, Peter asked Jana, "What would you like?"

You, but that's not possible. Jana said to the waiter, "I'd like the Coquilles Saint-Jacques appetizer and Sole Meuniere for the main course. Thank you."

Peter looked like a lost tourist in the French Alps. "I'll have what she's having."

"Very well." As the waiter took back their menus, he asked, "Excuse me, are you Jana Lane?"

Jana smiled. "Yes. What's your name?"

"Marco."

"It's nice to meet you, Marco." She shook his hand.

"It's even nicer to meet you." The older man blushed. "My daughters loved your old movies."

"Which was their favorite?" Peter asked, unleashing his dimples.

Marco replied, "*The Tiny Eskimo*, where you rode on the wolf to save little Timmy from the hunter. No, the *Jungle Girl*, where you wrestled the ape to save little Timmy. Or maybe *The Pirate Princess*, where you fought off the pirate king and steered the boat back to your father."

Peter laughed. "It sounds like *you're* a fan of Jana's old movies yourself."

He nodded. "They don't make movies like that anymore."

"Except for *His Obsession* and *Madam Senator*," Peter said.

Marco looked confused. "I didn't see those."

Jana offered a smile. "Thank you for liking my old movies, Marco. Please give your daughters my best wishes."

"I will. Thank you, Miss Lane. And your dessert is on us."

Once Marco left humming the theme song to *Young Mermaid*, Peter said, "You must get that a lot."

She nodded. "You will, too, when your movies are released."

"I have to be cast in them first."

Jana asked, "Have you auditioned for any films?"

He sat back in his chair. "Three so far."

"And?"

He shrugged his broad shoulders. "I got an offer, but my mother didn't like the script."

Probably because there wasn't a role for her in it. Jana took a sip of wine. "What was it about?"

"It was a low budget independent film. I would have played a police officer who falls in love with the woman he's protecting."

"Careful not to get typecast."

His green eyes glimmered in the candlelight. "I would have done the film if you were my leading lady."

Jana looked at her wedding ring. "Peter, I hope this isn't too personal, but why aren't you married?"

He laughed. "Is thirty-six over the hill?"

"Of course not, but someone with your looks, charm, and talent should have been nabbed by now."

"I got nabbed a few times, but it didn't take."

"How come?"

"My mother didn't like two of them."

"And the others?"

"They didn't like me."

They're fools! They drank their wine. Mesmerized by Peter's strong nose, square jaw, and strapping build, Jana put down her wine and spilled it on the table. Marco patted dry the white silk tablecloth and brought Jana a new glass. When they were alone again, she said to Peter, "I apologize."

"No harm done."

Ready to come clean, Jana asked, "Peter, can I be honest with you?"

"I don't think Jana Lane could be anything but honest."

She swallowed hard. "I like you."

"I like you, too."

"And I'm attracted to you."

"I'm attracted to you, too."

"And this is a problem since I'm happily married with three children. We shouldn't be having dinner together."

"What's wrong with dinner?"

"You know what I mean."

He took her hand. "Jana, I know you're married. And I understand what that means. But since you've been honest with me, let me return the favor. I have never been more attracted to a woman than I am attracted to you. When we met, it was like I found a lost treasure. I know we've only known each other one day, but I like being with you. It feels comfortable and right. If it never gets beyond the friendship and colleague stage, I'll be disappointed, but I can live with that."

Jana exhaled for the first time that evening. "Peter, I feel the same way about you. When we're together, it feels...right." She smiled. "Maybe we were lovers in another lifetime?"

"Too bad we can't recall our past lives."

Marco served the appetizers, then Jana dug into a warm, creamy, scallop. "Based on her behavior at rehearsal today, it's obvious your mother doesn't approve of you spending time with a married woman. I can't say I blame her."

Peter speared a scallop. "Mom has always been a doting mother. It drives me a little crazy, but I like knowing she still cares so much."

"Were you close to your father as well?"

"Unfortunately, no. He was away a lot on business." His handsome face saddened. "And as I mentioned, he died of cancer when I was a kid."

Jana squeezed his hand. "My mother died of cancer when I was a girl. It's something I'll never forget either."

"But you were close to your father. You did *Sweet Nothings* on stage together, and all those films in Hollywood with him."

"I adored him, and I wanted to be just like him."

"Is he still alive?"

Jana shook her head no.

"I'm sorry."

Let's change the subject. "Were you close to your mother's *third* husband?"

"No. He didn't stick around very long."

"When I worked with your mom in *Sweet Nothings*, I was only five years old, and she was twenty-three, but I remember her as a fun-loving woman who enjoyed playing games with me in her dressing room."

"That sounds like Mom."

"But it doesn't. Not today anyway. Savannah seemed...preoccupied and on guard."

Peter sighed. "Mom's been going through a lot lately."

"Do you mean Stanley not casting her unless she invested in our show?"

He nodded. "And her realization that she's become a character woman."

Jana wiped her mouth with her silk napkin. "Peter, there's something I don't understand. Bella told Dwayne that Stanley left Bella and Katrina a fortune in cash, stocks, bonds, cars, and property."

"That makes sense. Stanley seemed to adore his granddaughter, and Katrina is his old friend and theatre partner."

"But if Stanley had all that money, why did he pressure Savannah to give him money to produce our show?"

"Most producers have a firm policy of not putting their own money into their shows. This way if a play flops, the producer keeps his or her assets—and still gets a salary as producer."

"But Katrina's plays weren't flops—except for the last two. The other eighteen were hits. Katrina must have plenty of money. So if Stanley needed capital to produce *China Doll*, why didn't Katrina contribute? Why pressure your mother into investing?"

"Mom, Katrina, and Stanley are old friends. Maybe Stanley was trying to help my mom."

"How so?"

"Mom invested in the show. So she owns shares. If the play is a big hit, she'll get a windfall." He winked at her. "And how can it not be a smash with Jana Lane as our star?"

The busboy cleared their empty plates, then Jana said, "There's something else that's strange, Peter. When Dwayne, Tony Cuciolli, Sally Chen, and I were talking in Sally's dressing room about Sally's disappointment with the size of her role, Katrina told us she knows about Sally and Tony's affair."

"What!"

Feeling like a gossip columnist, Jana said, "Katrina said she didn't care if Tony had a wandering eye. As long as he comes home to her at night. Isn't that archaic?"

Peter's eyes widened. "Or modern—if Katrina's dabbling on the side as well."

"At eighty years old?" *And in poor health?*

"As they say, you're never too old to tango."

Jana sighed. "When we did *Sweet Nothings*, I thought Katrina and Stanley were kind, wonderful people."

"And now?"

For some reason I feel I can trust you. "I don't approve of the way they treated people today."

"You mean my mom?"

"And Sally and Gary. I understand a playwright puts her heart and soul into her work, but Katrina and Stanley didn't have to be so harsh when Sally asked if her role could be lengthened, and Gary gave them his thoughts about B.J.'s role."

"It is funny that your nanny thinks he's a theatre critic. And even though Katrina says it doesn't bother her about Sally and Tony, my bet is she gave Sally a small role as payback."

Jana leaned forward. "Worst of all is the way they treated Tate. He's struggling with a serious illness. Rather than helping Tate play his role, they fired him due to their religious beliefs! I have religious beliefs of my own, and none of them include firing people who are trying to do their job."

"So, why don't we do something about it?"

"I've already said publicly I'll quit if Tate is fired."

"I'm thinking on a larger scale." Peter unleashed a devilish, adorable grin. "You've sponsored two AIDS benefits. Why not do one on Broadway—with the performers from the current shows?"

I really like this guy. "Will you help me?"

"Of course."

They finished their dinners and desserts—vanilla

crème brulee—then left the restaurant.

Peter walked Jana to the doorway of her suite. "I had a great time."

"Me, too."

He chuckled like a teenager on his first date. "I'd love to come inside."

"Not a good idea."

"I understand." He kissed her forehead. "Get some rest."

"See you in the morning at rehearsal."

He called from down the hallway. "Can't wait to rehearse our scenes."

Upon entering her suite, Jana passed through the living room and found Brad's bedroom empty. *He's no doubt out somewhere with Bella.* She read a bedtime story to B.J., tucked him in, then said goodnight to B.J. and Gary.

Jana washed and dressed for bed, then lay in her twilight-blue satin nightgown on the white silk sheets of her brass bed. She called Brian back at his hotel in Las Vegas. "Is this the best mall designer in the country?"

"Only the *country?* Why not the world?"

They shared a laugh.

Her husband said, "Hi, beautiful. How's the Big Apple?"

Jana sighed. "I wish you were working on a mall project here."

"Vegas is wild and wacky enough for me."

"Things aren't going well?"

"I don't want to bore you with my work problems."

"Bore away. What are wives for?"

"It's the usual stuff. Budget issues. Holes in the designs. Permit delays. My brother champing at the bit to start construction."

"You solved those problems before, and you'll do it again."

He chortled. "So says my wife."

"So says the woman who knows you."

He yawned.

"Am I boring you?"

"It's been a long day."

"Tell me about it."

"Is B.J. bouncing off the walls?" he asked.

"B.J. is fine. He took to the stage like his grandfather, his mother, and his cousin."

"Uh-oh."

"And Gary is a good nanny—and somewhat of a theatre critic."

"What do you mean?"

"Gary told Katrina her play wasn't very believable."

"Is it?"

"Not terribly, but it's well written."

"Who do you play?"

"An amateur sleuth who figures out her neighbor murdered the woman's husband and his ex-wife for money and revenge."

"Type casting. How's the rest of the cast?"

"Nice." *Time to change the subject.* "The hotel suite is gorgeous."

"And?"

"The food is terrific."

"And?"

"It was interesting seeing Stanley, Katrina, and Savannah again."

"You might as well tell me, or we'll be up all

night."

Here it comes. "A piece of scenery from the show fell on Stanley and killed him."

"I knew it!"

"Dwayne thinks it was an accident."

"Not if Jana Lane Otley was anywhere nearby. And who's Dwayne?"

"Detective Douglas."

"Of course."

"He and I questioned everyone in the cast, since we were all moving around Stanley on stage when the set piece fell on him."

"Here we go again."

"And I'm the Equity Deputy. And I'm convinced Stanley was murdered."

"Jan, quit the play and come home right away."

"I'll do no such thing."

"How many times do you have to get caught up in murder?"

"*I* didn't murder anyone."

"No, but you're determined to figure out who did it. And once you start asking questions and talking about your old movie plots, the murderer will come after *you*."

"Peter is watching out for me."

"And Peter, whoever he is, is no doubt in love with you?"

"Peter Stevens is Savannah's son. He plays the police detective and my love interest in the play."

"Are there kissing scenes?"

"Just one...or two at most. And in real life he's only kissed me on the forehead after we went out to dinner."

"Jan, babe, please don't get involved in this. For B.J.'s sake. For my sake. Please go home."

"B.J. is having the time of his life. And so am I."

He sighed. "Of course you are."

"Besides, Tate needs me."

"And Tate is?"

"Tate Moonglow. He plays the murderer's husband. Her first husband. Brad plays her second husband, which is fitting since I caught them in Brad's bed tonight."

"Brad and Tate?"

"No, Brad and Bella. Aren't you listening? Tate has AIDS, and Stanley and Katrina tried to fire him. But I wouldn't let them."

"That's my girl."

"Peter and I are going to sponsor an AIDS benefit on Broadway. I'm going to call Simon and Cornelius to help."

"Sure you are." After a pause, Brian said, "Wait a minute. If Stanley Rothman was killed, who is going to produce the show?"

"Katrina, I guess. She and Bella inherited Stanley's money. Katrina's second husband, Tony, is directing— sort of. He's less than half Katrina's age, and he's openly having an affair with Sally Chen. Sally plays Tate's first wife. She isn't happy about the size of her role. And Savannah is putting in a bunch of the money, which seems strange to me since Stanley and Katrina are loaded."

"Jan, I'm not even going to try to understand all this. Please, come home."

"Brian, trust me. I need to be here. For my career…and for me. Come visit me as soon as you can."

Brian groaned. "All right. I give up. Star in your play. Find your murderer. But promise me you'll take care of yourself, babe. I couldn't live without you."

"You mean you don't want to have a wife *and* a girlfriend like Tony Cuccioli?"

"I *have* a wife and a girlfriend, and it's you, babe. Tell that to Peter and Tony and any other guy who comes near you."

"There's only one guy for me."

"It better be me."

"Sure. As I said in my old movies, 'Always and forever.'"

"Right back at you. Be careful, babe. Don't go anywhere alone. And if you trust this Peter guy, stay close to him."

"I love you, Brian."

"You're my life, babe."

I'm a lucky woman indeed.

Jana hung up the phone and rested back on her large silk pillow. She read the Equity Handbook, then reached for her script on the night table to study her lines. Soon her eyes grew heavy.

****

Jana Lane stumbled and fell on the floor of the dark stage. With her heart pounding in her ears, Jana scrambled to her feet and ran in the opposite direction of the footsteps. She crashed into something. Holding her throbbing leg, Jana made her way around a chair with the menacing footsteps growing louder and louder until—

Jana jumped up in bed with a scream. Realizing she was awake, she held onto the brass headboard and took in some deep breaths. Looking at the clock on the night table, she noticed it was time to get out of bed. So, she showered in the master bathroom's all-glass and gold shower, then hurried to the walk-in closet in the master bedroom to put on mint slacks and a rose scalloped-collared blouse. Sitting at the vanity, she applied mint eye shadow and rose rouge and lipstick. After teasing and layering her hair around her face, Jana added gold shell earrings, and of course her wedding ring.

Upon entering the living room, Jana breathed a sigh of relief to find Gary had gotten B.J. up and dressed in blue-green matching polo shirt and pants. Gary was in his usual white button-down shirt, buttoned to his neck, and black slacks. Brad entered from his bedroom, combing his hair and pulling up the collar of his skin-tight lemon polo shirt. Since Gary had ordered breakfast from room service, the extended family sat at the white table in the living room, looking out at the city that never sleeps, while wolfing down eggs, potatoes, and fruit. When everyone was fed, they hailed a taxi to the theatre.

Rehearsal began as Tony, in his mesh black shirt and black jeans with a dangling gold necklace, stood center stage and called for a moment of silence to honor Stanley. The actors all sat quietly in the front of the house, while Katrina wept openly in her same seat in the front row. Then Tony said, "Since the show must go on and all, Kat and me will produce. I'm still the director too, and youse are all still in the show, hah?"

Tate raised his hand then stood on long, shaky legs. "Am I still in the cast?"

Jana rose. "Of course you are, Tate."

Jose said from the stage manager's console off

stage, "Break in an hour-and-a-half, Tony."

"Yo, let's get to work, youse guys."

Jose had set chairs on stage to represent Sally's apartment. Tony asked Tate and Sally to come up on stage to rehearse the scene where Tate woos Sally into marrying him.

As Tate, Sally, and Tony rehearsed on stage, B.J. ran away from Gary in the house and plopped himself in his mother's arms. "Mommy, Bella is cold. She sits and shivers."

"What?"

Brad appeared and affectionately messed B.J.'s hair. "Bella's sitting shiva at her parents' place for Stanley. She said over the phone that she'll try to get away as soon as she can."

"I want to sit and shiver!" B.J. said.

"Come over here and sit with your cousin."

Brad and B.J. sat together a few rows back, as Gary sat next to Jana up front. "I guess I'm no longer barred from the theatre."

Jana whispered, "Just stay clear of Katrina and Tony."

"My pleasure."

When Gary went off to sit with Brad and B.J., Jana smelled a familiar mint scent as a warm breath grazed her ear. "Get a good night's sleep?"

Jana looked up to find Peter Stevens, looking good enough to eat in a tangerine T-shirt, blue jeans, and a lime blazer. "I'm glad things are back to normal."

"As normal as can be in the theatre." He sat next to her.

"Where's Savannah?"

"I just left her in her dressing room replenishing

her makeup. Jose knows where to find her when Tony needs her."

Jose moved the furniture on stage to represent Bella's apartment. Tony asked for Bella's understudy to come up on stage. Standing next to Sally far stage left, Tony blocked the scene where Tate's character talks Bella's character into aborting their baby. Though Bella's understudy seemed nervous, Jana noticed that Tate did a fine acting job, giving a layered performance even in rehearsal. The character's greed, regret, fear, and concern for Bella's character were all evident in his reading.

Jose moved the furniture back to Sally's apartment, and they rehearsed the next scene where Bella's character holds a bottle of digitalis behind her back, as Sally's character has a heart attack and dies. When the scene was finished, Sally stormed off the stage and slammed her dressing room door. Tony followed her, and Jose called for the first break of the day.

As Tate walked down the stairs from the stage to the house, Katrina met him near the orchestra pit. Wearing a plum business suit with shoulder pads and gold rope jewelry, she looked the role of famous playwright. "May I speak with you a moment?"

"Of course." Tate stood next to her.

Katrina took a step back. "I thought you did a nice job with your scenes."

He smiled. "It has to be on the page before it's on the stage."

"Thank you." Katrina rubbed her necklace. "I want you to know that you are on probation."

"Probation?"

"With Stanley...gone, I've decided to let you stay

in the cast. However, I will be watching you vigilantly to see if you can physically handle the role, and to make sure your presence doesn't upset the other cast members."

Probation! Jana stood on the other side of Katrina. "As the Equity Deputy I need to inform you there is no such thing as a producer putting an Equity member on probation."

Katrina's eyes narrowed. "There is in *this* production."

"Then I have no recourse other than to phone Equity."

Katrina held Jana's arm. "I don't think you understand who the victim is here."

"And who is that, Katrina?" Jana stood with her hand on her hip.

The wrinkles on Katrina's face hardened. "When Tate auditioned for this role, he made no mention of being a homosexual…or of having AIDS."

Tate replied, "Do you talk about your sexual orientation and medical status when you apply for a job, Katrina? Oh, that's right; you don't have to apply for work."

Katrina said to Jana, "I am willing to go against my religious beliefs, and my better judgment, as long as Tate is well enough to do his job." She glared at him. "And as long as he doesn't push himself on others in the cast."

"How exactly would I push myself on others in the cast, Katrina?"

Katrina grimaced. "I know what you people do."

"So, all gays are predators?" Tate asked incredulously.

"My religious beliefs—"

"Katrina, your religion doesn't seem to have served you well."

"And why is that, Jana?" Katrina asked. "Because as a Christian I stand against sinners?"

But not against your second husband and his girlfriend? "I'm a Christian, too, Katrina. And it looks like you missed the story about Jesus cautioning the people of his time not to throw stones."

"Sin is sin," Katrina stated.

Jana replied, "Many so-called religious people believe mystery stories, and theatre for that matter, should be banned as sinful, Katrina."

Katrina locked eyes with Jana. "Don't push me too far, Jana. I said I would allow Tate to stay in the role— for now!" Katrina sat in her seat. "I liked you better as a little girl." She took her fountain pen from her purse, and wrote on her script.

Jana walked down the theatre aisle with Tate. "I'm sorry you have to go through this."

"Thank you for what you did."

Jana smiled. "This is just the beginning."

"You look like you did in *Sugar and Spice* when you had the idea to ride a horse down the cliff and save Timmy. What are you planning?"

Jana laughed. "I'll let you know after lunch."

Bella returned wearing a black lace midriff blouse and skirt. Brad raced over to her, and the young couple kissed in the rear of the house.

"What a trooper you are," Brad said, squeezing Bella into his muscular chest.

"I didn't want my understudy to get accustomed to playing my role." Bella glared at the young woman

110

reading the script in a theatre seat nearby. "Or get accustomed to playing opposite you."

"There's no substitute for you, Bella."

Bella and Brad kissed again.

Jose called Bella on stage to give her the blocking for the scenes she missed. Then he released Bella's understudy.

Jana stood in the aisle and watched as Jose asked the arriving workmen to place the new set pieces in the basement for safekeeping. Then the stage manager moved the stage furniture on stage back to Bella's apartment, and called for everyone to return from break.

Tony came out of Sally's dressing room and continued the blocking rehearsal. Bella and Tate rehearsed the scene where Bella pretends to console Tate for Sally's death. Then Tony called Savannah and B.J. up to the stage to rehearse the scene where B.J. overhears Bella and Savannah discussing how Sally really died, and planning Tate's murder.

As they rehearsed, Jana took a seat up front next to Peter, and beamed at B.J.'s performance. "He did exactly as Tony instructed."

Peter grinned. "He's a chip off the old theatre block."

"So are you." Jana was being kind. Though Savannah fit her role well and was once a strong actress, Savannah seemed void of energy while playing the scene.

When the scene ended, Tony said from the down left corner of the stage, "Yo, Savannah, bring it up a notch, hah?"

Standing center stage, Savannah looked at Katrina in the front row. "I will if my role is brought up a notch."

"Your role is fine as written," Katrina replied, waving her fountain pen at Savannah like a teacher with a pointer.

"It is most definitely *not* fine as written," Savannah said.

"I'm not rewriting a word, Savvie," Katrina replied with an icy stare.

"Aye, you heard the playwright, hah?" Tony said. "Let's move on to the scene where Bella and Savannah catch B.J., and ask him to keep his trap shut about what he heard from the hallway of the apartment building, hah?"

B.J. did the scene off book. Jana's eyes filled with tears as he said his lines loudly, clearly, and with conviction.

Peter whispered in Jana's ear. "You may not be the only award-winning actor in your house for long."

Jana squeezed his hand.

Katrina walked up the stage steps and gave Tony new script pages for the scene. Once she returned to her seat, Tony consulted with the three actors on stage.

"I hope the rewrites don't throw B.J. off too much," Jana whispered to Peter.

Peter replied, "It'll throw my mother off more than B.J."

Jana was happy to see Peter was right. Gary ran up on stage and read B.J. his new lines. B.J. handled the line changes like a pro, even memorizing them on the spot. However, Savannah still seemed unwilling to sink her teeth into her role.

"The scene didn't work before, Kat, and it still doesn't work," Savannah said on stage.

Kat replied from her seat, "You'll make the scene work, Savvie, or you won't be working in this show."

Jose called for a break, and Savannah stormed off to her dressing room with Peter excusing himself and following her.

B.J. raced off the stage into Jana's arms. "How was I, Mommy?"

Jana hugged her son to her chest. "You were wonderful, honey!" Then she looked around the house at the rest of the company.

Gary approached Katrina, still sitting in the front row with her fountain pen and script in hand. "Thank you for not following Stanley's orders to bar me from the theatre." Gary pushed the glasses up the bridge of his nose. "And for taking my suggestion about Bella and Savannah trying to bribe and bully B.J. into submission. I think the scene works better now."

Katrina nodded. "You were right, Mr. Royale."

"I've had a lot of experience."

"Yes."

"Will you change the ending, too, and have Jana and Bella cut a deal for the money?"

Give it a rest, Gary.

Katrina offered him an icy stare. "No."

Tate pulled Gary away from Katrina, and the two men sat near Jana. "Better not push your luck with the dragon lady," Tate said.

Gary replied, "I've been a nanny for many years. I'm just trying to help make the play realistic."

"Don't ask Katrina for co-billing as playwright."

Gary laughed. "That was funny."

"Thanks."

"Given your...condition, I'm sure it's hard to make

jokes."

"Actually, it helps." Tate buttoned his beige sweater. "They say laughter's the best medicine." His handsome face saddened. "It's sure working better than anything else."

Gary asked, "How are you feeling?"

"Better today than yesterday."

Gary slid to the edge of his seat. "I heard what Katrina said to you about being on probation. That wasn't fair."

"Life isn't fair."

"But you're a nice guy. All you want is to do your job."

Tate smiled. "I'm surprised."

"About what?"

"I thought you didn't like me."

Gary did a double-take and had to replace his glasses. "I like you a great deal. I just don't want you...or anyone to think I'm a homosexual, because I'm not."

"Whatever you say."

Gary's stomach growled loudly.

Tate said, "You want to get some lunch? I'm up for anything. All food comes out of me pretty quickly these days anyway."

"You mean, get lunch...together?"

Tate nodded.

Gary's face paled. "I don't think that's a good idea."

"I mean when Jose calls lunch."

Gary blurted out, "Tate, I thought I made myself clear."

"About lunch?"

"About *me*."

Tate sighed. "Gary, I know, you say you aren't gay."

Gary groaned. "I say I'm not gay, because I'm *not* gay."

Tate put his arm around the back of Gary's chair. "Gary, you're middle aged. You're a good guy. You deserve to be happy."

"I am—"

"Not just as a nanny. As a man. Be gay, straight, bi, whatever you want to be. But don't hole yourself up on an island. Life's too short to hide from other people."

"Look what opening yourself up to other people did to you." Gary covered his mouth.

Tears filled Tate's eyes. "Okay, Gary. I get it." He rose from his seat.

Gary followed Tate into the aisle. "I didn't mean it that way."

"Then how did you mean it?"

"I didn't mean to offend you. I'm awkward around people."

"You're a person, too, Gary."

"Sometimes I don't feel like one. I had a messed up childhood. It left me afraid to talk to people." He blushed. "And frightened of being…intimate with anyone."

"I wasn't asking you to have sex with me, or even to date me. I just thought we could be friends."

"I don't know if I can do that."

Tate responded, "You can do it, Gary. If you want to."

Gary looked down at the floor and his glasses fell

into Tate's hand.

Tate returned the glasses. "It's your call."

Give it a try, Gary.

Jose rearranged the stage furniture for Jana's apartment, then called everyone back from break. Bella and Brad sat in the audience together. Up on stage, Tony rehearsed Jana and B.J. in the scene where B.J. tells his babysitter what he overheard from Bella and Savannah. Again Jana marveled at how naturally her son took to the stage. She was also pleased to see they had a great rapport on stage.

Next, Tony blocked the scene where Peter, as the detective, speaks with Jana in her apartment about what B.J. told Jana. The chemistry between Jana and Peter was sizzling. It was as if a ball of fire bounced back and forth between them. *It's just acting, girl.*

When the scene ended, Jose called for lunch. Still in one another's arms, Jana didn't want to let go. Jose reminded them they had only one hour, and they finally left the stage.

Bella and Brad fled for Bella's parents' brownstone, Savannah and Sally headed for their dressing rooms, Tony and Katrina went downstairs to their office, and Tate, Gary, and B.J. left for B.J.'s favorite deli. Then Jana and Peter headed to Broadway's most famous restaurant.

"Why isn't Jana Lane's portrait on this wall?" Simon Huckby adjusted his chartreuse scarf over his peach and fuchsia jumpsuit as he hollered at the waiter.

Sitting across from her agent, Jana Lane replied, "Because *China Doll* is only my second Broadway play."

Simon shouted at the waiter, "And it doesn't matter

that she starred in twenty-four films?"

The frightened young waiter said with a quivering voice, "Would you like anything else besides four chicken Caesar salads?"

Simon erupted like a volcano. "I want Jana Lane's picture on your wall!"

Peter Stevens smiled at the waiter. "We're fine. Thank you."

As the waiter sheepishly walked away, Cornelius Chamberlain, at nearly seven feet tall and thin as a breadstick, wrapped his long arm around his partner. "It'll be all right, Simon."

Simon waved his tiny arms. "How can it be all right when the next generation doesn't know the greatest star in the heavens?"

Jana raised her eyes to the mini chandeliers. "Simon, please calm down."

Her agent dabbed his napkin into his water glass and placed it on his forehead—smudging his makeup. "How are rehearsals going, baby doll?"

"B.J. is wonderful," Jana said,

"So is his mother," Peter added.

"How large is your role?" Simon asked.

Jana replied, "I discover the murderer—or rather murderers."

"Just like in real life," Simon said with a wink.

"And I play the detective on the case. But more importantly, I'm Jana's love interest."

Staring at Peter, Simon said, "I always said Jana should marry someone in the business."

Jana spit out her water. "Simon, Peter plays my love interest *on stage*. As you well know, in real life I'm married to Brian."

"And Farrah Fawcett was married to Lee Majors," Simon said with a smirk.

Peter put his arm around Jana. "I like your agent, Jana."

Ignoring Peter's minty smell and adorable eyes, she said, "Peter and I have become fast friends."

Simon nudged his partner's side. "So I see."

Jana looked at Cornelius. He took the hint. Pressing his thumbs between his emerald shirt and burgundy suspenders, Cornelius said, "Let's talk about the AIDS fundraiser."

"It was Peter's idea," Jana said.

"I doubt Brian would have thought of it," Simon answered, followed by a tap on the wrist from his partner.

Peter said, "There's a young guy in our cast, Tate Moonglow. He plays Sally's then Bella's husband, but in real life he's gay."

"As so many husbands are," Simon said.

Peter said, "And he has AIDS."

Simon's grin turned into a groan. "I'm so sorry."

"We are, too." Peter continued. "And it got me thinking that there must be other actors in Broadway shows who have AIDS, or have family members, friends, and neighbors stricken with the disease." He covered Jana's hand with his. "I remembered reading about Jana's fundraisers for AIDS in upstate New York and in Washington, DC. So I thought, why not on Broadway?"

"Since our elected officials aren't doing anything, it's up to us," Jana said. "We can have actors from the different shows do musical numbers, recite monologues, or answer questions from the audience."

Peter added, "And we can do it at the largest Broadway theatre, and charge two hundred dollars a ticket."

"All the money will go to AIDS research and patient care," Jana said.

Simon said, "I think it's a wonderful idea."

"Me, too," Cornelius said.

"Who's going to produce it?" Simon asked.

Jana swallowed hard. "You are."

"What?" Simon held onto his partner as if they were on a roller coaster.

Cornelius interceded. "Simon, we did it in Washington, DC."

"That was different," Simon replied. "You're a musician. You called in most of your friends to play and sing. We'd have to reach out to people in Broadway shows."

"I know most of the show pit players," Cornelius said. "I'm sure they'll volunteer their services for a Sunday evening when their shows are dark. And I bet they can enlist the actors in their shows."

"Then it's settled," Jana said. "How about this Sunday?"

Simon turned green. "Are you kidding? We need to book the theatre, arrange for the entertainment, and do the publicity. There's no way we can do all that in less than a week."

"Even for *me*?" She unleashed the famous Jana Lane smile.

Simon melted like a candle. "All right. But Jana Lane will be the master of ceremonies."

"Co-hosting with Peter Stevens," Jana replied.

"I'll drink to that." Peter started and the others

raised their water glasses for a toast.

The salads were served by the frightened waiter, then Simon speared a piece of chicken and asked, "How's your mother, Peter? She had some career." He winced. "Before the sitcom."

Peter picked up his fork. "I'm sorry to say she's going through a rough time."

Jana added, "Savannah didn't look well at rehearsal this morning, and she escaped to her dressing room the minute her scenes were over." She asked Peter, "Is she still upset about being a show angel without script approval?"

Peter shrugged. "She took a tranquilizer and fell asleep."

Simon chomped on his lettuce. "I read in the newspaper about Stanley's...accident. Of course I know better. He was murdered."

"How did you know?" Jana asked.

"Baby doll, murder follows you like a stray cat follows a leaky garbage truck. So who did it?"

Jana said, "We were all moving around the bookcase when it fell on Stanley, so anybody could have tipped it over."

Simon gave his croutons to Cornelius. "What are the motives?"

Moving her fork through her salad, Jana replied, "Stanley left half his money and possessions to Bella."

"Hm, is life imitating art?" Simon said.

"And he left the other half to Katrina," Peter added.

"But Katrina must have plenty of money of her own," Jana said.

"Money can come and go." A tear brimmed in Simon's dark eyes. "When my baby doll left me, I went through tough times."

"I was eighteen and left the business," Jana said. *Leaving us both millionaires.*

Simon blew a kiss at her. "But you came back to me!"

Peter said, "Stanley tried to fire the director, Tony Cuccioli."

"He tried to fire Katrina's studly young husband from the Bronx?" Simon asked in shock.

"And Tate." Jana added, "And Stanley tried to bar Gary from the theatre."

Simon sniffed. "I can't blame Rothman for that. Nobody in the closet should be allowed in the theatre—except for the cloak room."

Jana said, "And Sally Chen, who is Tony's girlfriend, is unhappy her character gets killed in the end of Act I."

"I don't think that's a motive for murder though," Peter said. "Mom doesn't like her role either."

"Well B.J. likes his role, so he's off the suspect list," Jana said.

"And I like mine, too," Peter said, exchanging a warm smile with Jana.

Simon squeezed Jana's hand. "Baby girl, if anyone can figure it out, you can. Now let's have cheesecake."

After lunch, Jana and Peter took a taxi to Bella's parents' brownstone for Stanley's shiva. While paying their respects to Bella and her parents, Jana noticed Brad never left Bella's side, and Bella never spoke or made eye contact with her parents.

When Bella headed for her parents' kitchen with empty trays of food, Jana excused herself and joined the young woman.

"Jana? Do you need something?"

"I haven't had the opportunity to tell you how sorry I am about your grandfather."

"Thanks." Bella opened the refrigerator and brought containers of cold cuts and salads to the table.

Jana stood next to her. "Can I help?"

"Sure."

Refilling the trays with food, Jana said, "This must be hard on you. I know how much you liked your grandfather, and how much he adored you."

"Yes, but he was an old man."

"We can miss old people when they pass on."

Bella got herself a glass of water from the sink. "True, but life goes on for the living, doesn't it?"

Especially when they inherit large sums of money. "Bella, I'd like to be honest with you if I may."

"Okay."

"You don't seem very upset that your grandfather passed away. Why is that?"

Bella put her glass down on the table. "I'm an actress, Jana, like you. I could clutch at my chest, pull out my hair, rant and rave, and cry so much we'd need buckets to bail out the house. But it won't bring Grandpop back. The show my parents are putting on out there is a circus. They never cared about Grandpop when he was alive, and they don't care a lick about him now that he's dead." She gripped the edge of the table. "None of the pomp and circumstances can change the fact that the only person on this planet who loved me is gone. And now I'm totally alone."

Jana held Bella's arm. "I think Brad cares about you, Bella, and he would like to be a part of your life."

For the first time, Bella's hard shell cracked. "Do

you really think Brad likes me? For more than sex? And more than my money?"

"I think so, Bella." Jana smiled. "Underneath Brad's ego and ambition is a young man with a kind heart and a good soul. If you let him, I think Brad will be there for you." Jana wiped Bella's tears away with a napkin, then lifted the serving trays. "Come on, let's go back out there and let him prove it to you."

The moment they reached the living room, Brad approached them. "Bella! I was worried about you. Where were you?"

"I had a talk with Jana."

"I hope it was about me," Brad said with a wink.

"You could say that," Bella replied, cuddling up to Brad's welcoming arms.

Jana and Peter left the brownstone and taxied back to the theatre, where they found more set pieces being delivered to the basement. Upon entering the theatre house, they noticed Jose had the chairs set up on stage for Bella's apartment. Not seeing B.J. or Savannah, Jana and Peter walked through the house, up to the stage, into the wings, and to the dressing room area. Peter went into his mother's dressing room. Standing just outside, Jana heard loud voices. Since Peter had closed the door, she couldn't make out what Peter and Savannah were arguing about. Recalling a scene in her *School Spy* movie, Jana hurried into Brad's empty dressing room next door, climbed up onto a stool then onto the makeup table, and placed her ear next to the vent.

"Dinner last night, and lunch today?" Savannah said. "That doesn't sound like a casual friendship to me."

"Mom, I like her. Jana's a terrific actress, a great person, and a real humanitarian."

"And she's married."

"So, she's married. That means she can't be my friend?"

"I remember some of the women you brought home, Peter."

"What do they have to do with—?"

"And what happened with each one of them."

"What happened was you scared them all away."

"Stop telling tales."

"Mom, I'm not a child anymore."

"Then don't behave like one. Jana Lane Otley has three children. You know the power you have over women. Stay away from her. Now, I want to talk about your character in the play."

"Mom, I appreciate all you've done for me. I love you very much. I know this a rough time for you. I would do anything for you. You know that. But I'm thirty-six years old."

Jana heard Jose call for the cast to come back from lunch. So she jumped down from the makeup table to the stool to the floor. As she left Brad's dressing room, she bumped into Katrina in the backstage hallway. "My apologies, Katrina." Jana noticed the eighty-year-old woman seemed out of breath. "I hope I didn't startle you."

Katrina wiped her forehead with a lace handkerchief. "I felt a bit flushed. I went to the ladies' room."

"I hope you feel better."

"Thank you." Katrina walked past her.

When Jana reached the stage, B.J. ran into her

arms. "I ate a white fish, Mommy!"

Gary explained, "He ate white fish on rye at the deli."

Tate added, "And a milkshake."

Jana laughed.

"I like Gary and Tate," B.J. announced.

Gary and Tate beamed like headlights.

"We like you, too," Gary said.

B.J. pushed Gary's glasses up the bridge of his nose. "Do you like Tate?"

Gary blushed.

"Of course Gary and Tate like each other, B.J.," Jana said. "We're all friends."

"Yeah!" B.J. shouted.

Tony stood center stage. "Listen up, all a yiz. I need Bella and Brad on stage to block the next scene, hah? The rest of youse can take a break. But don't go nowheres. I may need yiz."

Jana sat in the front of the house between B.J. and Peter. They watched the scene where Bella, now wealthy from her inheritance, talks Brad into marrying her. *Art really does imitate life.* Jana marveled at the unbridled passion between the two young people. *They've known each other only two days. Just as long as I've known Peter.* Though the scene called for one kiss, Brad and Bella kissed again and again throughout the scene.

"They're doing a nice acting job," Peter whispered to Jana.

Jana replied, "I don't think they're acting."

Sitting in the row in front of them, Gary asked Tate, "How are you feeling?"

"About as well as one can feel after eating borsht

and chopped liver."

They shared a laugh.

Gary replied, "The food was really good."

"So was the company," Tate said.

"Yeah, it was."

Watching the young lovers on stage, Tate said, "That's the one thing I regret."

"What?"

"Not having anyone to love…and to love me…at the end."

"You don't have to talk about—"

"No, it's okay. I've come to terms with dying young."

"How did you do that?"

"I moved from fear to disbelief to shock to anger to blame to resentment and now acceptance." Tate shifted in his seat to face Gary. "If they find a cure, I'll be the happiest guy in the world. But if they don't, I think I'm okay with that. No more nausea, weakness, shooting pains, blurred vision, diarrhea, and fatigue. But dying will also mean I'll never love anyone again, or be loved. That's what hurts the most." Tate wiped a tear off his cheek. "I'll never hear anyone say he loves me. Or have the feeling of being held in someone's arms."

Gary's Adam's apple bobbed over his collar. "I've never had that."

Tate did a double-take. "You've never been held by anyone?"

Gary shook his head, then replaced his glasses.

"I'm sorry, Gary. For both of us."

"Me, too."

Me, too.

"Yo, Jose, change the furniture to Jana's

apartment, hah? Jana and Savannah, youse two are up. Bella don't go nowheres. Brad, you can take a load off." Tony moved to far stage left and blocked the scene where Jana confronts Bella and Savannah with what B.J. told her, leading to Jana and Bella's final showdown.

Jana felt all eyes on her as she told Bella what she knew. When Bella attacked her, Jana used a move—from *Jungle Girl*—to turn the tables and pin Bella to the sofa. Jana's monologue about good and evil felt riveting. When Savannah entered and Jana exposed her as selfish, manipulative, and psychotic, there were gasps from those watching. *That was fun!*

Tony gave the actors notes on stage. As Jana went back to her seat, she heard Gary say to Tate in their audience seats, "That was ridiculous."

Tate replied, "I thought the scene was good."

"I told Katrina the more believable ending would be for Jana and Bella to split the money, but she wouldn't listen to me."

Tate laughed and put his arm around Gary. "Maybe you should be a playwright." Tate was sitting very close to Gary. "Is this all right?"

Gary nodded. "You're easy to talk to."

"So are you," Tate replied.

Gary said, "And guys put their arms around each other all the time. That doesn't mean they're gay. Right?"

"Right."

"Straight men are affectionate with one another in Europe. They sit like this together all the time."

"True."

"And just because we're sitting close together, that

doesn't mean I'm gay." Gary rested his head on Tate's shoulder.

"Whatever you say, Gary."

How sweet.

Savannah walked down the stairs and headed for Katrina. "Kat, we need to talk."

"Not now, Savvie." Sitting in her front row seat, Katrina wrote notes on her script with her fountain pen then fanned herself with her handkerchief.

"Are you all right?" Savannah asked.

"It's probably just a hot flash," Katrina answered.

At eighty? Is that what I have to look forward to?

Peter congratulated Jana on her scene with Bella and Savannah. Then Tony called Jana and Peter on stage to block their last scene. Savannah sat in the seat across the aisle from Katrina to watch.

The two actors made the scene shine. Peter, as the detective, told Jana how worried he was about her. She thanked him for watching over her. Standing downstage center, they declared their love for one another. As the play came to a close, Peter took Jana in his strong arms, and they shared a long kiss.

Acting is the best profession in the world.

When he released her, Jana took in Peter's chiseled features, mountainous shoulders, and fresh scent. His eyes radiated adoration as he said, "Good job, partner."

Jana sounded like a soprano. "It was very nice working with you, Peter."

Sally clapped her hands in an exaggerated fashion, then walked from the wings to Tony, still standing on the side of the stage. "And by now the audience will have forgotten all about the *China Doll*."

"I ain't forgotten about you, Sal," Tony said with a

smile.

Katrina buried her head in her script.

"I just phoned my agent," Sally said. "Unless I get more time on stage, I'm out."

Katrina rose from her seat on shaky legs and waved her fountain pen at Sally like a baton. "Not another word of this script will be rewritten."

Savannah glared at Katrina. "You're making a huge mistake, Kat."

Gary stood at his seat. "I'm sorry to bring this up again, but I agree with Sally and Savannah. The script needs work, especially the big confrontation scene."

Tate pulled Gary back into his seat.

Thanks, Tate.

"This is *my* play. My *twentieth* play," cried Katrina. She struggled for air. "And the script is *my* domain...and *mine* alone! If—" Katrina gasped for air, clutched at her heart, and fell on top of her script.

Chapter 5

"What's xylene?"

Jana Lane Otley sat on a stool at her dressing room makeup table across from musical theatre buff Detective Dwayne Douglas. "Xylene is a chemical found in small quantities in ink and paint."

The detective scratched his curly dark hair. "And how did it kill Mrs. Cuccioli?"

Jana explained, "A large amount of the chemical was injected into the ink in Katrina's fountain pen. As Katrina made notes on her script, did rewrites, and gestured with her pen, the vapors got into her lungs." She slid to the edge of her stool. "When I ran into Katrina going to the ladies' room, she was feeling ill. By later in the day, she was gasping for air and clutching her heart."

Dwayne said, "Mrs. Cuccioli was eighty years old. Writers work with fountain pens all the time. Couldn't she have died from a heart attack?"

Jana shook her head. "It was a large amount of xylene."

"And how exactly do you know this?"

"From my old movie."

"You're kidding."

Jana explained, "In *The Cutest Scientist* the villain placed a large amount of xylene in paint. When little Timmy inhaled it while painting his red wagon, Timmy passed out and was taken to the hospital. As a young scientist, I tested the paint in my school science lab and came up with the cause—and eventually the culprit—by finding the xylene in my neighbor's workshop."

Dwayne started to write a note on his pad and stopped. "I still don't follow how this applies to Mrs. Cuccioli."

Jana paced the dressing room. "After Katrina fell to her death, Gary checked her vitals and pronounced her dead. Jose called for the ambulance. Sally comforted Tony." *Just like Bella comforts Tate in the play after she kills Sally.*

"I still don't get it."

"I bent over the body, and I smelled something very sweet."

"And xylene has a sweet odor?"

"Exactly. And the pen was right near Katrina's body."

"Why would someone put a large amount of xylene in Mrs. Cuccioli's fountain pen?"

"Obviously to kill her."

Peter Stevens entered Jana's dressing room. "Jana, are you all right?"

Jana nodded. "How's Tony?"

Peter rubbed the back of his neck and his bicep nearly ripped open his blazer. "Jose phoned Tony at the morgue. He said Tony was shaken but able to make arrangements for the burial."

"Are the cast members in their dressing rooms as I asked?" Dwayne rose.

Peter's dimples appeared. "Everyone except me." His eyes softened. "I was concerned about Jana."

"Since you are here, Mr. Stevens, where were you

when Mrs. Cuccioli passed away?"

Peter replied, "I was on stage with Jana. We had just completed our scene." He winked at her. "And it went very well."

"Where was everyone else?"

Jana stood between them. "Dwayne, it doesn't matter where everyone was at the time of Katrina's death."

"Did you learn that in *The Little Detective*?" Dwayne asked.

Very funny. "It takes time for even a large amount of xylene to kill someone." *Though not as long if someone is terminally ill.*

"And you learned that in *The Cutest Scientist*?" the detective asked.

Jana nodded. "Whoever killed Katrina probably took Katrina's fountain pen in the *morning* when Katrina was in the ladies' room or in her office downstairs. Each of us moved freely throughout the theatre the entire day. Any one of us could have done it."

Dwayne exhaled loudly. "I sent the pen out to the crime lab for testing. Of course the place where Mrs. Cuccioli fell is taped off for further examination. I'll let you know what comes up." He walked to the doorway. "In the meantime, it looks like I need to talk to everyone. You can go, Mr. Stevens. I'd like *The Little Detective* to assist me with the interviews again."

"I'll wait for you in my mother's dressing room, Jana."

Once Peter was gone, Jana said, "Dwayne, there's something you should know. Katrina was ill from cancer."

"But that didn't kill her?"

"No."

"All right. Let's get started. I hope we finish the interviews by curtain time for *My One and Only*. I don't want to miss the overture."

Lead on, Singing Detective.

Jana and Dwayne walked into Savannah's dressing room and found the aging actress sitting on the easy chair with Peter standing at her side.

"I won't keep you long, Miss Stevens," Detective Douglas said.

Savannah wiped the tears from her eyes. "Thank you."

Peter patted her shoulder. "Are you up for this, Mom?"

"I'm all right." Savannah sat back in her chair. "Ask me your questions, detective."

Dwayne said, "Where were you when Mrs. Cuccioli took ill?"

Savannah replied, "I was right across the aisle from her."

"Did she say anything before she died?" Dwayne asked.

Savannah shook her head no.

"Did you see, hear, or smell anything peculiar?"

"No." Savannah blew her nose.

"You and Mrs. Cuccioli were old friends?"

Savannah sighed. "Another pal from the old neighborhood gone. I know she was ill and eighty years old but…she was a part of my past."

"I'm sorry for your loss. Thank you for speaking with me." Dwayne started to leave.

Jana held Dwayne's arm steady. "Savannah, what

percentage of the production do you own as an angel?"

"An angel?" Dwayne asked.

"Someone who gives the producer money to produce the show," Peter explained.

Dwayne rubbed his strong chin. "In community theatre, everyone involved in the production is an angel."

Savannah replied, "My share is twenty percent."

"But you also wanted script approval, and you didn't get it," Jana said.

Savannah patted down a hair that was already in place. "I understand an actress who is…of a certain age is relegated to playing the mother role." She looked at Peter. "On stage and in life." Her jaw clenched. "But I don't see why the mother in this play, and her daughter for that matter, are so vicious and despicable." Her eyes fastened on Jana. "Kat certainly wrote *your* role quite likeable."

"Savannah, have you ever heard of xylene?" Jana asked.

"No. Is it a new cosmetic?" Savannah asked.

"I believe it's what killed Katrina," Jana replied.

"After some testing, we'll see if Jana is right. Thank you both," Dwayne said.

Jana and Dwayne found Bella's and Tate's dressing rooms empty. They walked into Brad's dressing room, and B.J. threw himself into his mother's arms. "I'm hungry, Mommy."

"We'll eat dinner soon, honey," Jana replied with a kiss to the top of her son's head.

Noticing Brad at the makeup table, Jana asked, "Where's Gary?"

Brad scratched his washboard abdominal muscles.

"He asked me to watch B.J. for a bit, then he disappeared."

B.J. plopped himself on Brad's lap. "My cousin Brad!"

"That's right, little man." Brad hugged B.J. to his chest.

"Is Bella back at Stanley's shiva?" Jana asked.

Brad nodded. "First Stanley. Now Katrina. It's crazy. Do you think Tony will become the producer of the show?"

My nephew, always the practical thinker. "I imagine so."

"Good. As they say, the show must go on."

Dwayne asked, "Mr. Lane, Miss Tarnowsky had mentioned Stanley Rothman's inheritance was divided between herself and Mrs. Cuccioli. I did some checking. As I understand it, with Mrs. Cuccioli deceased, your girlfriend gets the whole windfall."

Brad looked like a homeless man cashing in a lottery ticket. "That's terrific!" Jana looked at him in shock. Brad said, "I mean, it's nice to know that Stanley's wishes are being honored."

"I don't suppose you saw anything suspicious before Mrs. Cuccioli came to her death?" Dwayne asked.

Brad replied, "I'm afraid not. Bella and I were...preoccupied in the wings."

"Thank you, Mr. Lane."

Jana said to Brad, "I'll be through shortly, and we can all go back to the hotel together."

"Sorry, Aunt Jana. Bella and I are going to Studio 54."

Bella is going to a nightclub after she sits shiva for

her grandfather? "B.J., stay with cousin Brad. I'll be back soon."

Since Sally's dressing room was empty, and the detective wanted to have dinner out with his wife before seeing the show, he promised to keep in touch with Jana about any developments, then left the theatre.

Jana heard voices coming from the green room. As she entered the place where actors wait for their cues to come on stage, she saw Tate lying on the sofa with his head on Gary's lap.

"Are you feeling better?" Gary asked, moving the hair off Tate's forehead.

"I am now." Tate smiled up at Gary. "This is nice."

"You're nice."

"So are you."

Upon seeing his boss, Gary jumped up, nearly giving Tate whiplash. "Tate was feeling nauseous and dizzy. I told him to lie down in here."

Jana said, "Gary, I—"

"But Tate and I aren't…. I'm not—"

"Gary, it's all right." Jana took Tate's hand. "How are you feeling?"

Tate replied, "The room has stopped spinning, and my breathing and heartrate are back to semi-normal."

"Good," she replied.

Gary kneeled at Tate's side. "Are you hungry? Thirsty?"

"I'm fine. Thanks."

"Is it time for your pill?" Gary rose. "I can go to your dressing room if you need it." He turned to Jana. "But that doesn't mean Tate and I are…. I've never been with…. It's not what you think, Jana."

Jana took Gary's hand. "I think it's nice that you

and Tate are friends. I think it's very nice. For both of you. Do you understand what I'm saying to you, Gary?"

Gary nodded his head.

Jana added, "But what I find peculiar is how you keep giving your critiques of the play at rehearsals. It upset Katrina."

"No worries about that now."

Tate and Jana looked at Gary in shock.

"I mean, since Katrina passed away...tragically," Gary said.

Jana replied, "And I'm sure Tony will want us to continue with the play—just as Katrina wrote it."

"The ending isn't right," Gary said. "You and Bella should agree to split the money."

I have the feeling Bella would never agree to split the money—except perhaps with Brad. "Gary, I'm going to give you some advice, as your employer and as your friend. Keep your critiques of the play to yourself. Spend your time taking care of B.J."

"And me," Tate said.

Jana smiled. "And Tate. Can you do that, Gary?"

Gary sat on a chair and sighed. "All right."

"Thank you." Jana patted Tate's shoulder. "Do you need help getting back to your apartment?"

"I don't want to bother anyone." Tate sat up slowly on the sofa.

"It's no bother. Gary, can you please take Tate home?"

Gary's eyes bulged. "You want me to go to Tate's apartment?"

"That's generally how you take someone home," Jana answered.

Tate stood on shaky legs. "You don't have to do that, Gary."

"No, I want to." Gary swallowed hard. "I just don't want anyone to think that I'm—"

"Helping a friend home?" Jana asked.

Tate stood next to Gary. "Thanks, Gary, but I'll be fine."

Gary put his hand on Tate's forehead. "You seem a little warm. I'll take you home, get you some soup, and make sure you get into bed." He said to Jana. "Alone!"

As the two men left, Gary said, "Lean on me for support."

"That sounds good," Tate replied.

"That sounds good to me, too," Gary said. "But don't lean on me too much or people might think…"

When they were gone, Jana walked down the hallway and found Sally Chen talking on the payphone.

"It sounds like everything is going according to plan." After a pause, Sally added, "I love you, too." She hung up the phone.

"Was that Tony?"

Sally noticed Jana standing opposite her. "Yes."

"How is he?"

"Exhausted."

"I'm not surprised. When will he be through?"

Sally shrugged her small shoulders. "He identified Katrina's body, signed all the papers, and arranged for the burial."

"There must be more legal issues to resolve."

"Such as?"

Thanks for taking the bait. "Katrina's will."

"She didn't have one."

An eighty-year-old famous millionaire didn't make

a will! "I wonder why not?"

Sally said matter-of-factly, "Tony said Katrina wanted everything to go to him."

"She could have put that in a will."

"No need. Tony was her husband. She doesn't have any children."

B.J. ran down the hallway with Brad chasing him. "B.J.'s hungry!"

"Excuse me, Sally." Jana put one arm around her son and the other around her nephew. As they passed by Savannah's dressing room, Jana poked her head in. "Hi, care to join us for dinner in a restaurant, then a taxi back to the hotel?"

Peter's dimples bulged out of his cheeks. "We'd love to."

Savannah stood next to her son. "Thanks, Jana, but I'm not up to it. I'd like to go to the hotel and rest." She looked at Peter. "Will you take me, honey?"

"Of course, Mom. Sorry, Jana."

"I hope you understand, Jana." Savannah batted her eyelashes.

Jana replied, "I certainly do. Good night."

"I have to beg off, too," Brad said. "I'm having dinner with Bella."

"Enjoy," Jana said to Brad's back.

As Jana and B.J. left the theatre, Rollo R. Rorro met them outside. "Jana, who do you think killed Katrina Wright?"

Jana sighed. "Please speak to Detective Douglas."

Roll rubbed his large stomach. "Hello, B.J."

"Hi!" B.J. replied.

"It must be fun to be in your famous mom's play, just like your mom's famous dad put her in his play when she was a kid. Pity other kids who have to audition, huh?"

Before Jana could respond, B.J. said, "B.J. knows his lines!"

Which is more than I can say for many of the actors I've worked with over the years.

Jana and B.J. had dinner at B.J.'s favorite Jewish delicatessen. Upon sitting at his usual table by the window, B.J. shouted to the waiter, "Hiya, Mort. Matzo ball soup and pastranami on rye!"

Back at the hotel, Jana got B.J. ready for bed, read him a bedtime story, then kissed him goodnight. Once she had changed into her silver satin nightgown, Jana lay on the brass bed and phoned Devon and Ed. When she was caught up on her sons' fishing, basketball, arts and crafts, and campfire activities, Jana kissed the mouthpiece of the phone, and told them how much she missed them and loved them.

Just as she had slid down on the white silk sheets and buried her head into the fluffy white pillow, the phone rang.

"How's my beautiful wife?"

"She misses her hunk of a husband."

"Hi, babe."

"How are things in Vegas?"

Brian exhaled so loudly, Jana moved the earpiece from her ear. "We're running into some environmental issues."

"In Las Vegas?"

"Yup. And we can't break ground until things are cleared up."

Jana sighed. "Does that mean you won't be home in two weeks?"

Brian laughed. "*You* won't be home in two weeks either."

"I can't wait until next month when we're both home together again."

He snickered. "You'll be commuting on the train to your show."

"And you'll be designing your next mall project."

"But we'll be home together," they said in unison, followed by a laugh.

Brian asked, "How's B.J.?"

"Sleeping soundly."

"I called him at the theatre today. He's pretty excited about the show. He kept saying, 'Daddy, B.J.'s on stage!'"

"He loves it," Jana replied. *Just like his mother.* "Brad loves it, too, but he seems to love Bella even more."

"After only two days?"

"I fell in love with you when I met you."

"It took me longer."

"It did?"

"About five minutes." He laughed. "How's your boyfriend?"

"*You're* my boyfriend."

"I mean on stage."

"Peter is a very generous actor. Our scenes together really took off."

"Uh-huh."

"And he's very sweet to B.J."

"Uh-huh."

"And good to his mother, who seems to be struggling with the effects of being an aging actress." *Maybe I should take lessons for the future.*

"How was your love scene?"

Uh-oh. "It took me a while to find my motivation, and for Peter and me to get the rhythm of the scene."

"I'll bet."

"But Tony worked with us, and the scene should be fine."

"I'm sure."

"Brian, stop being jealous. I'm an actress." *Thank goodness for that.* "It's part of my job to play love scenes. Peter is an attractive guy, but there's nothing between us. Except—"

"Here we go."

"Listen to me, Brian. With everything going on at the theatre, I appreciate Peter watching out for me. He seems to be protecting me in a way. We've formed a kind of…bond."

"That's what I was afraid of."

"It's not like that."

"Did you have dinner with him again tonight?"

"No, Peter ate with his mother."

"Are they close?"

"Not close actually. More like dependent upon one another. Probably because Peter's father died when Peter was a boy, and Savannah went through three husbands pretty quickly."

"Unlike Jana Lane."

"Who has her hands full with one husband."

He asked, "How's Gary doing as B.J.'s nanny?"

Jana rubbed her toes against the silk sheets. "Fine. I think Gary's in love."

"With *you*?"

"No! With Tate Moonglow."

"I thought Gary was in the closet, and Tate

Moonglow has AIDS."

"Thankfully most people come out of the closet when they fall in love. And people can love people with AIDS."

"Does Tate have karposi sarcoma?"

"I haven't seen any lesions, but his breathing is labored. I hope he doesn't get pneumocystis pneumonia."

"How's the benefit coming?"

"Ask Simon. I basically dumped the whole thing on his and Cornelius' capable laps."

"Good move."

Jana took a pad and pen from inside the night table and wrote a note. "I have to remember to invite the cast."

"Can they afford the admission price?"

"Bella certainly can. With Stanley and Katrina gone, Brad's girlfriend is a wealthy woman. She seems to—"

"Back up a minute. 'With Stanley *and Katrina* gone?'"

Here goes. "Katrina was murdered today from a large amount of xylene in her fountain pen."

"That's it. Take our son, and get on the train and go home right now."

"No."

"Jana—"

"Brian, Dwayne needs me to help him solve the case."

"He *needs* you? What kind of detective *is* he?"

"One who loves musical comedies."

Brian groaned.

"Like Stanley, Katrina was murdered in the theatre

with all of us present. So any one of us could have done it." She sat up cross-legged. "Katrina was willed half of Stanley's money. Plus she was a wealthy and successful playwright. So with Katrina dead, Bella and Tony are rich. Tony's girlfriend, Sally Chen, must be happy about that. But happy enough to kill for it?"

"Babe—"

"And Sally, Savannah, and Gary, of all people, are unhappy with the script. They might have thought Tony would be more approachable about script changes than Katrina."

"Jan—"

"I just realized, with Katrina gone, Tony is now our producer, director, *and* he owns the copyright on the play."

"Jana—"

"And don't forget both Stanley and Katrina threatened to fire Tate."

"Okay, I get it! You love acting, and you love sleuthing."

"And I love you."

His voice softened. "But please be careful, babe."

"Always."

"Look behind both shoulders."

"Of course."

He said, "I must be out of my mind to let you stay there."

"I'm out of my mind in love with you."

"Protect yourself and our son."

"I will."

"Think about me while you sleep, my love."

"Every night."

"Call me if you need me."

"Always."

Jana hung up the phone, and spent most of the night lying in bed thinking about who killed Stanley Rothman and Katrina Wright. *And why I feel so happy when I'm with Peter Stevens.*

****

Not only Jana woke groggily having not had enough sleep. Upon throwing on her robe and venturing into the living room, she found out Brad had spent most of the night helping Bella move into Stanley's duplex, and Gary had picked up takeout dinner, then spent all night on Tate's sofa.

Jana dressed and fed her men breakfast from room service—B.J. requested pastrami, but Jana ordered banana pancakes—then their taxi driver dropped them off in front of the theatre. Jana noted more set pieces were being delivered by truck to the basement.

The rehearsal began as Jose asked the cast to sit in the front of the house. Jana sat between B.J. and Peter in the second row.

Wearing a black sweatshirt and chinos, Tony stood center stage sporting a forlorn look. "As youse all can imagine, I'm still in shock about losing Katrina. My wife was a great playwright, and a great human being, hah?" He wiped a tear off his Roman nose. "I hope yiz can all join me at Katrina's funeral tomorrow, hah?" He blew his nose on a white handkerchief then stuffed it back into his back pants' pocket. "But Katrina would want us to continue. And that's what we're gonna do. Katrina will live on through this play. And youse guys will make it happen on this stage. As producer, director, and owner of the play, I will make sure not a word of what Katrina wrote is altered in any way by any of youse guys."

Sitting next to Tate farther down in the second row, Gary rolled his eyes to the chandelier.

Across the aisle, Savannah said, "Kat was doing rewrites before she passed away, Tony."

"I seen them, and there ain't nothing substantial," Tony said. "So youse all learn your lines exactly like Katrina wrote them for yiz." Tony shuffled from one large foot to the other. "I am making one small change though." He gazed at Sally Chen sitting in the front row, wearing a short, tight, low-cut black dress with white pearls. "I'm adding a few speeches for Sally at the start of the play and throughout Act II. See Sally and me come up with a new idea I know my Katrina would have liked. The play will be from Sally's perspective like—as a ghost. So after she's murdered and all, as narrator, Sally will talk to the audience like about what Bella and Savannah done to her, hah?"

Wearing a canary-yellow midriff blouse and short skirt, Bella rose from her seat next to Brad's in the front row. "That will make Sally's role the focus of the play."

A few seats away, Sally grinned like the Cheshire Cat. "I guess it will, Bella. Maybe now the title of the play will make sense."

Brad stood and put his arm around Bella. "What doesn't make sense, Tony, is rewriting Katrina's play."

Jana asked, "Tony, who wrote Sally's new monologues?"

Sally looked down at the carpeting.

"Sally and I wrote them last night," Tony explained.

Peter whispered to Jana, "I wonder if Sally will start her first monologue with, 'Youse guys, listen up, hah?'" Then Peter replied to Tony, "Don't you think that's unfair to your wife's talents?"

B.J. jumped up from his seat. "B.J. wants up on stage!"

Clearly relieved at the diversion, Tony said, "The kid is right. Let's start rehearsing, hah? Sally, you come center stage like. Yo, Jose, we'll need a spotlight on her, hah?"

Sitting at the stage manager station just offstage, Jose wrote a note on his script. "Got it, Tony."

Jana cringed as Sally read her opening speech to the audience from center stage. "I am a specter. I see everything. I hear everything. I know everything. Diabolical people may snuff me out like a candle, but I remain alive in the smoke."

Peter whispered to Jana, "Katrina must be rolling over in her grave."

Jana couldn't stifle her giggle.

When Jana and the other cast members were called up on stage by Tony, they rehearsed their scenes with Tony giving them directions like, "Get closer to him, hah?" and "Do it more upset like, will yiz?" When they got to Act II, Sally performed her new ghostly monologues to audible moans and groans from the other actors. Jana's love scene with Peter went well again. *Let's keep rehearsing it until we get it right.*

If the actors weren't needed on stage, they either retreated to their dressing rooms, complained to their agents on the backstage phone, or watched from the front of the house. Jana phoned Dwayne from backstage to see if there was any news about the toxicology report on Katrina and her pen. While it was too early for any results, Dwayne promised to call her as soon as he received them.

During a break, Jana stood on stage and invited everyone to the Broadway benefit for AIDS. They all seemed happy to attend and support the worthwhile cause. *There's no people like show people.*

When Jana left the stage to go to the ladies' room, Savannah stopped her backstage. Dressed in a low-cut blueberry dress with her hair teased high and her diamond necklace on display, Savannah said sotto voce, "Can I speak to you?"

"Of course."

The two women sat on a sofa in the green room.

Savannah said, "With all that's been going on, we haven't had a chance to talk."

"Yes, it's been rather hectic."

"And though I've been grumpy about my role, I want you to know that I'm glad we're working together again, Jana."

Jana smiled. "So am I, Savannah."

The aging actress regained her youth. "I have so many fond memories of *Sweet Nothings*."

"So do I."

Savannah giggled. "Remember how your father kept forgetting his exit line at the end of the first act? And he'd stand on stage looking at us like we forgot to give him his cue?"

Jana felt like a little girl again. "I remember!"

"And that time you were late for your cue at the top of Act I, because I was beating you at checkers?"

Jana laughed. "Yes."

"And when my blouse ripped on that nail in the bar on stage, and I stood behind the sofa until the end of the scene?"

They shared a laugh.

Savannah's face sobered. "And now all these years later we're working together again. And with my son as well."

"It's amazing.'

Savannah crossed her still shapely legs. "Speaking of Peter, I see how you two always sit with your heads together at rehearsals. I know you like him, and he likes you. When I was critiquing his acting during the break, I told him how happy I am that you and he get along so well."

"I'm happy about that, too."

"Good." Savannah's face hardened. "But don't get any ideas about him."

Jana nearly fell off the sofa. "What on earth do you mean?"

"Come on, Jana. You're not a child anymore."

"Peter is my love interest—in the play."

"You sure it's only in the play?"

"Savannah, I have no designs on your son."

"Good. Let's keep it that way." She rose and started to walk away but stopped. "I hope I wasn't too blunt. I prefer honesty to beating around the bush."

Jana stood. "Since you like honesty, Savannah, I'll be honest and tell you that Peter is a thirty-six-year-old man. You are more possessive of him than I am of B.J. who is only three."

"Don't mock me for caring about my son."

"Caring and smothering are two different things."

"I've had a tumultuous life with many highs and lows. People came, and people went. My son is the only one who didn't leave."

"I hope Peter stays, Savannah, but trying to run his

life may push him away."

"Isn't that easy for you to say at the height of your career with a husband and three young children." Tears filled Savannah's eyes. "When you get older and you're at the end of your career, and you have no one but B.J., then you'll understand." Savannah left her dressing room.

Jana walked down the backstage hallway. When she came to Sally's dressing room, she stopped in the corridor.

"You've been my rock, baby," Tony said, sitting Sally on his lap in the easy chair.

"And you've been mine. I love my new scenes, Tony."

"And I love you, hah?" He kissed her cheek.

"Bella was jealous of my new speeches."

"Everybody's gonna be jealous of you, baby. You got it all."

Jana continued down the hall to Brad's dressing room.

"I never thought I'd find the perfect guy for me," Bella said with her thin arms wrapped around Brad's wide back

"But you have." Looking handsome in a raspberry polo shirt and beige slacks, Brad kissed his beloved.

"Do you like the duplex?" Bella asked.

"I love it. Just like I love you."

They kissed again, then Bella said, "I'm meeting with Grandpop's lawyer tonight to go over everything. I hope I can take it all in. I have a terrible head for figures."

"I'm great with figures." Brad said, "Numbers, too! Would you like me to come?"

"Would you?"

"Sure."

"We're such a good team." After another kiss, Bella said, "When *China Doll* is over, maybe we can produce a show together—starring you and me."

"Sounds like a plan." He winked. "We'll have the money."

Bella cooed. "Right!" Then she pouted. "But in the meantime, what do we do about Sally's role in *this* show?"

Jana heard coughing from the next dressing room. Upon entering, she found Tate sitting on the easy chair, bent over his knees. "Tate, are you all right?"

"I…can't…stop…coughing."

Jana hurried out to the water cooler in the hall and returned quickly with a paper cup filled with water.

Tate took a sip and immediately coughed it up.

Jana felt his forehead. "You're burning up. You have to go to the hospital."

"If…I…leave…Tony…will…fire me." He gasped for air.

Jana kneeled at Tate's side. "Tate, listen to me, you have to get help."

"I'll…be…okay."

"Not if you don't go to the hospital."

"I…can't."

"Tate, I think you have pneumocystis pneumonia."

Gary entered the dressing room. "Jana, Jose called for you. B.J.'s on stage."

"Tate needs to go to the hospital," Jana said.

Tate continued coughing.

Jana handed Gary some money. "Take Tate by taxi."

"Of course." Gary helped Tate out of his chair.

Jana said, "After we rehearse, I'll ask Brad to watch B.J. then I'll get to the hospital as soon as I can."

Gary nodded. With his arm around Tate's waist for support, Gary led Tate out of the dressing room and out the stage door.

Jana rehearsed her scenes then left B.J. with Brad in Brad's dressing room. She joined Tony and Peter, standing in Tony's usual spot far downstage left. "Tony, will I be needed again today?"

"Nah, youse two are done for the day. Good work. The both of yiz." Tony scratched at his dark mane. "You two got real chemistry, hah?"

Peter put his arm around Jana's waist. "Jana's my favorite leading lady."

Jana laughed. "I'm sure you say that to all your leading ladies."

"Actually, he does." Savannah stood next to her son.

Peter blushed. "That's not true, Mom."

"Sure it is," Savannah replied. "I was at each rehearsal for every one of his Off-Broadway plays—to give him acting notes." She came face to face with Jana. "The actresses nowadays are quite brazen. Very different from how we behaved in my day. Those dames swooned over him. They made their intentions quite clear. Peter didn't hurt their feelings. My son is a gentleman. He played along, and they thought he was interested."

"Mom, you're exaggerating."

"I am not."

While Savannah and Peter argued, Jana said, "Tony, may I leave for the day?'

Tony shrugged his large shoulders. "Sure. See ya tomorrow, hah?"

"Thank you, Tony."

Peter turned away from his mother and held Jana's arm. "Is everything all right?

Jana replied, "I want to check up on Tate."

"Where is he?" Tony asked.

"He finished his scenes," Jana said.

"That ain't what I asked."

Jana looked down at the stage floor. "Gary took him to the hospital."

"Why?"

"I told him to go. He didn't look well," Jana explained.

"That does it." Tony walked offstage. "Jose, call in Tate's understudy. And tell his agent he got the part permanent like."

Jana was at his heels like a bloodhound. "That's not fair. Tate may be perfectly fine."

Tony cornered her against the curtain rope. "You know and I know that Tate ain't 'perfectly fine.'"

"I'm going to visit him now. I'll call you if he will be out tomorrow."

"Don't bother. He's out *today*."

"As the Equity Deputy, I'd like to remind you that you can't fire an Equity member without just cause."

Peter said, "Tate has been nothing but professional, and he's very good in his role."

"I agree with my son," Savannah said.

Tony glared at them. "Tate goes." He walked on stage with Savannah following him.

Peter put his arm around Jana. "I'm sorry to hear Tate isn't doing well."

Jana couldn't resist leaning on Peter's strong shoulder. "Me, too."

On stage Savannah yelled, "So you can rewrite the play to give Sally more to do, but not to make my and Bella's characters more likeable?"

Tony replied, "You got it. Your characters are fine. And what do you care about Bella anyways. You her agent?"

"I play her mother."

"That's like make believe, Savannah. You're *Peter's* mother in real life, which you never let us forget."

"My son and I are very close," Savannah said.

Tony replied, "Maybe you and Bella can be 'more close' on stage. I nearly fell asleep watching your scene today."

Savannah's eyes were on fire. "No director has ever told me my acting was boring."

"This one just did."

Savannah glared at him. "I was making movies when you were a child."

"Then maybe it's time you retire, hah? Stanley and Kat only cast you 'cause you was old friends—and because you put up some dough."

Peter walked on stage. "That's not fair, Tony."

"What? Are youse two like ganging up on me now?"

Peter said, "We are fortunate to have my mother in our play. Katrina and Stanley knew that, and you should, too."

"Yeah, yeah. Blah, blah, blah."

As Tony, Savannah, and Peter argued, Jana slipped out the stage door.

"Is it true that Tate Moonglow has...the gay plague?"

Jana came face to face with Rollo R. Rorro. "Since you are interested in AIDS, please tell your listeners Peter Stevens and I will be hosting a fundraiser for AIDS, featuring the stars of Broadway. It's this Sunday evening."

Roll picked at a pockmark on one of his chins. "You and Peter Stevens! That sounds cozy."

"Just Peter, me, the top entertainers in New York, and hundreds of audience members filling the largest theatre on Broadway. See you there, Roll." Jana jumped into a taxi, and sped to the hospital.

Upon entering the emergency room, Jana spotted Gary sitting on a sofa with his head in his hands. She took the seat next to him. "How's Tate?"

Gary's eyes were wide and questioning. "I don't know. They won't let me see him." He grimaced. "They told me, 'family only.'"

"Where is he?"

"I was with him in a cubicle down the hall. We waited for quite a while. Tate kept coughing and gasping for air. I was finally able to get an intern to examine him, then an orderly wheeled Tate upstairs, but I'm not sure where." Tears filled his dark eyes. "Nobody will tell me anything."

Jana rose and asked an elderly, overweight nurse at the nursing station, "Excuse me, I would like a report on Tate Moonglow."

"You, too? The skinny guy asked me five times in the last hour." The nurse moved her stringy hair behind her ears. "Hey, you're Jana Lane, right?"

"Yes. I am very concerned about Tate Moonglow.

Can you tell me where he is?"

The nurse rested her chart on the desk. "I lost a hundred dollars because of you." She ignored her ringing phone. "I bet on Meryl Streep for the Best Actress Oscar last year in the hospital drawing. When you won for *Madame Senator*, I was so angry, I wanted to pull the plug on somebody."

"Can you please tell me how I can visit Tate Moonglow?"

The woman's back arched. "Hey, no need to get snippy. I'm just trying to do my job."

Then do it. Jana looked at the nurse's nametag. "Hannah, I am very worried about my friend."

The woman smiled, revealing dentures too large for her face. "You said that just like in your old movies when you were worried about little Timmy."

"Now I'm worried about Tate Moonglow. Hannah, can you please help me?"

"You look smaller in real life." Hannah opened a file drawer. "And you're a regular person. Not like the snobby actresses who come in here after their botched facelifts and tummy tucks. And I like how you do those fundraisers for AIDS. If I was a rich, beautiful movie star like you, I'd sit in my mansion by the pool and never leave home. It's nice how you care about people." Hannah opened a file folder. "You can't see him."

"Why not?"

"His file is marked, 'family only.'"

"What's his condition?"

Hannah looked inside the folder and shook her head from side to side. "That information is for family only."

Jana sighed. "Tate's family isn't in New York. I'm working with him on a play. If you ask him, I'm sure he will want to see me."

"Sorry." Hannah closed the folder and leaned over the counter. "We have contests for the Tony Awards, too. You think you'll win this year?"

I hope I do so you can lose another hundred dollars.

Jana headed back to the sofa, and found a young orderly with curly blond hair standing over Gary.

The man said, "I heard you ask at the nurse's station about Tate Moonglow."

Gary jumped out of his seat like a rocket. "Is he all right?"

The orderly spoke softly. "Are you his lover?"

Gary gasped. "Why do you ask?"

"Only family can see patients in the AIDS ward." The orderly sounded like a secret agent. "But some of us...bend the rules for the patients' lovers."

Gary said, "And you want to know if I'm Tate's lover, so you can help me see him?"

The orderly looked both ways. "Are you?"

Gary took in a deep breath and proclaimed, "Yes."

"You're lucky. He's really cute."

"Thank you."

"Follow me."

As she did in *Girl Detective*, Jana walked behind them, leaving enough space for them not to notice her.

When they arrived on the top floor of the hospital, Jana stood behind a column and watched the orderly give Gary a mask and gloves.

"I'm not afraid of catching anything," Gary said.

The orderly replied, "This is to protect your lover.

He's very vulnerable to infection right now." He led Gary inside Tate's room. "I'll be back for you in ten minutes."

The orderly left. Jana stood to the side of the doorway and watched Gary sit in the chair next to Tate's bed. Gary blinked back tears as he gazed at the various tubes attached to Tate's nose, mouth, and arms.

Tate looked frightened. Upon seeing Gary, he smiled.

Gary smiled back.

"Aren't you...afraid the orderly...will think...you're gay?" Tate asked.

Gary replied, "Not only does he think I'm gay, he thinks we're lovers."

Tate laughed and coughed. Once he settled down, Tate said, "And you're...okay with...that?"

"I was afraid at first. But when the words came out of my mouth, I felt...relieved." Gary squirmed in his seat. "Tate, there's something I need to tell you."

"I'm sick. I know."

"Not that." Gary took in a deep breath and closed his eyes. "I'm...gay."

"I think I know that."

"You do?"

Tate nodded.

Me, too.

"I guess now I know it, too."

Tate smiled. "And so...does the orderly."

"Yeah."

Tate sighed. "I wish we...had met sooner."

"How come?"

"It would have been...nice."

"What?"

"To be…lovers."

Gary said, "Nobody's ever said that to me before."

"I'm saying…it now."

"If we were lovers, what would we do?"

"Lots of things…together."

"Like what?"

"Cooking and…eating together. Shaving…together. Walking in the…rain. Going to…restaurants and…theatre. Taking…vacations. Cuddling in bed…and…waking up…in each other's arms."

"It all sounds amazing, except for the last one. I snore like a bear."

Tate laughed, which led to more coughing.

Gary pointed to a magazine on the tray table. "What's this?"

"That's me…in an Off-Broadway show I did…last year. A nurse…asked me to…autograph it."

Gary held up the cover, a photo of Tate wearing an Elizabethan white tunic and sky-blue tights.

"You're really beautiful."

I'll say.

"Not anymore."

"That's not true." Gary took Tate's hand. "I like the way you look."

A tear appeared in Tate's eye. "Gary, thanks…for coming."

"I was worried about you. So was Jana."

"Jana's…a terrific…woman."

"She sure is."

Tate began coughing.

When the coughing continued, Gary said, "Should I call a nurse?"

Tate shook his head no.

"Do you want me to call your parents, or another family member?"

Tate stopped coughing. "My family's...already here."

Gary rested a hand on Tate's shoulder. "And I'm not going anywhere."

"Good." A tear dropped down Tate's cheek. "I'm...scared, Gary."

"Me, too."

"It's...pneumonia."

"I know."

"This...isn't...fair. I just...found...you." Tate gasped for air. "I wonder...how long...it will be."

Clearly not an actor, Gary feigned optimism. "Plenty long. You have to get well to come back to the show."

"I'm sure...Tony won't...allow that."

"I'll deal with Tony."

Me, too.

Gary added, "And the benefit is coming up on Sunday night."

"I guess I won't be performing."

"Of course not. You'll be coming...as my date."

Tate looked up at Gary. "In front of all those people?"

Gary nodded. "With my head held high."

"Now I have...to get well."

Gary smiled. "Tate, there's something else about me that I haven't told you."

"You're a...Mormon with...two wives?"

"Seriously, I—"

Jana noticed the orderly coming down the hallway.

She snuck behind a supply cabinet and listened.

Tate said, "That's…amazing, Gary. I have…so many…questions!"

"Save them for next time."

Tate said, "I will. Thanks for letting Gary see me, Barry."

The orderly replied, "Don't mention it. Literally. Now kiss your lover on the forehead."

Jana heard the sound of a kiss, then Gary say, "I'm proud to be your lover."

Tate replied, "And I'm proud to be yours."

When they were outside of the room, Gary gave back the gloves and mask, and Barry gave him the phone number for Tate's room.

Gary pushed his glasses up his nose. "Thank you, Barry."

Barry winked. "You two guys make a great couple."

"We sure do," Gary said proudly.

They walked down the hallway, and Jana raced down another staircase. When Gary found her back at the waiting room sofa, she pretended not to be out of breath. "How's Tate?"

Gary replied, "He has pneumonia. He's hooked up to so many tubes and machines."

Jana put her arm around Gary. "How are *you* holding up?"

Gary replied, "I think I'm okay…for the first time in my life."

"I think you're okay too." Jana held Gary in her arms, and he wept on her shoulder.

Once back at her hotel suite, Jana phoned the three men in her life, then called room service. When the dinners arrived, she joined Gary, Brad, Bella, and B.J. at the living room table. Enjoying the panoramic view of the city, Jana bit into her crabmeat stuffed flounder. Then she turned to Bella. "Again my condolences for the loss of your grandfather."

"Thanks, Jana," Bella replied as if Jana had commented on a worn out sweater being thrown into the trash.

"How are things going with the probate of Stanley's will?" Jana asked.

Bella moaned. "It's taking forever."

"But Brad said he helped you move into Stanley's duplex."

Bella smiled at Brad. "I had the key."

"And me as the workman," Brad said chewing his prime rib.

"Strong man!" B.J. swirled his carrots and peas around his mashed potatoes.

"That's right, B.J." Brad flexed his biceps.

"How did the rest of rehearsal go today?" Jana asked before taking a sip of herbal tea.

Bella groaned. Staring down at her lobster, she said, "Sally acted like a prima donna. Her ridiculous ghost monologues got torturously longer. She's also getting a different costume for each scene. How does a ghost change clothes?" Bella slid to the edge of her seat. "And she said Tony is going to give her the last curtain call."

Simon will wave my contract in Tony's face like a flag.

"The play is about *your* character, Bella." Brad turned to Jana. "No offense, Aunt Jana."

"None taken," Jana replied.

"Bella's the murderer." Brad looked adoringly at Bella. "And Bella is terrific in the role."

Bella blew him a kiss. "You're not so bad yourself, Bradsky."

Brad-sky?

"Tony is an awful director," Bella said. "And he's an even worse playwright. The new lines are laughable. Somebody needs to stop him before he destroys the show—and all of our careers."

Brad and Bella left for Stanley's, rather Bella's, apartment. Jana got B.J. into his pajamas and off to bed. As she read him a bedtime story, Gary sat in the living room and phoned Tate. Then Jana studied her lines in bed until her head hit the satin pillow, and she fell into a deep asleep.

****

Jana Lane raced toward the ghost light on stage. The footsteps behind her grew louder and more persistent. With her heart pounding in her ears, Jana's scream for help echoed through the empty theatre. She ran toward her dressing room and finally exhaled once her door was in view. But someone reached out for her from behind.

The star of *China Doll* awoke in her king-sized bed, rested her head on her palm, and took in some deep breaths. *It's only a dream.* She showered then put on an amaranth angora sweater with an ivory skirt and gold heart necklace. Sitting at the vanity, she teased her hair in layers and applied her makeup. Then Jana herded her troops to the table for breakfast—French toast with honey—and into the taxi to the theatre.

Jana and her entourage passed the workmen loading the remainder of the set into the basement.

Upon their entry into the theatre, Jose asked everyone to sit in the front rows. Jana sat in the second row between Peter and Brad with B.J. on her lap. Next to Brad sat Bella. Savannah was next to Peter. Sally sat alone in the front row, and Gary was the only one in the third row. Jose was stationed at the stage manager console just off stage.

Looking fetching in an olive polo shirt with beige slacks and sandals, Peter leaned in toward Jana and his bicep bulged out of his shirt. "Are you okay?"

Jana sighed like a soap opera heroine. "I had a rough night."

"Bad dreams?"

She nodded. "All about me."

"I dreamt about you, too." His dimples appeared. "But *my* dreams were terrific."

I wish you were in my dreams.

Once the cast was settled, Tony took center stage in his usual all-black attire. "How yiz all doin'? Before we start rehearsal, I want to invite each of youse to honor Katrina's memory on Saturday afternoon at the funeral home around the corner, hah? A right. I got a couple of things to say about the show now."

So much for the grieving widower.

"First, Tate Moonglow is in the hospital," Tony announced.

"Is Tate all right?" Bella asked, wearing a marigold lace midriff blouse and skirt.

Tony replied, "He still ain't feeling so good. So Tate's understudy is taking over the role." Tony pointed to a tall, thin young man sitting alone house left.

Gary rose from his seat in the audience and pushed his black glasses up the bridge of his nose. "I phoned

Tate this morning, and he's doing better. There is every reason to believe he will be back before opening night."

"No there ain't. Tate's no longer with the show," Tony said.

Gary's cheeks turned crimson. "That's unfair."

Tony walked to the apron of the stage. "And what are you gonna do about it, Mr. Nanny Critic, hah?"

Jana gave B.J. to Brad. "Tony, Tate is ill, however, if his doctor believes he will get better soon, I recommend you leave Tate's employment open ended." She looked at Tate's understudy. "If Tate isn't well enough to go on, it's nice to know he has a competent and well-rehearsed understudy."

"Tate's out," Tony said.

Jana replied, "I will be phoning Equity at our first break."

"You do that."

"B.J. has to go!" Jana's son proclaimed to the balcony.

Gary took B.J. and headed for the bathroom.

Tony continued. "Another thing. I seen Sally's new monologues at the last rehearsal." Sally and Tony shared a smile. "And they're good. So I added three more of them into the script."

Savannah, wearing a pearl-colored blouse and peach skirt and blazer with shoulder pads, said, "Why not make the whole production a one-woman show where Sally plays all the roles?"

"Don't tempt me," Tony replied.

The muscles in Brad's back contracted under his turquoise polo shirt. "This isn't fair to Bella." He put his arm around her.

"Life ain't fair, kid," Tony answered.

Bella added, "Grandpop wanted to produce Katrina's play, not yours."

"I know what my wife would have wanted, hah?" Tony said. "And one last thing."

You're going to bulldoze the theatre?

Tony said, "The theatre marquee is being changed this afternoon."

As if on cue, Simon Huckby, wearing a vermillion and lavender jumpsuit with a gold fanny pack, stormed into the theatre. Standing in the aisle, the elderly little man shouted up at Tony as if David confronting Goliath. "This is an outrage!"

"Simon!" Jana shouted. "What's going on?"

"What's going on"—Simon replied with his eyes bulging out of his small head—"is this poor excuse for a director and producer has broken our contract."

"Aye, I did not." Tony waved his large hand.

Simon pointed at Sally Chen as if she was the murderer in a television crime drama. "*She* will be getting the last curtain call in the show? And *her* name will be over the title on the marquee?"

"The play *is* called *China Doll*." Sally folded her arms over her chest.

Simon scowled. "And your boyfriend will be called 'finished in this business' if he violates my client's contract!"

"Yo, calm down before you burst a kidney," Tony said. "I ain't violating no contract."

"Based on the memo I received from your office, you most certainly are!" Simon screamed.

"Let me explain something to yiz all." Tony sat at the edge of the stage. "Jana's contract says her name goes above the title, and she gets the last curtain call.

Jana's name stays over the title, and she gets the last curtain call." Tony winked at Sally. "Only Sally joins her in both. No contract violated." Tony smiled proudly.

Simon looked like a bull in a fire pit. "Mark my words. You won't get away with this. You're finished!" Then he stormed out of the theatre.

"Aye, have we had enough theatrics?" Tony asked as he came to his feet. "Are youse all ready for rehearsal?"

"Everyone on stage, please," Jose shouted.

Tony met Jana downstage left as she entered the stage. "Aye, no hard feelings, hah?" Tony said.

Jana replied, "Tony, I don't care anything about billing and curtain calls, but I do care about fairness. And I will fight you to the Supreme Court if necessary on firing Tate."

"You threatening me, Jana?" Tony asked with an oily smile.

Jana's eyes met his. "No, Tony, I'll let Equity's, Simon's, and *my* lawyers do that."

Sally performed her agonizing opening monologue, then the cast rehearsed the scenes in Act I under Tony's directions—"yo, bigger" and "louder, hah?"—between Jose's calls for breaks.

When Jose announced lunch break, the lighting technicians arrived and began focusing the lights on stage. Tony and Sally headed downstairs. Gary hurried off to visit Tate in the hospital. Brad and Bella hugged and kissed with Brad calling out over his shoulder their plans to have lunch at a local bistro.

B.J. shouted, "B.J. wants lox and potato latke!" So B.J., Jana, Peter, and Savannah ate takeout lunch from the deli, curtesy of Peter, in Jana's dressing room. Savannah complained about her role in the play for nearly the entire hour. Peter sat at her side and listened sympathetically. *What a loyal son, being attentive to his mother this way. I wonder if B.J. will do the same if he and I share the stage in twenty years.*

When Jose called everyone back from lunch, Tony directed the scenes in Act II—"aye, faster," and "like slower, youse guys." Even Jose couldn't help from groaning when Sally performed her ghost monologues, which seemed to grow like weeds in an overwatered garden. Jana and Peter were pitch perfect in their love scene. *My favorite scene.* And Jana felt on top of her game in the final showdown scene with Bella and Savannah. Bella seemed up for the exchange, but Jana noticed that Savannah appeared sluggish and distracted.

When they finished rehearsing the scene, Savannah walked over to Tony on the left side of the stage. "Do you really think an audience is going to sympathize with two such one-dimensional, vile characters?"

"Why should the audience sympathize with youse two?" Tony asked.

"Because it's *our* story," Bella said.

"Not no more." Tony winked at Sally standing next to him, wearing a low-cut emerald cocktail dress.

Savannah didn't give in. "Can't Bella and I improvise our scenes for you, and show you how our characters could be more layered and interesting?"

"Improvise!" Tony raised his eyes to the stage lighting. "You sound like Stanley."

Savannah sat down hard on the stage sofa. "I can't believe I left Hollywood for *this.*"

Tony stood over her. "You didn't leave

Hollywood, Savannah. It left *you*. And if you don't want to keep being a has-been, you'll do your scenes like my Kat wrote them, hah?"

Gary called out from the house, "The ending doesn't work, but it's not because Bella's and Savannah's characters need to be more sympathetic."

Not again, Gary.

Gary put B.J. in Brad's charge and walked up the stairs onto the stage. "Even as calculating as Savannah and Bella are, why would Jana turn her good friend in to the police?" Gary stood next to Tony center stage. "No matter how attracted Jana was to Peter."

Jana felt herself blushing.

Tony gritted his teeth then said to Gary, "Yo, I'm only gonna tell you this one more time. You say another word about the plot of this show, or one more syllable about your pansy boyfriend, and you're out of here on your nelly ass! You get me!"

Gary's body stiffened, and his face turned beet red.

Before Jana could defend Gary, B.J. asked from his seat in the house, "What's a, 'nelly ass'?" Brad put his hand over his cousin's mouth.

Simon stormed into the theatre. Standing at the orchestra pit, the emaciated little man waved a piece of paper at Tony like a ransom note. "I have a court order stating you may not replace the marquee."

Tony laughed. "Tell it to the marines, hah?"

"I am dead serious, Mr. Cuccioli," Simon said.

"Me too. Now get the hell out of my rehearsal."

"You'll be hearing from my lawyer," Simon said with sneer.

"I look forward to it." Tony called out, "A right, let's rehearse the last scene, hah? Jana! Peter!"

Jana and Peter took their places center stage as the other actors made their way to their seats in the house. Gary and Simon stood in the aisle seething with rage.

Standing at his usual place far downstage left, Tony shouted, "Hit it, hah?"

Jana said her first line in the scene, then she heard a loud crash. Peter put his arms around her, as they looked at Tony lying on the floor with a floodlight next to his head.

Chapter 6

Jana sat in the theatre house and looked up at the stage sealed with yellow tape, looking like a huge wrapped gift. She had watched Tony Cuccioli's body being taken away by the paramedics with Sally Chen sobbing after them, and the fallen floodlight bagged and taken to police headquarters by one of Detective Douglas' officers. She had heard Dwayne interview Simon, Jose, the lighting technicians, and Tate Moonglow's understudy and released them. Sitting in the second row next to Jana were Peter on one side with his mother, and B.J. on the other with Gary. Bella and Brad sat in front of them with their bodies entwined like teenagers at a movie theatre.

Standing in front of the orchestra pit, Dwayne said, "Ladies and gentlemen, it looks like we are here again."

"Is Tony dead?" Bella asked as if she was asking about the weather.

"I'm afraid so," Dwayne responded. "And once again I will need to speak with each of you before you can leave."

"Detective Dwayne!" B.J. said.

Dwayne smiled. "That's right, B.J. You can be first. But before we begin, I'd like to talk to your mother."

A few minutes later, Jana sat next to Dwayne on the sofa in her dressing room. "Dwayne, I'm getting quite concerned for my son—and for all of us."

"You should be."

Jana did a double-take. "You kept telling me the deaths were theatre accidents."

"Not anymore." He pulled his pad out of the breast pocket of his suit jacket. "You were right about the ink in Mrs. Cuccioli's pen."

"There was xylene in it?"

He nodded. "Enough to kill her."

"I knew it!"

"So we have at least one murder," the detective said. "And a new suspect. When I talked to your agent, he was pretty hot under the scarf."

"Simon would never hurt anyone."

"Even to protect your star status in the play?"

"Simon wasn't in the theatre when Katrina was killed."

"Neither were the technicians or Tate's understudy. I released them for now."

"I believe we have *three* murders." Jana slid to the edge of the sofa. "There's no way that bookcase would have fallen on Stanley unless someone had pushed it. And the floodlight could not have fallen without tampering."

Dwayne flipped through the pages of his notes. "That's what the lighting technicians said earlier. They swore it was hung securely."

"It was."

"How do you know?"

"Their union is quite closed. Those technicians have been hanging lights for many years. They know what they are doing, and they don't take shortcuts. Besides…"

"Besides what?"

"When I did *The Tiny Eskimo*, the snow machine fell into the igloo set."

"Okay?"

"Thankfully nobody was hurt. The technicians had secured it properly, but the cleaning woman moved it while she was cleaning."

"So you think a cleaning lady killed Mr. Cuccioli?"

"No, but I believe *somebody* loosened the floodlight during the lunch break. Somebody who knew Tony always stood on stage in that exact spot while he directed, and who assumed the light would fall on Tony before the end of rehearsal. The only people who had this information, and had access to the theatre, besides the techs, were the cast members. This is true for each of the three murders. I think one of the cast members murdered the producer, playwright, and director of *China Doll*." *Think, girl.* "But why would someone in the cast want to stop the show? They may complain about their roles, but they all want to open in a Broadway play by Katrina Wright."

Dwayne put his pad back inside his jacket pocket. "I don't like non musicals, but I wouldn't kill the people putting them on, especially if I was in the cast." The detective scratched his short curly hair. "This reminds me of that mystery where each person is knocked off one at a time."

Thanks for reminding me.

"They should make that into a musical."

Jana froze. "That's it."

"What, making a musical?"

"Getting all the suspects together like in an old mystery novel." She rose and paced the room. "Please ask everyone to sit in the green room. We'll ask them questions, and see how they answer—with everyone listening."

Dwayne shrugged his broad shoulders. "What do we have to lose, *Tiny Eskimo?*"

Hopefully not our lives.

Five minutes later, Jana sat on a sofa in the green room with B.J. on her lap and Peter and Savannah sitting next to her. The sofa opposite was occupied by Brad, Bella, and Gary.

Douglas sat on an easy chair nearby. "The reason I asked you all back here is to discuss what happened today to Mr. Cuccioli."

Gary raised his hand.

"Yes, Mr. Royale?" Dwayne said.

Gary scratched at the Adam's apple over his closed shirt collar. "I don't think B.J. should be present." He rose and stood next to B.J. on the sofa. "May I take him back to the hotel?"

"I would like for you both to stay, Mr. Royale." Dwayne turned to B.J. "You want to stay, don't you, B.J.?"

"B.J. likes Detective Dwayne!"

Gary stood in front of the detective. "You should consider the boy's mental health, detective."

"I have experience questioning children," Dwayne replied. "Besides, he's three years old. How much of this will B.J. remember in time?"

"A great deal of it," Gary said. "I've read articles about this."

Jana put her arm around B.J. "Gary, I appreciate your concern, but I'll look after B.J. Dwayne, can we get started. B.J., and all of us, have had a long day."

"Of course." Dwayne pulled out his pad and pen. "Can each of you tell me where you were when the light fell on Mr. Cuccioli?"

Gary stomped back to his seat. "We were all sitting in the house."

"Except for Peter and me. We were on stage," Jana said. "But it doesn't matter where we were, the floodlight was tampered with before that. Probably during lunch when all of us walked freely through the theatre."

Dwayne asked, "Did any of you see anybody near the floodlight at any time during the day today?"

"I did." Everyone looked at Gary. "The technicians."

"Besides them?" Dwayne asked.

"Cousin Brad on the ladder!" B.J. pointed to Brad. "I like cousin Brad!"

All eyes were on the juvenile actor.

Brad squirmed in his seat. "One of the lighting guys asked me to come up and hold a light for him while he screwed it in."

"That's against Equity rules," Jana said. "He shouldn't have asked you to do that, Brad."

"And you shouldn't have done it," Peter added.

Brad shrugged. "I was helping the guy out."

"B.J.'s tired!" He rested his head on Jana's chest and quickly fell asleep.

Jana asked, "Does anyone have any idea why someone would want to kill the creative team of this show?"

Peter asked, "With Tony, Katrina, and Stanley deceased, who owns the show?"

Brad hugged Bella to his chest. "As Stanley's only

living heir, Bella takes over the contract to produce *China Doll*."

Savannah replied, "The producer options the show, but the copyright of the play is owned by the author."

Bella said, "But Katrina is dead."

Brad added, "And now so is Katrina's only living heir."

"But Tony's heir is very much alive." Sally Chen entered and sat on an easy chair.

"Please elaborate, Miss Chen." Douglas said.

"It's not Miss Chen. It's Mrs. Cuccioli. Tony and I were married last night."

Brad, Bella, and Savannah shouted at the same time.

Like flies around a dead bird.

"Please, listen!" Silencing the hysteria, Peter said, "A man has been killed. The third person in our company in only four days of rehearsal. Any one of us could be next. I recommend that each of us calms down and answers the detective's questions." He looked at Sally. "We can figure out the future of *China Doll* later."

Sally glared at her cast mates. "The future of *China Doll* is alive and well."

And starring Sally Chen.

Sally dabbed a handkerchief at her dry eyes. "Unlike my poor Tony who I miss so much."

"My condolences for your loss, Mrs. Cuccioli," Dwayne said in official detective mode. "Thank you for coming back."

"I did everything I could for poor Tony," Sally wailed.

Peter whispered to Jana, "I can see why she won

that Tony Award."

Dwayne said, "Mrs. Cuccioli, we were discussing why someone might kill Stanley Rothman, Katrina Wright Cuccioli, and Tony Cuccioli."

Bella glared at Sally. "Maybe to take over the copyright of the play."

"Or to try to get her role rewritten," Sally said with dagger eyes at Bella and Savannah. Then she turned toward Jana. "Or save her star billing."

Savannah crossed her shapely legs. "This all seems like a power play to me."

"Explain," Dwayne said, taking his seat.

Savannah pursed her lips. "I remember Kat as fun-loving, talented, and incredibly determined to find success."

"She sure didn't seem fun-loving to me," Gary said.

Stop being a theatre critic, Gary. Jana said with B.J. sleeping on her chest, "Savannah, do you think Katrina killed Stanley?"

Savannah nodded without mussing her high-teased hair. "And I believe Tony killed Kat. And Sally killed Tony."

All eyes were on Sally.

The young actress jumped to her feet and pointed at Savannah. "If you think this is all a power play, let's talk about the cast member who owns shares of the show!"

Peter held Savannah's hand. "My mother is only an investor in the production."

"Can you elaborate?" Dwayne asked.

Peter replied, "Once the show…hopefully makes enough money to cover all the salaries and expenses, it breaks even. After that, the investors get a return on their money. It's like making interest from a bank account. But Mom doesn't own or control the show in any way. That's the *producer's* role."

Everyone looked at Bella. "So I own the production, and Sally owns the copyright?"

Dwayne rifled through his notes. "That's the best I can figure out at this point."

Bella smiled like the Cheshire Cat. "Then we go back to the original script, marquee, and curtain call order."

Sally stood and stomped her foot on the concrete floor. "I'll pull the rights!"

"Then you'll pull yourself out of a show." Brad sneered at her. "And given your reputation for being a prima donna, you might not get another one."

"Who says I'm a prima donna?" Sally shrieked.

Brad grinned. "I do. To every producer I meet from now on."

Sally lunged at Brad as she screamed and cursed. Dwayne and Peter brought Sally back to her chair, where she took out her handkerchief and wept on cue. "Brad's trying to destroy my career! You all hate me because you think I used Tony."

B.J. stirred in all the excitement, so Jana laid him on her lap.

Peter whispered in Jana's ear, "That's the first thing Sally has said that I agree with."

Sally hunched over and rocked back and forth. "But I loved him so much. Tony meant everything to me."

And to his dead wife.

"I don't know how I'll go on without him." Sally

sobbed. "I just want to die."

Peter whispered to Jana, "I wouldn't say that around here."

That minty smell, those muscular shoulders, and that gorgeous face. Remember the investigation, honey. "Sally, are you dropping out of the play?"

"No." Sally resumed her performance. "I would drop out, but I know Tony would want me to continue." She lifted her head high. "So my performance will be dedicated to my husband."

Of one day. Jana looked at her cast mates. "Peter is right. Three people have been murdered. If this play continues, there may be a fourth. And it will be one of us. Whatever you know, no matter how inconsequential, please tell Detective Douglas. Please, don't let anyone else die."

When nobody stirred, Bella said, "As producer, I ask everyone to go home, get some rest, and be back here at nine am ready to go back to the original script." She held Brad's arm. "I'm going to call my acting teacher. I think he will make a great director."

"Is he open to script revisions?" Savannah asked.

"I own the copyright to the script," Sally said, looking exhausted.

"We are going back to the original script that Grandpop licensed from Katrina," Bella said.

"Will Tate be allowed back in the company?" Gary asked.

"Just as soon as he's well enough," Bella said.

Brad put his arm around Bella. "This production will once again be *China Doll* starring Jana Lane with Savannah Stevens. Also starring Peter Stevens, Tate Moonglow, Brad Lane, Sally Chen, B.J. Lane." He kissed Bella's cheek. "And Bella Talloway as the featured ingénue."

Hearing his name, B.J. woke up. "We rehearse!"

"Not now, B.J." Dwayne rose from his seat. "If anyone has anything to tell me. Please do so now. Otherwise, I'm sure I will see you again."

As everyone filed out of the green room, Peter squeezed Jana's elbow. "Would you like to have dinner?"

"Sure," Jana replied.

"Good. Put B.J. to bed. I'll get Mother her tranquilizer and night mask, then I'll knock on your door at seven o'clock."

"Perfect."

Peter led Savannah out.

Gary asked Jana, "Is it all right if I visit Tate again?"

Jana put a hand on his shoulder. "Of course. Please give him my best."

Gary smiled. "The best from the best." And he left.

Brad hugged Bella to his side. "I'll be at Bella's duplex tonight, Aunt Jana. See you in the morning."

Sally was the last to leave. Clutching at Dwayne's arm, she said, "Please find whoever killed my husband." She left weeping.

Dwayne walked Jana and B.J. out of the green room. "My staff will examine the floodlight, the stage area, and the body." He took her arm. "Please be careful."

Jana and B.J. taxied back to the hotel, then Jana ordered room service for B.J.—blueberry blintzes, his choice—and changed into a powder-blue silk dress with sapphire earrings and necklace. She finished reading

B.J. his story and tucked him into bed just as Gary returned from the hospital. Closing B.J.'s bedroom door, Jana met Gary in the living room. "How's Tate?"

"He's breathing better," Gary replied, looking exhausted. "He was able to eat something, too." He smiled. "He spelled my name with grapes."

Jana sat him down next to her on the white sofa. "You like Tate a great deal, don't you?"

"We're just—"

"You can tell me, Gary."

He exhaled. "I like Tate more than I've ever liked anybody, including myself." His eyes filled with tears. "And I'm so afraid of losing him."

Jana put her arm around him. "Gary, look at what's happening in the theatre. All of our lives are transient. Each day is a gift." She squeezed his shoulder. "And love is the greatest gift of all. Enjoy every moment you have with Tate, and make each day count."

He nodded and dropped his glasses.

Jana retrieved them and handed them to him. "And while you're taking care of Tate, don't forget to take care of yourself."

Nodding, Gary rose then went into his and B.J.'s bedroom as Jana heard a rap at the front door.

She opened the door to Peter, wearing jeans and a blue and green rugby shirt.

"You look gorgeous," he said. "Now change into something comfortable."

"Aren't we going to dinner in the hotel restaurant?"

"Not tonight." He pinched her nose. "Time for a costume change."

Jana hurried into her bedroom and changed into an off the shoulder tea rose blouse and white slacks. Then she raced to her vanity, and applied tea rose lipstick, rouge, and eye shadow. After grabbing a white compact purse, she met Peter in the living room and followed him out the door to the elevator.

Once they were in front of the hotel, Jana asked, "Where are we going?"

"You'll see."

A taxi pulled up. Peter ignored it.

"Peter, here's a taxi."

"I have a different idea." Peter led Jana into a horse drawn open carriage. "I hired a driver from the station at Central Park South."

When they were settled comfortably in the rear of the carriage, Peter whispered something to the driver up front then handed him a wad of cash.

As the horse galloped through the streets lined with tall buildings, Peter put his arm around her. "Beautiful night. Just like you."

Jana looked out at the clear azure sky. "What fun!"

They passed by Rockefeller Center with its proud statues, the famous Radio City Music Hall, various museums, the Broadway district with its glowing marquees, and Macys' elaborate store windows.

Jana took in the view of the city. "I feel like a princess in a fairy tale."

"I guess that makes me the prince."

"Perfect casting," Jana replied.

"I'll have my mother read the script and get back to you."

Jana giggled.

When they reached Gramercy Park, the carriage stopped, and Peter helped Jana onto the pavement. Then they walked hand in hand through the cozy park lined with trees and bushes.

"How's your mother doing?" Jana asked.

Peter replied, "A drink of scotch stopped her from complaining about her role in the show. The tranquilizer ended her fears about which of us will be murdered next, and if I will ever leave her. And the sleep mask and ear plugs finally did the trick and sent her to sleep."

"Why is Savannah so unhappy with the script? I know Sally's new monologues were ridiculous, but we're going back to the original script written by Katrina. I think it's pretty good."

"Especially our love scenes."

Jana felt her cheeks turn the color of her blouse. "Why is your mom so determined to get her role rewritten?"

Peter sighed. "It's not an easy lot for an older actress. Mom yearns to go back in time when she played the leading lady. She can't seem to accept that those days are over, and enjoy playing the character roles—even if they are villainous."

"I no doubt will be joining her one day."

"Never! Jana Lane will always be the young and beautiful heroine."

They sat on a bench next to the statue of British actor Edwin Booth as Hamlet.

"Now there's an actor for you," Peter said.

"You aren't so bad yourself," Jana said.

"Thanks. Everyone in our cast is terrific." Peter's face saddened. "I don't want to put a damper on the evening, but I'll admit I'm worried about our company."

Jana rested back on the bench. "Me, too."

"I wonder why Detective Douglas doesn't close down the show."

"He didn't believe Katrina was murdered until today."

"Why would anyone want to kill Stanley, Katrina, and Tony?"

"Good question." *Is that my stomach growling?*

His dimples made an appearance. "Discussion to be continued."

Peter led Jana back into the carriage. They rode down the narrow village streets past quaint boutiques and cafes to Little Italy, where the carriage stopped in front of a green awning. Peter helped Jana out of the carriage then led her through a small restaurant to a fenced-in courtyard lined with small trees covered with tiny white lights. They sat in the corner next to a marble fountain at a little table with a white and red checkered table cloth. A heavyset, elderly woman wearing a dress sporting multi-colored flowers kissed Peter on both cheeks, greeted Jana, brought them two glasses of red wine, and told them what to eat. Since Italian love songs were playing over the outdoor speaker, Peter took the restaurant owner in his arms and they danced.

When the song ended, Jana applauded.

Alone at their table, Peter took a sip of his wine then said to Jana, "I hope you like what Mama Yolanda selected for us."

"I do! She must be psychic."

"Only when it comes to Italian food."

Jana sipped her wine. It tasted sweet as candy. "I didn't know you were such a good dancer."

He winked. "There's a great deal you don't know about me."

"Let's fix that tonight." Jana looked around the festive patio. "Starting with, how did you find out about this place?"

"It's one of Mom's favorites. We came here all the time when I worked Off-Broadway. Mom sat across from me and gave me acting tips during the entire meal. Of course I did what she said. She's an amazing actress. And I could never say no to Mom."

"Has Savannah critiqued your acting after rehearsals for *this* show?"

"Not as much as usual. She's been too upset about her own role."

Mama appeared with Antipasti and Tri Colori Salad then wished them, "Buono Appetito."

Jana took in the scent of the cold meats, fish, olives, and cheese and bit into the crunchy salad drizzled with olive oil and lemon. "What was it like growing up with a famous mother?" Jana asked.

Peter grinned. "Are you concerned that B.J. will have psychiatrists' bills when he grows up?"

"Especially after doing *this* show," Jana said.

Peter's pectoral muscles nearly burst out of his shirt as he leaned in to her. "Jana, B.J. will be fine. I know Gary said his research showed we store memories starting at three years old, but I believe kids remember things as they want to remember them. B.J. is a fun-loving kid who is having the time of his life. He seems not to be phased at all by the grim realities of our company. And as for your other concern, growing up with a famous mother is no different from growing up with a not famous mother."

"Was your mother out a lot when you were younger?"

"She was around more than you think. As I mentioned, my father was away on business a lot. I remember Mom teaching me how to tie my shoe, tell time, say my nursery rhymes, even play baseball."

"Wasn't she needed on the set of her movies?"

"She often took me with her."

"How about when she did the television show?"

"I was older by then, so I visited the set a lot." He smiled. "It was a great experience for a wannabe actor."

Jana washed down her salad with more wine then said, "You said your mother's third husband wasn't around for too long. Did they argue?"

"Not that I heard. He was a nice guy. A businessman. I think she just grew tired of him, since he wasn't in show business." He winked at her. "We thespians need to stick together."

You sound like Simon.

As Mama cleared away the empty plates, Jana and Peter assured her they were the best appetizers they had ever eaten. Moments later, Mama appeared again with their pasta dish—Gnocchi alla Sorrentina then disappeared.

Jana plopped a warm, potato wonder into her mouth and savored the delicious tomato sauce and Italian herbs. "This really is the best pasta I've ever tasted."

"Tell Mama. She will love you forever." Peter took a bite of his gnocchi and moaned in delight. "This is my mother's favorite."

Jana said, "Do you think Savannah will ever remarry?"

"It's possible. Look at Katrina. At eighty years old, she married Tony. Mom has twenty years to go."

"Savannah seemed quite upset about losing Stanley and Katrina. As the saying goes, there are no friends like old friends."

Peter swallowed then said, "Mom has never had many close friends. Neither have I."

She took his hand. "You have one now."

He squeezed her hand. "So do you." Peter wiped his mouth with his napkin. "And speaking of you, tell me about *your* younger days."

"There isn't much more to tell other than what you've probably read in the magazines."

Peter's eyes narrowed. "There must be more than ex-child star and daddy's girl."

Jana turned back the pages of time. "I was two years older than B.J. when I appeared on Broadway in *Sweet Nothings*. It was all so exciting. The lights, the crowds, the make-believe world on stage, and working with captivating people like Savannah Stevens." She smiled. "I remember telling my father I wanted to be just like Savannah when I grew up."

"You and Mom." He laughed. "I can't think of two more different people."

"Maybe we're not so different."

"What do you mean?"

"I did quite a lot of movies like your mom. I got married and had a son—three actually. And my son, and my nephew, are appearing in a play with me."

"But Mom began working at twenty-two. You stopped working at eighteen."

Jana felt her heart racing. "It was a terrible time for me."

"I know. I read about it. I'm so sorry that happened to you."

Jana exhaled. "But thanks to my amazing husband, my best friend Jackson, and Simon, I bounced back."

"And unlike Mom who had three husbands and one son, you have three sons and one husband."

They laughed as Mama cleared their plates, quickly replaced them with broccoli rabe smothered in olive oil and garlic, then moved on to another table.

Peter asked with a sincere look on his handsome face, "Is your marriage a good one?"

"Very good. Brian and the kids are my life. I wish he didn't have to go out of town so much."

"What does he do?"

"Brian is an architect. He designs malls all over the country. His brother manages the construction."

"That sounds quite different from what you do."

"They say opposites attract."

Mama brought their Sole Francese and white wine, bowed to their applause, and left them.

The mouthwatering tender fish covered with a thin coating of egg, butter, olive oil, and lemon melted in Jana's mouth.

"What does he look like?" Peter asked.

"Who?"

"You forgot him already? Your husband."

She smiled. "Brian is very handsome." *Almost as handsome as you.* "You'll meet him on opening night. I'm forcing him to attend."

"Isn't Brian interested in show business?"

"Not in the least. Simon needles me about that constantly."

"Simon doesn't like Brian?"

"Simon doesn't like anyone not in show business."

Peter licked a bit of olive oil off his thick thumb.

"He sure seemed upset at Tony today."

"Simon has been looking out for me like a guard dog since he discovered me in *Sweet Nothings*. I owe my career to him then and now." She whispered, "Don't tell anyone, but Simon's bark is far worse than his bite."

Jana held her expanding tummy, as Mama cleared their plates then replaced them with Chicken Napolitano. The dish filled their nostrils with the smell of sweet basil. Jana and Peter tasted the warm, delicious thinly breaded chicken smothered with bits of tomatoes, mushrooms, and olives and moaned in ecstasy. Mama served more red wine, blew them kisses, and was gone.

"I may never eat hotel food again," Jana said.

"Then we'll just have to come back here soon."

"Deal."

They continued enjoying the mouthwatering entrée.

Peter said, "I wonder what will happen tomorrow at rehearsal."

"I imagine Bella will introduce us to our new director."

"He couldn't be worse than our old director."

Jana couldn't help herself from giggling.

"Not to speak ill of the dead, but, 'aye, do it louder like, hah?' isn't directing." He took a sip of wine. "I wonder if Sally will calm down."

"That's doubtful."

"Will Tate be back?"

"Not yet. But hopefully soon."

"Good. I want our whole company together—unharmed."

"I feel the same way. Dwayne and his team are

investigating. I guess we have to put our faith in him."

"But *you're* investigating, too."

"Not really. I'm just helping Dwayne."

He pointed a finger at her. "I've watched you, Jana Lane. You're questioning suspects, and using the 'little gray cells' to try to figure out whodunit."

"I've had a bit of experience, but—"

"And you're using it—right now. Jana, I'm flattered that you agreed to have dinner with me, but I know your real motive was to question me about my mother. Is she your favorite suspect?"

Jana put down her knife and fork. "Peter, please don't take this personally, but I have to do everything I can to try to figure out who is doing this and why."

"And you think Mom is our murderer because she doesn't like her role in the play? Wouldn't it be easier for her to quit the show rather than kill three people?"

"To be honest, I don't know what I think. But I know the murderer is in our company."

"And everyone seems to have a motive."

"Exactly. Because of the murders, Bella, and Brad by association, are the producers and get to pick the new director. Sally owns the copyright for the play. Tate is allowed to come back when he is discharged from the hospital."

Peter did a double-take. "You don't think Tate killed Stanley, Katrina, and Tony?"

"No, but someone who loves him might have done it for him."

Peter's eyes doubled in size. "Your son's nanny? The skinny guy with the glasses who thinks he's a theatre critic?"

"I know it sounds ridiculous. It all sounds

ridiculous." She sighed. "There is something I'm missing, but I can't figure out what it is."

Mama cleared their plates amidst praises and bravos, then brought them cappuccino and assorted Italian pastry. Peter indulged, but Jana kindly refused. *I don't want my costumes to rip.*

When Mama had gone, Peter took a sip of the hot Italian coffee. "I'm worried about you."

"Why?"

He took her hand. "Jana, playing detective can be dangerous. Experienced or not, by sniffing around after clues and interviewing suspects you're putting yourself in harm's way." He swallowed hard. "I know I've only known you four days, but I'm—fond of you. I've never felt this way about anyone before." He smiled. "You make me laugh. You understand my sense of humor. It feels...right when we're together. I know you feel it, too. It took me thirty-six years to find you, and I don't want to lose you. I try to look after you as much as I can, but, though I'd like to, I can't be with you every moment." He ran a thick hand through his wavy hair. "Please stop working with Douglas. I don't know what I'd do if anything happened to you."

Tears welled up in Jana's eyes. "Peter, I feel the same way. I love being with you. And when we're apart, I think about you. I feel the bond between us like electricity. But there are two things you need to understand. I'm happily married. So nothing can happen between us. As much as we may want it to. And whatever it takes, I'm going to do everything I know how to find and stop the murderer."

His eyes looked sad and wounded. "Then be careful."

She squeezed his hand. "I will."

Peter paid the bill, thanked Mama again and again, and promised to come back soon. Then Jana and Peter walked off their dinners under the cobalt star-laden sky.

"Little Italy is adorable," Jana said.

"So are you."

They shared a smile.

"Are you ready to co-host the AIDS benefit with me Sunday evening?" Jana asked.

"Sure. What do I have to do?"

Jana replied, "Wear a tux, look handsome, be charming, and stand next to me."

"Is that all?" He laughed. "Is there a script?"

She shook her head. "Simon and his partner Cornelius are booking the entertainment. They'll give us the list of performers when we arrive. I'll make a brief introductory speech, then we'll introduce the talent."

"I hope we have good rapport with some banter between the acts."

"That's pretty likely," she replied.

When their legs grew tired, they took a taxi back to the hotel, and Peter walked Jana to her door. "What an amazing night."

Jana replied, "I had a terrific time. Thank you for everything, Peter."

"My pleasure."

"Mine, too."

Peter bent over, put his hand on the back of her head, leaned in, and gently kissed her lips.

Enjoying Peter's minty breath, strong arms, and soft lips, Jana wanted to surrender to his kiss. *Brian. Remember him? Your soulmate who you adore.* Instead, she placed her hands on Peter's strong chest and pushed him away.

"Peter, what are you doing?"

Jana and Peter nearly got whiplash as they turned to face Savannah Stevens, wearing a chocolate silk bathrobe and silver high-heeled slippers.

"What are you doing here, Mom?" Peter asked.

"Looking for you," Savannah replied. "I woke up and you were gone."

"Jana and I went out to dinner."

Jana took in a deep breath. "Savannah, would you like to come inside for coffee or tea?"

"They keep me up at night," Savannah said.

Peter looked at Jana. "Mom gets terrible insomnia. I should get her get back to bed."

"Of course." Jana came shoulder to shoulder with Savannah. "This isn't what you think."

Savannah locked eyes with her. "When you were a little girl, you always told the truth. When did that change?"

Before Jana could respond, Peter said, "Goodnight, Jana. We'll see you in the morning." He put an arm around his mother and led her to the elevator.

Jana let herself into her hotel suite. Since it was too late to call Devon and Ed at camp, she looked in on B.J., noticed Brad was still out at Bella's, washed and put on a lavender satin nightgown, then phoned Brian. Propped up in bed on her silver satin pillow, Jana asked, "How's Viva Las Vegas?"

He exhaled. "I nearly murdered the owner of the mall chain."

"I'll get my nail file for my prison visit."

Brian said, "I'm going crazy without you. I'm a

lunatic all day, then I lay awake thinking about you at night."

"Come visit me."

"I wish I could. I'm booked at meetings…or should I say, *battles* for the next few days. How's B.J.?"

"Still having the time of his life."

"And his mother?"

Jana picked up her script from the night table and tossed it onto the bed. "Nearly off book."

Brian asked, "Any more murders?"

Jana closed her eyes and said a silent prayer. "Only one."

"What!"

"A floodlight fell on our director."

"Where were you and B.J.?"

"I was on stage, and B.J. was in the audience."

"That's not safe, Jan!"

"Brian, please stop shouting."

"What am I supposed to do when my wife and son are in danger?"

Jana sat yoga style. "Please calm down."

"What's the detective doing?"

Jana groaned. "Probably listening to the cast album of *Bye Bye Birdie*."

"Where's Brad?"

"At Bella's duplex." *No doubt planning to take over Broadway then the world.*

"What about the guy you like with AIDS?"

"He's in the hospital, but he's getting better. Gary is taking care of him."

"I thought Gary was taking care of B.J."

"He is." *Between making recommendations for script changes.*

"What about your boyfriend in the show?"

Try to sound casual. "Peter and I had dinner in Little Italy tonight."

"That sounds *festive*."

"We went by horse and open carriage. The food was amazing. And don't worry, he walked me right to my door."

"Did he kiss you goodnight?"

I can never lie to you. "Yes."

"What!"

"It was just a little goodnight kiss from a friend."

"I don't kiss *my* friends goodnight."

"Jackson would like to kiss you goodnight."

"This isn't about our friend Jackson, or about me. What the hell is going on, Jan?"

"Somebody…or somebodies killed Stanley, Katrina, and Tony."

"And the play is going on?"

"With Bella as producer, Sally Chen as the estate owner of the play, and Bella's acting teacher, whoever he is, as director, I think."

"Three murders! And you have no idea who committed them?"

Jana rubbed her forehead. "I'm totally stumped."

"That doesn't sound like Jana Lane Otley."

"I know what each person in the cast has to gain by killing Stanley, Katrina, and Tony, but it doesn't all fit together. Why would Bella kill her grandfather? I know she inherits his estate, but he adored her, and he was featuring her in his show. And Stanley was in his seventies. He would have died from natural causes soon enough. And even though Sally is quite self-absorbed like Bella, I believe she loved Tony, so why kill him and Katrina? They cast Sally in their play, even when Katrina was aware that Sally was her husband's mistress. And why would sweet Gary kill them to get Tate reinstated in the show? I had already laid down the ultimatum, threatening to leave the show if they fired Tate. And if Savannah doesn't like her role, or Bella's role, or my role for that matter, Savannah could quit the show and try to get another show. Why kill three people?"

Jana came up for air, and Brian said, "I don't know what you're talking about."

"Sorry."

"But it sounds like you need to check into everyone's past, like you did with the suspects in *Girl Detective*. Figure it out before whoever killed Stanley, Katrina, and Tony comes after you—and our son."

"Brian, I know there's a missing piece to all this. I *have* to find it."

"Don't get killed looking."

She heard muffled voices from the receiver.

"I have to go, babe. Look all around you. And look after B.J. I'll tie things up here and get there as soon as I can."

"I'll be waiting." *I wish I could reach through the phone and be in your arms.*

"You're my reason for living."

And he was gone.

Jana hung up the phone, studied her lines, and fell asleep with her arms wrapped around her script— pretending it was Brian. At three in the morning, she jumped out of bed. *Check into their pasts. Of course. I love you, Brian.*

****

Jana Lane hid behind the sofa in her dressing room, terrified of the shadow above her. When the dark shadow faded, she leapt up and raced out of the dressing room with her heart pounding in her chest. Heavy footsteps followed. When she reached the stage, two hands reached for her neck and she screamed.

Trying desperately to regulate her breathing, and her pulse, Jana sat up in bed and slowly inhaled through her nose and exhaled through her mouth. Soaking wet, she rose on shaky legs and headed for the bathroom. She showered and dressed in a teal suit with shoulder pads and a navy scarf, then teased her hair and applied her makeup—highlighting the teal eye shadow.

By the time Jana reached the living room, Gary and B.J. were up and dressed.

"Gary, please order breakfast for you and B.J., then take him by taxi to the theatre."

"B.J. wants lox and eggs! Oye vey!" Jana's son rubbed his stomach.

She kissed the top of his head, and remembered Brian's chestnut hair. "And please tell our new director I'll be a bit late. It shouldn't be a problem since I'm not in the first two scenes."

Gary buttoned the top collar of his white shirt. "Is something wrong?"

What could be wrong? Three people died in our company. "I need to run an errand."

Gary shrugged his narrow shoulders. "Okay."

"Thanks."

Jana taxied to the midtown New York Public Library. She walked through the marble maze of rooms and asked two staff members for directions until she reached the Microfilm/Microfiche room, where an

African American woman near Jana's age stood behind the circulation desk.

Jana took off her sunglasses and approached the desk. "Hello, I'm hoping you can help me."

The woman clutched the chest of her magenta cotton dress. "Little Jana Lane in my circulation room. Be still my fluttering heart!"

Jana smiled. "That's very nice of you. I'm looking for—"

"Where's your father?"

"He's no longer with us."

"How about little Timmy?"

"He lives in California. And he's not so little anymore."

The woman smiled nostalgically. "Remember when you were the Indian princess, the young mermaid, the pirate princess, the pink ballerina, the sweet candy striper? How I loved those movies. They got me through puberty. I told my mother I wanted to be just like Jana Lane. You were always so kind and helpful to everyone."

"Thank you. I—"

"I heard on TV that you're back in the movies, but with three kids I don't get out to the movies much."

"I'm here today—"

"What are your new movies about? Is little Timmy in them?"

"No." Jana looked at the woman's nametag. "Elmira, I'm doing a play on Broadway."

"I don't get out to see many plays. The kids keep me hopping. Do you have kids?"

"Three. Elmira—"

"What's your play about?"

"Greed, murder, and revenge. I—"

"It *is*? I would never have thought that. You're so sweet and innocent. Who do you play?"

"The neighbor who uncovers the truth. I need to do some research for the play. I'm thrilled my old movies helped you, Elmira. Now can you please help *me*?"

"Say, 'let's be friends,' like you did in your movies," Elmira asked with joy filling her face.

Glancing at her watch, Jana said, "Let's be friends?"

"You got it, honey!" Elmira wept tears of joy.

Jana asked Elmira for any newspaper or magazine articles from the past that might shed light on her company members, listing them by name. Miraculously, Elmira found more information than the F.B.I.

After signing an autograph, posing for a picture, and singing the theme song from *Girl Astronaut*, Jana was finally seated in a corner table with a microfilm machine in front of her and a stack of microfilm boxes at her side. She perused the information on her cast-mates for over an hour.

Jana looked at her watch. *There's no way I can read all this and get to the theatre before lunch.* She printed the documents, then asked Elmira at the desk for a box to carry them.

"Thank you, Elmira."

"Thank you, Jana Lane!"

Jana dropped off the box at the hotel then taxied to the theatre's front lobby, where she was met by Roll, his microphone, and his sneer. "Another death! Jana Lane, your theatre is turning into a graveyard!"

"I'm late for rehearsal, Roll."

He stood in front of the inner lobby door. "Is it true your producer, playwright, and director met with foul play?"

"You'll have to ask Detective Douglas."

"Peter Stevens was out here a moment ago looking for you. Your fans want to know if Peter will be husband number two, and Brian will be husband number ex."

Jana's eyes narrowed. "Husband number one is coming to visit me soon. When he does, I suggest you stay clear of him, or you'll be reporter number ex."

Jana passed through the inner lobby and found the theatre in pandemonium. Dwayne stood on stage in his suit. A Hispanic man she had never seen before was in front of the orchestra pit wearing a lemon tunic and black slacks. The cast members were huddled together in the front of the house. B.J. ran into her arms to greet her. She kissed his cheek and asked him what was going on. He shrugged. *I'm with you, B.J.* With everyone shouting and waving their arms, Jana couldn't make out what anyone was saying.

"Hold it!" Dwayne got everyone's attention. "As I was saying, our testing showed Mrs. Cuccioli's fountain pen and the floodlight that killed Mr. Cuccioli were tampered with. So for the safety of everyone in this theatre, and so we can further investigate, this theatre is closed until further notice."

"Where are we supposed to rehearse the show?" Bella adjusted her vermillion midriff blouse.

"How will we be ready for opening night?" Brad asked in a matching polo shirt and white parachute pants, putting his arm around her.

"Tony would have wanted the show to continue."

Sally wiped her dry eyes then placed her handkerchief inside a designer black bag that matched her designer black chiffon dress.

"And I need to talk to all of you again about your relationship with the deceased," Dwayne said.

Savannah looked stunning in a white form-fitting dress with white pearls and earrings. "We need to rehearse to work out some script changes. I don't care who owns the show, who is in love with whom, or who has AIDS."

Gary's jaw dropped. "What a vicious thing to say."

Savannah's eyes doubled in size. "What did you call me?"

"I said you're *vicious*. And I meant it," Gary replied.

Peter stood between Savannah and Gary. Towering over B.J.'s nanny, Peter's muscles bulged out of his aqua polo shirt. "You've said enough."

"I've just begun." Gary said with rage in his eyes.

Calm down, Gary. She didn't mean to insult Tate.

The man Jana didn't know said, "Detective Douglas, can't you just station an officer in the theatre each day while we rehearse?"

Dwayne shook his head. "Two, probably three murders were committed in this theatre over the week. The only responsible thing to do is close the theatre."

More pandemonium ensued. This time Jana quieted everyone down. "Everyone. Please. Detective Douglas is right. It's no longer safe—for any of us to be here. But that doesn't mean we can't put up our show—and open on time."

"How?" Sally asked.

"By catching the murderer," Jana replied.

"You've had experience in that arena, Jana." Sally reapplied her blood-red lipstick. "What's taking you so long?"

Jana replied, "I promise each of you that I will work with Detective Douglas to find whoever is responsible for these heinous crimes against our company members. Then, in the names of our deceased colleagues, we will open our show—on time."

"How are we going to do that without a theatre?" Brad asked.

Jana walked with B.J. down the aisle. "Dwayne, I certainly understand your concern." *I was the one who convinced you they were murders and not accidents.* "But we're all here now. Won't you please allow us until lunchtime to meet and plan the next step for the production?"

"All right," Dwayne said. "Have your meeting in the greenroom. But everyone needs to be out of the theatre by noon. Jana, can I speak with you?"

Jana handed B.J. over to Brad then met Dwayne on stage.

"This has moved into full investigation mode," Dwayne said with a worried look on his face.

"I understand."

"Good, because I need you to help me."

"Do you want to conduct interviews in the dressing rooms again?"

"I'll do the interviews at police headquarters. I'd like *you* to talk to your coworkers. And if you uncover anything suspicious, give me a call right away."

"All right."

He squeezed her arm. "And take care of yourself." Dwayne left the theatre house to speak with his police officer in the lobby.

Jana walked down the stage steps and extended her hand to who she assumed was the new director. "Hello, I'm Jana Lane."

The tall, handsome, dark-haired man with a large mustache shook Jana's hand. "I'm Manuel Martinez. It's my pleasure to meet you."

"I apologize for being late."

"No harm done."

With Brad playing tag with B.J. around the theatre house, Bella approached Manuel and Jana. "I'm glad you two met."

Manuel put his arm around Bella and squeezed her into his chest. "Here's my girl." He kissed her cheek. "This young lady is going to be the biggest star on Broadway."

Bella giggled and cooed as her cheek rubbed against the black chest hair peeking out of his tunic. She said unconvincingly for an actress, "Stop, Manuel."

"We are so lucky to have such a beautiful ingénue in our show." Manuel turned to Jana. "And such a beautiful star."

Jana unleashed a strained smile. "Thank you. Would you like me to ask the cast to assemble in the green room?"

Manuel put his other arm around Jana. "Jose can take care of that. I'd like to spend some time getting to know my leading lady."

"Excuse me." Jana ducked out of his grasp. "Bella, may I speak with you a moment?"

"Sure. See you later, Manny."

"That you will."

Jana walked Bella to a corner toward the rear of the

theatre house. "Is Manuel just your acting teacher?"

"What do you mean?" Bella repaired the scrunchie in her hair.

"You two seem to be more than just teacher and student."

Bella pulled up her lace gloves. "We were together for a short time."

"Manuel is your ex-lover?"

"You say that like it's a bad thing. Manuel is a total hunk. I notice the way you look at Peter Stevens." Her eyes wandered over to Peter sitting with his mother. "Not that I blame you. I wouldn't kick *him* out of bed."

This isn't about Peter and me. "You and Manuel seemed pretty friendly."

"Manuel is a good acting teacher. I think he will be a good director, too."

Bella started walking away, and Jana pulled at her arm. "Are you sure whatever you had with Manuel is over?"

Bella smiled. "Manny's fun and sexy. I don't regret being with him. But your nephew and I are the real thing."

Jana followed Bella to the green room, where everyone sat on sofas and chairs. Bella stood opposite them. "We need to talk about the future of the show," Bella said.

Brad put his arm around Bella. "Everyone listen to our new producer."

Manuel stood on the other side of Bella. "Our *beautiful* producer and ingénue."

Sitting on a sofa with B.J., Jana said, "Our set is in the basement. Most of the lights are hung and focused. We're all off book."

"B.J. knows lines!"

"That's right, B.J.," Jana continued. "Today is Friday. Perhaps by Monday, Detective Douglas will reopen the theatre. If not, we can rent a rehearsal hall."

"That sounds like a good plan." Peter beamed at Jana with pride.

Jana said, "Let's all clear out what we need from our dressing rooms. Please go to the police station during the time Dwayne tells you, and be as forthcoming as you can about anything you might know."

As everyone headed for his or her dressing room, Peter rested a hand on Jana's shoulder. The room smelled of fresh mint. "Jana, now you can let Douglas and the police investigate, and come back to the hotel with Mom and me."

As difficult as it was, Jana pulled away. "I appreciate your concern and your friendship, but I'm not going to stop trying to put the pieces of this puzzle together."

Jana walked into her dressing room, and screamed at the words written with lipstick on her makeup mirror, 'Stop, Jana. Or we'll stop you!'

Chapter 7

Peter Stevens rushed to Jana's side. "Are you all right?"

Jana nodded, unable to stop looking at the blood-red lipstick on her makeup mirror.

Putting his arm around her, he said, "This is what I was afraid of."

Dwayne stood next to Peter and looked at the mirror. Then he turned to the group. "I need to frisk each of you, then I want you to follow me to police headquarters for fingerprinting and interviewing."

"Frisk us?" Bella clutched onto Brad's arm.

"I just got here," Manuel said, taking Bella's hand.

"Nobody is frisking *me*," Savannah said.

"Fisking!" B.J. giggled.

"Everyone, please quiet down," Dwayne said. "I need to determine if the lipstick on Jana's mirror belongs to any of you."

"No need, Dwayne." Jana pointed to her dressing room mirror. "It's Sally's shade of lipstick."

Sally's eyes ignited. "You're not going to pin this on me, Jana! Why would I write that on your mirror?"

Jana bent down and held up the small garbage can under her makeup table. "Here's the lipstick, Dwayne. There won't be any prints on it. The murderer—" She looked at the mirror. "—or murderers are too smart for that."

Dwayne used his handkerchief to put the lipstick into a plastic bag. "Can everyone please follow me back to the station?" He turned to Jana. "You should go to your hotel and get some rest."

As they were leaving, Peter said to Jana, "Call me tonight?"

Jana nodded.

Once everyone had gone, B.J. said to his mother, "Why did they go?"

Jana used her acting skills to smile. "Dwayne needs their help with something."

"Dwayne needs help!"

That's for sure.

Jana and B.J. left the theatre, picked up sandwiches—sturgeon on pumpernickel bread, B.J.'s choice—and taxied back to their hotel suite. Gary returned from the police station and joined them at the living room table.

"How did things go with Dwayne?" Jana asked.

Gary helped himself to a sandwich. "I've never been fingerprinted before."

"I want my fingers printed!"

"Finish your lunch, B.J.," Jana said.

"Dwayne asked me where I was this morning," Gary explained.

Everyone had free reign of the dressing room area. Anybody could have done it.

Gary continued. "Is it all right if I visit Tate at the hospital after lunch?"

"Sure." Jana put down her sandwich. "How is he doing?"

Gary breathed a sigh of relief. "Much better. He should be released really soon." His face lit up. "When

I visited him yesterday, I brought him a red rose. Tate said that's his favorite flower."

Jana squeezed his hand. "Buy him a bouquet on me."

"Thanks, Jana." A tear welled up in his eye. "You're a good woman."

"Mommy's good!" B.J. shouted. "B.J. wants to play!"

"Okay, honey. Your blocks are still out," Jana said.

Once B.J. was in his room, Gary said, "You're different from the others."

"What others?" Jana sipped her tea.

"The other women in the show."

She wiped her mouth with her napkin. "I heard you and Savannah arguing at rehearsal."

Gary groaned. "She acts like she's so high and mighty."

"She was a big movie star."

"So are you, and you don't act that way."

"Everyone's different."

"Savannah's no different from Katrina."

"What didn't you like about Katrina?"

He replied, "She acted so holier than thou. What a hypocrite."

"Don't worry. I won't let anyone fire Tate from the show." She sighed. "If we have a show."

Gary took another sandwich. "The break might be good for the play."

"How do you mean?"

"Maybe Bella and Sally will take another look at the script. It needs work."

Everybody's a critic. "I thought you were happy when Katrina rewrote B.J.'s scene for Bella and

Savannah to bully and bribe him to keep quiet about what he heard them say."

"That scene is better. It gives B.J. so much more to play as an actor."

He's three years old!

Gary pushed his glasses up the bridge of his nose. "But the second to the last scene still needs work." Gary spoke like a Broadway producer. "The writing is fine, but the tempo, relationships, and motivations are wrong."

When did you get your degree in theatre criticism?

"Why would you turn Bella over to the police detective? You've already seduced him into submission. Why not split the money with Bella and her mother and live happily ever after?" Gary was on a roll. "By the way, your love scenes with Peter Stevens are totally believable." He pushed his empty plate away and wiped his mouth with his napkin. "I guess spending so much time with him helped."

Jana choked on her tea. "There is nothing going on between Peter and me, if that's what you mean."

He peered at her over his glasses. "It doesn't look that way."

"Then look again. We're co-stars and friends. Nothing more."

B.J. shouted from his bedroom, "Gary play with B.J.!"

"Duty calls." Gary went into the next room to play with B.J.

Jana looked out the window at the New York skyline and thought about Peter.

The star of *China Doll* spent the rest of the day exercising in the hotel gym, talking to Devon and Ed on the phone, and studying her lines. Since Brad was with Bella, Jana had dinner in the suite with B.J. and Gary, then she answered Brian's phone call, conveniently leaving out the lipstick and mirror incident.

Jana changed into a maroon satin nightgown and matching robe, then settled down on her bedroom chaise to read her research materials from the library. After reading only one sentence, the phone rang.

"I thought you were going to call me."

Could any man's voice be more sexy? "Peter, I'm sorry. I got tied up.

"Are you okay?"

"A little lipstick on my mirror won't get me down."

"Good."

"How did things go with Dwayne at the station?"

"They went."

"Did he take everyone's fingerprints?"

"Mm, hm. Even Jose's." He chuckled. "The female police officer lingered a bit too long with mine."

I'm not surprised.

"Douglas looked frustrated. I got the feeling our answers didn't help much. I heard him playing the *King and I* soundtrack on his office tape player as we all left."

They shared a giggle.

Peter said, "Good detection about Sally's lipstick shade. Though Sally wasn't too happy about it."

"The girl who played my older sister in *Pink Ballerina* wore the same shade. I always admired it but thought it wouldn't work on me."

"Anything would work on Jana Lane."

"I doubt Sally would agree with you."

"Do you think Sally wrote that on your mirror?"

"No. Sally is a bright young woman. If she wanted to warn me to stop investigating the murders, she wouldn't use her own lipstick. Somebody took it."

"And that's exactly what it was, a warning. Whoever killed Stanley, Katrina, and Tony means business. I'm worried about you."

Jana leaned back in the chaise. "I have something up my sleeve."

"Do tell."

"I took out some research materials from the library, and I intend to spend the evening pouring through them."

"Research on what?"

"You mean on *whom*? I have articles about everyone involved in *China Doll*."

"On me, too?"

"I'm afraid so."

"Hm, Jana Lane reading all about me. I like it."

"I don't." She looked down at the box on the floor. "There's a ton of papers here, and I don't relish reading all of them."

"Want some help?"

"Thank you, Peter, but this is something I need to do. There's got to be something in here that can lead me to the killer."

"Based on that message today, it sounds like there's more than one murderer."

"You may be right."

"Jana, I'll miss the show, but I don't want to miss you." His breath was heavy. "I know it's only been a week, but after this is all over I want you to be a part of my life."

"Peter—"

"I know you're married. And I understand your...priorities, but if nothing else, I hope we can be friends."

"Always and forever."

"Thanks, *Girl Detective.*"

Jana heard a noise on the other end of the phone.

"Mom's calling. She's in a bad way. I better go."

I hope you have some scotch.

"Take care of yourself, honey."

"I will."

She hung up the phone, then Jana stared into space thinking about Peter. *There's work to do, girl.* She climbed into bed and began reading the newspaper and magazine articles until she drifted off to sleep.

****

Jana's dreams were filled with grotesque images of Savannah throwing scotch and Sally hurling lipstick at her, Brian and Peter fighting over her, Brad and Manuel arguing over Bella, Stanley's ghost pulling Tate's oxygen hose out of the hospital's oxygen tank, Katrina's ghost and Gary arguing over script changes, and Dwayne performing "Broadway Baby" from the musical *Follies.*

When Saturday morning finally came, Jana shakily rose from bed, showered, put on a black linen dress with matching shoes and white pearls, applied her makeup—including clown white to conceal the bags under eyes—and teased her hair into layers.

Happy to find B.J. and Gary up and dressed, she ate breakfast with them at the living room table—matzo brei and raisin toast, B.J.'s choice. "Gary, are you going to Katrina's and Tony's funeral today?"

"Hah!" Gary wiped his mouth with his napkin. "I wouldn't be caught dead there."

No pun intended.

"I couldn't stand either of them."

B.J. threw a raisin at Gary. "B.J. can stand!"

"Eat your eggs, B.J." She took a sip of lemon mint herbal tea then asked Gary, "Are you visiting Tate today?"

Gary shook his bed head. "They're doing some tests at the hospital. I'll call him later."

"Can you watch B.J. while I go to the funeral this afternoon?"

"Sure."

"I shouldn't be home too late."

B.J. shouted, "I want to rehearse!"

"Not on Saturday, B.J." *And maybe never again.*

With Gary watching B.J., Jana escaped to her bedroom to call Devon and Ed at camp, then spent a few hours reading more of her research.

When her eyes blurred over, Jana taxied to the funeral home. Upon entering the main room, she found Katrina's and Tony's mourners sitting quietly on sofas and easy chairs facing the two closed coffins up front. Most of the people in attendance appeared to be business associates of Katrina's or friends of Tony's. Since the deceased had no children and their parents were dead, Sally Chen played the role of the bereaved host. Peter, Savannah, Brad, and Bella sat on a large sofa toward the rear of the room in whispered conversation. Jana joined them, sitting on an easy chair nearby.

Sally, wearing a black gabardine gown and silver necklace, stood between the two coffins and addressed the small crowd. "Thank you all for coming. It is with great pain and heartache that I say goodbye to my dear, loving husband." Sally wept theatrical tears into her handkerchief. "Tony Cuccioli was a warm, fun-loving, kind, considerate, and intelligent—"

Really?

"—Broadway stage manager and director. He was also my husband, and my best friend. Tony Cuccioli saw only the good in everyone."

Except Tate Moonglow.

"He was honest and loyal."

To his two wives.

"Tony Cuccioli believed in the theatre, and he believed in the people of the theatre. Most of all, he believed in me." Sally broke down and wept over Tony's coffin.

Wearing a black suit that perfectly sculpted his muscles, Peter leaned into Jana and filled her nostrils with the scent of mint. "Should we applaud?"

When the crowd went back to their conversations, Sally miraculously composed herself and commanded their attention again. "I will never forget my husband. I know you won't either."

Peter whispered to Jana, "No way, youse guys, hah?"

Jana used her acting skills to keep a straight face.

"I cherish the brief time I had with my husband, and I will forever be proud to be Mrs. Tony Cuccioli." Sally walked from one side of the room to the other, playing to her entire audience. "Before his tragic and shocking death, my husband was directing me in *China Doll* on Broadway." Sally glanced at the other coffin. "Katrina Wright, the famous playwright, whose death we are also mourning today, wrote *China Doll*, her greatest play yet, as a star vehicle for *me*. Though the police have temporarily closed down our show, as we pray for my husband's dear departed soul to be resurrected into Heaven, I hope you will also pray that *China Doll* will be resurrected soon." As if an afterthought, she said, "And pray for Katrina."

That's big of her. As Tony's widow, Sally gets Katrina's money. Just like Bella's character in the play.

Sally gestured grandly to a tall, middle-aged man who entered the sitting room wearing a priest's collar. "And now Father…"

The priest mouthed his name.

"Samuel—," Sally said as if she'd known the man all her life. "—will say a few words about my husband, then lead us all in prayer."

Father Samuel stood next to Sally. "Dearly beloved, we are gathered here today to pay our last respects to—" He pulled an index card out of his jacket pocket. "—Anthony Cuccioti."

Sally whispered in his ear.

"Anthony Cuccioli, our dearly departed. Anthony was a good man. A fine citizen. And very much loved by his wife and everyone." He dropped the card.

"Let's all pray now, Father," Sally said.

As the priest led everyone in a prayer, Savannah, in a low cut gray satin dress, left the sitting room and headed for the lobby.

Obviously sensing something was wrong, Peter followed her.

Clearly losing interest in the prayer, Brad, in a navy blue polo shirt and chinos, and Bella, wearing a chocolate-colored midriff blouse and spandex pants, cuddled together on the sofa.

When the prayer was finished, Sally wept in the priest's arms and thanked him for the "beautiful, and heartfelt eulogy." The moment she paid him, he left.

Since Sally appeared not to know what to do next, Jana approached her. "Sally, my condolences."

"Thank you." Sally turned her back on Jana and sat on a sofa.

Jana joined her. "I know you didn't write those words on my dressing room mirror."

"Everyone else thinks it was me—thanks to you giving my lipstick to the detective."

"I believe somebody took your lipstick to frame you."

"Who?"

"I was hoping you could help me figure it out."

"I think they are all jealous of me because I own the copyright to the play script. They think I married Tony because he was the director, and because he had Katrina's money." Sally inched closer to Jana. "I know I come off as high strung." Real tears welled up in her eyes. "And I was frustrated that Tony stayed married to Katrina. But I loved Tony so much I was willing to take him on any terms, including Katrina's." She wiped the tears off her cheeks with a lace handkerchief. "I would never have hurt Tony. He was my love, and my life."

But would you hurt Katrina and Stanley? "Sally, we haven't gotten to know each other at rehearsals. I apologize for that."

"You're a big star. I'm sure you have better things to do than get to know me." She held her head high. "Even though I did win a Tony Award."

"I don't judge people based on their

accomplishments."

"Everyone does, Jana."

"*I* don't."

Sally sighed. "My parents back in China instilled in me the mantra of fortitude and perseverance. They made it crystal clear from my first memory that I had to succeed—whatever the cost."

"I'm sorry you were raised that way, Sally. No child should feel she needs to prove her self-worth to anyone, including her parents."

"Well, this child did. And I'm still proving it."

Jana sat back on the sofa. "You're an intelligent, successful Broadway performer. That must make your parents proud."

Sally laughed bitterly. "The only thing that would make my parents proud is my name over the title on a marquee."

"I'm sure that will happen for you someday, Sally."

"It can't happen soon enough."

"And Tony promised that to you?"

She nodded. "Every time he told me he loved me." She wailed. "But where is Tony now?"

Jana held Sally in her arms as Sally wept until Jana looked up to Savannah and Peter standing over her.

"Sally, I need to speak with you." Savannah sat on the other side of Sally.

Sally wiped away her tears.

"Peter and I are sorry for your loss," Savannah said.

"Thank you," Sally replied as if Joan of Arc.

Savannah leaned in closer to Sally. "With poor Tony gone, and you controlling the script, I hope we can discuss some revisions."

Jana stood and nearly bumped into Peter. *Not a problem.*

Peter whispered in her ear, "Mom is at it again."

Sally replied to Savannah, "You heard Bella say she wants to present the play her grandfather contracted."

As if on cue, Bella and Brad stood behind Sally and Savannah. "Do you want to speak with me, Savannah?" Bella said.

Savannah stood and faced Bella. "You know as well as I do our roles in the play need rewriting. Our characters are selfish, vindictive, and diabolical."

Bella replied, "That's because the play is a thriller."

Savannah looked at her cast mates. "You are all young and have your careers ahead of you. I have a name and a history to protect. Can we please discuss rewrites?"

As if filled with the spirit of her late grandfather, Bella said, "Grandpop contracted this script, and this is the script we are going to do."

"Bella, be reasonable," Savannah said.

Brad stood between them. "Maybe you should take your own advice, Savannah." Then he put his arm around Bella and they walked away.

Sally said to Savannah, "Unfortunately, our roles are frozen—just like Bella's heart." She held her handkerchief to her chest and walked toward a reporter.

Jana stood next to Savannah. "The audience will understand that you are playing a role, and it's not you on stage."

"There was no difference between the two in old

Hollywood, and you know that." Savannah held back tears.

Peter put his arm around his mother. "Please try to calm down, Mom."

Savannah sniffled.

He turned to Jana. "Would you like to join Mom and me for dinner at the hotel restaurant? You can help me cheer her up."

"I'm not feeling well, Peter." Savannah clutched at her son's arm. "Please take me back to the hotel suite. I'd like to order room service then go to bed."

With a bottle of scotch.

As Savannah walked away, Peter said to Jana over his shoulder, "Sorry."

"I understand," Jana replied.

He whispered, "I'll knock on your door after Mom falls asleep." And he was gone.

Jana said goodbye to her other cast-mates, then taxied back to the hotel. When she arrived at her suite, she found a note on the living room table.

Jana,

Took B.J. to Central Park then to his favorite deli for dinner. Be back soon.

Gary

Jana phoned Brian and hung up after ten rings. Then she welcomed home Gary and B.J. Once B.J. was in bed and Gary had left to visit Tate in the hospital, Jana ordered room service then ate dinner at the dining room table while reading more of her research papers. As she swallowed the last bite of her Greek salad, she heard a knock at the door. She quickly put the papers back inside the box in her bedroom then answered the door.

Peter stood in the doorway. His muscles bulged out of a twilight-blue T-shirt and gym shorts. "I just came from the gym. I'll never make it up to my suite without a glass of water."

She got him a glass of water from the bar, forgetting to close the front door.

Peter walked into the living room and downed the water. "Thanks. I needed that."

"So I see." She put the empty glass back on the bar. "How's Savannah?"

"She had eaten and was out like a light before I left our suite—thanks to a valium."

"Care to sit down?"

Jana and Peter sat on the sofa, and watched the sky turn into yarn of amber, scarlet, and mahogany.

She said, "At the funeral, Sally seemed genuinely upset about Tony's death."

He laughed. "I think she needed more rehearsal."

"Bella appeared to be channeling her grandfather."

He laughed again. "Is Brad with her?"

"Of course. And Gary's with Tate."

He leaned in closer. "Two romances courtesy of our show."

And there won't be a third.

"How are you doing on your research?"

"I'm about halfway through."

"Any leads?"

"Not yet."

He took her hand. "I was awake all last night worrying about you. I wish you would stop sleuthing, or at least let me help you."

Jana squeezed his thick, warm hand. "You're a good friend, Peter. But I need to figure this out."

"And I need to figure out why I care so damn much about you."

"Peter—"

He put his arm around her. "Jana, please hear me out. Being with you feels so…right."

So right, and so wrong. "Peter—"

He put his finger over her lips. "I just want to sit here with you. For a few minutes. To make sure you're safe. All right?"

"All right."

They sat with his arm around her. Jana rested her head on his wide shoulder.

He said, "I adore you, Jana Lane."

"Your door was open."

Jana and Peter looked up to see Savannah standing in front of them.

Jana jumped up. "I didn't realize." She closed the door. "Sit down, Savannah. Would you like something to drink?"

"When I woke up and found Peter gone, I knew he was here." Savannah's eyes glazed over. "I was afraid this would happen."

"Afraid what would happen?" Peter asked, as he led his mother to sit next to him on the sofa.

Savannah buried her head in her manicured hands. "I tried to warn you. I tried to stop you."

"Warn us and stop us from what?" Jana asked, as she sat on an easy chair across from them.

Savannah sighed. "I saw you two…on the sofa…together."

"We were just—"

Savannah raised her hands. "Jana, I know what I saw."

"Mom—"

"Peter, I'm not a stupid woman. I know how you feel about Jana."

Peter said, "All right, I'll admit it. I love Jana."

Uh-oh!

Savannah whimpered like a wounded animal. "But you can't."

"I know. Jana's married."

Jana said, "Savannah, as I've told you before, Peter and I are not involved."

"But you will be if I don't put an end to it," Savannah said with tears staining her eyes.

Unable to stop herself, Jana said, "And even if we were involved, why is that a problem for *you*?"

Peter rested his hand on his mother's knee. "Mom, why are you so upset? Tell me what's wrong."

Savannah blew her nose then returned her handkerchief to the pocket of her Asian print robe. "I never wanted to tell you this."

"Tell me *what*?"

Jana started to rise. "I can go into the bedroom and—"

"Please stay." Savannah took in a deep breath. "You know my first husband died when he and I were quite young." Her face softened. "I think he was the only man I ever loved." She let out an ironic laugh. "I think I married my second husband out of fear of being alone. He must have sensed it, too, because he wasn't around much."

"Dad was away on business," Peter said.

"That's what I told you. I knew better." She walked to the bar and poured herself a glass of scotch. "I married him shortly before we started rehearsal for

Sweet Nothings. It was a huge mistake."

Peter asked, "Was Dad mean to you?"

"Yes." Savannah sat on the sofa and drank her drink. "But not in the way you think. It's worse to be ignored than to be chastised or demeaned. If someone yells at you, or even hits you, at least you know he *sees* you. I spent my whole marriage feeling invisible." Tears filled her eyes. "It's ironic that I'm crying now. I was the only one who didn't cry at his funeral. Everyone complimented me on being so brave. It wasn't bravery, it was relief."

Peter took his mother's hand. "Why are you telling this to me now?"

Savannah wiped the tears off her cheeks. "I was so excited when we started *Sweet Nothings.* Katrina was a promising female playwright. Stanley, an up-and-coming Broadway producer. We rehearsed all day then sat up all night in Katrina's apartment laughing, talking, and reliving every moment of our days in the theatre." She looked at Jana. "And the cast was amazing. You were only five years old and a stronger actress than most of them. And your father was dashing, charming, and the perfect leading man." She said through a tight throat. "On stage and off."

Oh my God! "You and my father weren't only lovers *on* stage?"

Savannah looked away.

Jana said, "Back then I sensed there was something between you two, but at five years old I didn't fully understand what it was. I only knew my mother wasn't around, and my father paid a great deal of attention to you."

"Your father was a special man," Savannah said.

"He sensed I was lonely, and he knew my self-esteem was in the toilet." She smiled in recollection. "Scott made me feel like I mattered. Like I was worth something. Like I was a woman."

Jana's mind raced as fast as her heart. "Thirty-seven years ago you and my father had an affair."

Savannah nodded.

Peter's my brother.

The blood drained from Peter's face. "And you became pregnant with *me*?"

Savannah nodded and wept. "Scott and I talked about what to do. An abortion was out of the question. We counted the months and assumed the play would close by the time I showed too much. We couldn't go public. We didn't want to hurt our spouses. So I told everyone my husband was the father of my baby."

"Including the baby," Peter said softly.

Jana said, "But years later when my mother died, and your husband died, why didn't you tell everyone then?"

Savannah wiped her eyes. "By then, Scott and I were both movie stars. During that time, it would have tarnished both of our images, and ended our careers."

"And your son knowing his real father didn't enter into the equation?" Peter asked incredulously.

She took his hand. "I wanted to tell you so many times, Peter, but what would have been the point?"

Peter replied, "The point would have been for me to know my real father." He turned to Jana. "And my half-sister."

Savannah rubbed her temples. "That's why I was so upset when I saw you two together."

"We aren't together, but we *could* have been,"

Peter said. "Mom, how could you keep this from me for so long?"

Tears streamed down Savannah's face. "Please don't hate me, Peter."

He paced around the room. "I don't hate you, Mom. You were the only one there for me when I was a kid. And I appreciate that. But what you did was cruel, and so unfair!"

"I deserved that. What I've done is inexcusable." Savannah wept bitterly.

Peter sat next to her. "Mom, please stop crying."

"I can't." Savannah continued crying.

"Mom, go back to our suite. Get some sleep."

Savannah rested her hand on his cheek. "Please forgive me for what I've done."

Peter said, "We'll talk more in the morning. Right now I want to talk to Jana. Please."

Savannah rose with slumped shoulders. She walked to the door, looked back at Jana and Peter, then left the suite.

He's my brother. That's why Peter and I have such a strong connection. "Are you all right?"

"I understand what she must have been going through. And she was the best mother a kid could have." He put his head in his hands. "But she should have told me!"

Jana sat next to him and put her hand on his back. "It's a shock—for both of us. But I have to admit—" She smiled. "—it makes me happy."

He looked up at her with tear-stained eyes. "Happy?"

"I always wanted a brother. I used to ask my parents for one all the time." She snickered. "That must have made my father uncomfortable."

"What was he like?"

"I adored him. I wanted to be just like him. Dad was the consummate actor, living from one stage or one movie set to the next. He loved life, and in his way, he loved me." She frowned. "We weren't on good terms for the last few years of his life. But I'll never forget his charisma, passion for life, and pride in me and my accomplishments." She blinked back tears. "And he had amazing green eyes—just like yours."

"I remember him in your old movies. He was a good actor."

"He sure was. He just wasn't always a good man."

"I want to hear all about him."

"I'll tell you everything I remember."

"And I want to be a part of your life, now more than ever."

Jana laughed. "I think I can arrange that." She took his hands in hers, scarcely believing her words. "Peter, you're my brother." Tears filled her eyes. "And I couldn't ask for a better one."

He looked like a little boy. "Jana."

They embraced and cried into one another's tears.

Chapter 8

Jana and Peter spent the night in Jana's living room, talking about Jana's father and Jana's childhood. When the sun wrapped a golden band around the New York City skyline, Peter and Jana shared a hug, and he left for his suite.

After sleeping for only two hours, Jana was woken by B.J. bouncing on her bed. As it was Sunday, once Jana, Gary, and B.J. dressed and had fruit and juice, Jana took B.J. to a nearby open and affirming church, while Gary picked up Tate, who was being released from the hospital.

Jana sat in a rear pew of the historic church, wearing a sea-blue dress, with B.J. next to her in a dark blue suit and red bowtie. She gazed at the beautiful stained-glass windows surrounding the church, as they told the story of the man who served outcasts, ate with the downtrodden, healed those shunned by society, and preached to love your neighbor as yourself and to judge no one. *How did that precious message become corrupted by some for political and financial gain to suppress women and persecute men like Simon, Cornelius, Gary, and Tate?*

Jana and B.J. joined in singing the hymns, accompanied by an antique pipe organ. Then they listened as the minister took to the pulpit with a true Christ-like message of love, forgiveness, and servitude to all.

When the service was over, Jana shook the minister's hand at the doorway to the church. The young pastor's eyes lit up and his dimples appeared. Looking under Jana's large hat, he said, "I didn't realize we had a celebrity with us today. Thank you for coming, Miss Lane."

"It's Jana. And thank you, Reverend Thomas, for that wonderful sermon."

"I like church!" B.J. said.

"I'm so glad." Reverend Thomas smiled.

"I'm B.J.!"

"Hello, B.J." The pastor shook B.J.'s hand. "Will we see you again?"

Jana replied, "Our church is in Hyde Park, led by Reverend Heather. B.J. and I are staying in New York City while we rehearse a play. I'm not sure how much longer we will be living here."

"Well, I sure hope to see you again."

"You can see me tonight if you like."

"Tonight?" the reverend said.

"I'm co-hosting a benefit to raise money for people with AIDS. My agent and his partner have arranged for members of the Broadway community to perform. Tickets are $200, but I would love for you to come as my guest."

He beamed. "I would be most honored."

Jana gave the reverend the address and time of the benefit. Then she took B.J. back to the hotel suite, where Jana, Brad, and B.J. had brunch. When they had finished the last blueberry pancake, poached egg, and bite of tuna salad with kosher pickle—B.J.'s idea—, Jana heard a knock at the door.

She opened the door to Peter, unshaven in an India-green T-shirt and black sweatpants. "You look tired."

"Is that any way to talk to your brother?"

They shared a smile.

"Come in. Can I order you breakfast?" Jana asked.

Peter followed her. "Mom and I already ate."

"How are you two doing?"

"We talked, and ultimately I forgave her." His face softened. "Mom's a good woman. She did what she thought was best for me."

"I'm glad you worked things out."

"Me, too."

Jana squeezed his shoulder then led him to the living room table.

B.J. shouted, "Peter!"

"Hi, Peter," Brad said, finishing his orange juice.

Jana took in a deep breath. "Brad, B.J., Peter and I found out something last night." She put her arm around Peter. "Something pretty wonderful."

"What?" B.J. screeched.

Brad pushed back his chair in full attention. "What's going on, Aunt Jana?"

Jana cleared her throat. "I'll explain the details to you, Brad, when we're alone. B.J., I'll tell you all about it in about fifteen years. For now, the good news is that Peter is your uncle."

"Yeah, Uncle Peter!" B.J. threw himself into Peter's arms.

Tears streamed down Peter's cheeks as he hugged B.J. to his stomach.

Brad rose from his chair and came face to face with Peter. "I didn't know I had an aunt in show business until a few years ago. Now I have an uncle who's an actor, too. I could get used to this."

Their green eyes made contact, then the two men shared a long hug with B.J. between them.

Jana wiped the tears from her eyes with the back of her hands.

"Why are you crying, Mommy?" B.J. asked.

Jana kissed her son's cheek. "Because Mommy's happy that Uncle Peter is her brother."

"I have two brothers," B.J. explained to Peter. "Devon and Ed."

Jana said to Peter, "You'll meet them when they come home from camp. And you'll meet Brian when he gets back from Las Vegas."

"I'm looking forward to it," Peter said.

"Uncle Peter, play with B.J.!" B.J. took Peter's hand and led his new uncle into his room.

Jana relayed Savannah's story to Brad, who replied, "I'm having lunch with Bella. I can't wait to tell her the news."

"Don't forget the benefit tonight."

"I wouldn't miss it."

Once Brad and Peter left, Jana phoned the hotel's babysitting service, checked in with Simon about the benefit and told him about Reverend Thomas, read more of her research documents, ate a light dinner with B.J.—chicken and matzo ball soup, and changed into a strapless, sequined silver satin gown with matching shoes, rope necklace, and eyeshadow.

When the babysitter and B.J. were settled in his bedroom, Peter knocked on the door, looking dashing in a twilight-blue pinstriped suit.

In the taxi on the way to the theatre, Peter said, "You look amazing, as always."

"Right back at you. Good thing, too. Simon said we're sold out."

"I know. I swung by the theatre earlier to see how things were going, and to drop off my mother."

"Was it a madhouse?"

"Totally. Simon was screaming at everyone, musicians were warming up, singers were vocalizing, dancers were stretching, technicians were hanging and focusing lights. And our cast-mates were there."

"They were?"

"They're doing a couple of preview scenes from the show."

"Which scenes?"

"Two scenes I recommended. Don't worry; they're not giving away the plot of the play."

"Brad didn't tell me."

"I guess he wanted to surprise you." He wiped the perspiration off his forehead. "Let's hope that's the only surprise of the night."

"Simon will have the introductions written out for us, and the performers waiting backstage. Cornelius will take care of all things musical. Just be your usual charming self."

He sighed. "I'm not worried about the benefit. I'm worried about *you*." He took her hand. "Jana, you're going to be up on stage in front of hundreds of people. Countless bodies will be milling around backstage. The word is out that you're helping Douglas investigate the three murders at the theatre. What if the murderer is there and takes a pot shot at you?"

She squeezed his hand. "My little brother will protect me."

Peter's eyes pleaded. "How about if I make an

announcement tonight that you are no longer investigating the murders?"

"No way! I'm still reading the research papers I got from the library."

"Have you found anything?"

"Not yet. I plan to finish going through them tomorrow."

"Promise me you'll tell me if you uncover something?"

"Right after I tell Dwayne. In the meantime, we have a benefit to host!"

When Jana and Peter got to the theatre entrance, Simon greeted them in near hysterics. "Where have you two been?"

Jana looked at her silver watch. "You told us to get here at seven, and it's six-thirty."

Simon waved his small hands in her face. "Never mind about that, baby doll." He adjusted the sleeves of his fuchsia jumpsuit then primped his tangelo scarf. "Cornelius has the musicians ready in the orchestra pit, and the actors are in their dressing rooms. Yours are the first two rooms. The audience will be arriving shortly." He handed them folded papers from his mulberry fanny pack. "Baby girl, you'll have to wing your opening and closing speeches. But I've written out the introductions of the performers for both of you."

"Thanks, Simon," Peter said with a wink.

Simon looked at them. "You two make such an adorable couple." He whispered to Jana, "Are you sure you don't want to dump what's-his-name for Peter?"

Jana whispered back, "Do I have a surprise for you."

"Not now, doll face! I have to browbeat the ushers

into submission."

Jana and Peter shared a smile then walked through the outer and inner lobbies into the theatre house. Jana marveled at the three giant crystal chandeliers, eight box seats, vast orchestra seating area, double balcony extending to the heavens, intricate gold molding, and ornate tapestries.

When they arrived at the orchestra pit, Jana kissed Cornelius' cheek. "Thank you for all you and Simon have done, Cornelius."

"Anything for Jana Lane," the tall and thin man said, as he popped the pumpkin-colored suspenders over his harlequin shirt.

"Cornelius Chamberlain, this is Peter Stevens."

The two men shook hands.

"Nice to meet you, Cornelius."

"Likewise, Peter."

"Peter is my co-star." She added, "And my brother."

Cornelius did a double-take.

She whispered, "I'll tell you and Simon all about it."

"We'll hold you to that," Cornelius replied.

Jana thanked the musicians for donating their talents, then she and Peter went backstage to welcome and thank the performers. When Jana and Peter got to the last dressing room, they heard familiar voices.

"Hi, Aunt Jana."

Brad, Bella, and Sally waved from their stools in front of the makeup table.

Standing at the doorway with Peter, Jana replied, "I didn't know you were doing preview scenes from the show tonight."

"It was Sally's idea," Bella said, in a nearly see-through lace jonquil dress.

Sally applied her blood-red lipstick, which matched her backless gown. "As producer and copyright owner of the show, Bella and I made a truce."

Jana and Peter looked at one another in surprise.

Brad explained, "Since we control the show now, we might as well all be friends."

We?

He stood up and bowed. "Do you like my tux, Aunt Jana?"

"You look very handsome," Jana replied.

"That's for sure," Bella said, salivating into her makeup.

"Is Manuel coming?" Peter asked.

Bella applied her jonquil eye shadow. "He'll be in the audience cheering us on."

At least, cheering you on.

"Well, have a good show everyone," Peter said, as he led Jana out of the dressing room.

As they walked down the hallway, Jana said, "Strange bedfellows."

Peter replied, "As they say, anything can happen in the theatre."

They stopped at their dressing room doors, and Jana said, "I put my makeup on at home."

"Me, too." He blushed. "Or rather Mom put it on."

"Where is Savannah?" Jana asked.

"She probably snuck out for something to eat."

Or drink.

"I'm sure she'll be back by show time." He smiled. "She's never missed a rehearsal or performance of mine yet."

Jana looked at her watch. "Let's take our places in the wings, and sneak a look out at the audience."

A few minutes later, the orchestra played an opening song while Jana and Peter stood backstage. Hidden behind a teaser curtain, Jana peeked out and located Simon, Savannah, Manuel, and Reverend Thomas in their orchestra seats. She was thrilled to see Gary and Tate arrive. Though Tate looked pale and thin, as he and Gary took their seats in the mezzanine, Tate seemed happy to be there. Jana breathed a sigh of relief when Dwayne took his seat in a box near the stage. *I'm sure he'll enjoy the musical numbers.*

When the overture ended, Jana said to Peter, "Wish me luck."

He kissed her forehead. "Knock 'em dead."

The curtain came up and Jana took the stage to welcoming applause. Standing center stage, she looked out at the audience and spoke from her heart. "Thank you all so much for coming to the benefit, and for opening your wallets…and your hearts for this worthy cause. I wish we didn't have to do fundraisers like this, but sadly our representatives in government have abandoned people with AIDS. But how fortunate we are that the stars of Broadway have said, 'that's not okay.' In an effort to help those living with AIDS, these amazing individuals have collectively pooled their talents on their night off to entertain you." When the applause died down, Jana said, "And every penny collected tonight will go to AIDS research and patient care." As the applause ended, Jana said, "Well, you didn't come here tonight to hear *me* talk."

A young man in the front row shouted, "I did!"

When the laughter ceased, Jana smiled. "Then

you're in luck, because I'll be back to introduce the second performer. But first I would like to introduce someone very special to me. He is not only my co-star in our upcoming Broadway play, *China Doll*, but I am proud to report, he is also my brother." Following the gasps and whispers, Jana said, "Ladies and gentlemen, Peter Stevens."

Peter entered the stage to swelling applause and stood next to Jana. "Thanks, sis." He said to the audience, "I guess I'll have to get accustomed to saying that." He winked at her. "Especially since I intend on asking you for a lot of favors."

"Don't get too accustomed to it."

The laughter ended, and Peter introduced the first performer.

Jana and Peter alternated introducing talented singers, dancers, actors, and comedians who received bountiful applause from the satisfied audience.

During intermission, the hosts stood in the wings, again peeking out at the crowd.

"Everyone seems to be having a good time," Peter said.

Jana nodded. "Especially your mother."

They looked out at Savannah holding court with Roll and three other reporters near the orchestra pit. Jana raised her eyes as Savannah, clearly relishing the attention, told the heartbreaking story of her forbidden, yet overpowering love for Scott Lane, and how she selflessly kept the secret of her son's paternity for thirty-six years in order to protect her son.

"It will be in all the newspapers tomorrow," Jana said.

"Fine by me." He tweaked her nose. "I'm proud

you're my sister."

The second act went as well as the first. Each performer delighted the appreciative audience with his or her talent, and Jana enjoyed her chemistry with her co-host. The last performance was the preview of *China Doll*. As Jana and Peter watched from the wings, Jana was proud of her young cast-mates. They fit their roles well, and their acting was believable and moving. The audience members seemed charmed by Bella befriending Sally—not knowing what lies ahead for Sally, and Bella and Brad's mutual attraction. It was clear that *China Doll* would be a hit. *If we ever get back to rehearsal.*

When the show concluded, Jana and Peter took center stage again. Jana said, "I hope Peter and I remind you that we are *all* brothers and sisters, and we all need to take care of each other. Thank you again for coming, and good night."

The curtain came down to wild applause, then audience members herded to the house exit doors. Jana thanked the cast on stage. Pandemonium ensued as Simon barked out orders to the stagehands, while cast members welcomed visiting friends and family pouring on stage from the stage door. Savannah, Gary, Tate, and Manuel joined Jana, Peter, Sally, Brad, and Bella on stage, congratulating them on a job well done. As Jana thanked them, through her peripheral vision she saw Peter running toward her. She screamed as he pushed her, and she landed on the stage floor folded in his arms. As everyone shouted and fled, Jana noticed a sandbag on the floor where she had been standing. Suddenly, the stage area grew fuzzy. Jana strained to see the blur and dimness in front of her. The noise in her ears softened, and the white dots in front of her turned to blackness.

****

Where am I? Jana woke lying on a sofa in her dressing room.

Peter sat next to her, holding her hand. "Thank goodness."

She took in a deep breath then slowly sat up. "What happened?" Before Peter answered, Jana said, "I remember. You saved me from the sandbag."

"And you fainted."

Dwayne entered the dressing room. "Feeling better?"

She took a glass of water from Peter. "Somebody pulled a rope that released the sandbag. It was meant to fall on me." She took a sip of water. "Peter pushed me out of the way."

"Even unconscious you figured out the mystery," Dwayne said with a smile.

"But who did it?" Peter asked.

Dwayne looked at Jana.

"There were dozens of people on stage and in the wings," Jana said. "It could have been anyone."

"How is my baby doll?" Simon bustled into the room.

"I'm all right, Simon."

"Thank goodness you're alive." He took her hand then turned to Dwayne. "What are you doing to protect my baby girl?"

"We taped off the area," Dwayne said. "My officers and I interviewed everyone in the vicinity of the sandbag."

"Did anybody see anything?" Peter asked.

Dwayne looked down at the floor. "I'm afraid not."

Brad, Bella, Sally, and Savannah appeared at the doorway.

"Are you all right, Aunt Jana?" Brad was noticeably shaken.

Jana held on to Peter's shoulder and stood up. "I'm fine, everyone. Really."

"Thank goodness," Sally said.

"We don't want to lose the star of our show," Bella said, sounding like her grandfather.

Savannah entered the dressing room and put her arm around her son. "Peter saved you."

"I always wanted a brother," Jana said with a smile. "Now I know why."

Simon said, "I don't care if my baby girl has a twin in Japan, I want her protected." He glared at Dwayne. "What are you doing to make sure the maniac who is after her doesn't succeed?"

Dwayne said, "Peter, please take Jana back to her hotel suite. Make sure she goes to bed."

"And I'll sleep on her sofa," Peter said.

"Good idea." Dwayne addressed the others. "The rest of you, please go home, but don't leave town."

"What about *China Doll*?" Bella asked.

Dwayne replied, "The play is still on hiatus until we find out who is behind this. Now, everyone please go. I'll contact you if I need you."

As Peter walked Jana and Savannah out of the dressing room, Dwayne called out, "Take care of yourself, Jana. I don't want another murder."

That makes at least two of us.

Jana and Peter taxied to the hotel, walked Savannah back to her room, then entered Jana's suite, where Jana paid and discharged the babysitter. She checked in on B.J. who was sound asleep. Once inside her bedroom, Jana changed into a satin peach nightgown and matching robe. When she climbed under the silk sheet and called him into the bedroom, Peter sat at her side and took her hand in his.

"I knew this would happen."

"You were right, Peter. The murderer or murderers found out I'm getting closer to the truth, and he, she, or they tried to silence me. But it didn't work. Thanks to you, I'm still here." She thought about her box of library papers inside the walk-in closet. "And now I'm even more determined to find out the truth."

A crease appeared between his dark eyebrows. "Jana, I may not be there to protect you the next time. Please think about—"

They heard a knock at the front door.

"I'll get it," Peter said. "Don't come out of this room."

Jana stood in the bedroom doorway and watched Peter take off his tie and jacket at the front door.

"Who is it?"

"It's Brian."

Peter opened the door, and Brian entered the suite in a wrinkled blue suit, looking as if he hadn't slept in days.

Brian looked at Peter standing next to him. "Who are you?"

Extending a hand, Peter said, "Peter Stevens."

Brian glared at Jana, standing in her nightclothes at the bedroom doorway. He asked in a rage, "What's *he* doing here?"

"I can explain," Jana said.

"Do you know what time it is?" Brian shouted.

"Yes, Brian—"

"Is this guy your lover?"

Jana replied, "No, he's my brother."

"He's your *what*?"

Jana and Peter sat Brian down between them on the sofa, and they filled her husband in on the last two days of events. Then the three of them sat in silence.

Finally, Brian said to Jana, "You're not doing that show."

"There's no show to do at present," Jana said.

Brian added, "And you have to stop investigating the backgrounds of the people in the play."

Peter replied, "That's what *I've* been saying."

"And you're right," Brian said to Peter.

Jana groaned. "Will you two stop ganging up on me? I'm fine. B.J. is fine. Brad is fine. I'll be more careful next time."

"There won't *be* a next time," Brian and Peter said in unison.

"Before you two start a brother-in-law fan club, I'd like to remind you that I'm a grown woman, and I am perfectly capable of taking care of myself."

"Unless someone's dropping a sandbag on you," Peter said.

Brian rose from the sofa. "I'm beat. I came straight here from a meeting in Vegas, and I worked on the plane. I have to call the mall company's New York office in the morning. Let's get some sleep and talk more about this tomorrow."

Peter stood up and said to Jana, "You don't need me to stay here with Brian back. I should check on my mother anyway." He shook Brian's hand. "Nice meeting you, Brian."

"I'm sure I'll see you again soon," Brian said.

"You can count on it," Peter replied with a smile.

When they were alone, Brian wrapped his arms around his wife. "That's better."

Jana kissed his neck. "Let's stay like this forever."

They walked arm in arm to the bedroom.

"Do you like your new brother-in-law?" Jana asked.

"I do, but I like you better."

Standing at the foot of the bed, Brian kissed her, then he kissed her again, then again. As he leaned her back onto the bed, he began taking off his clothes.

"I thought you were exhausted."

They kissed again.

"I'm never too exhausted for you, babe."

Jana threw her arms around her husband's V-shaped back, then worked her way forward to his melon-like pectoral muscles, and washboard abdominals.

As he kissed her neck then worked his way downward, Jana said, "Welcome home."

****

Jana woke the next morning in her husband's arms. They showered together, dressed, and entered the living room. Brian made his business call. Then B.J., wearing a polo shirt and shorts, threw himself into Brian's arms. "Daddy!"

Brad, also in a polo shirt and shorts, was right behind his cousin. "Uncle Brian!"

The four of them caught up on the last week over a buffet breakfast. Then B.J. jumped up from the table. "Daddy, the zoo!"

Jana, wearing a powder-blue blouse and jeans, looked at Brian for clarification.

Brian explained, "When we talked on the phone, I told B.J. I would take him to the Bronx Zoo when I got here."

"B.J. goes to the zoo!"

"Looks like he remembered," Brian said.

"It seems that way," Jana replied.

"You can get there by subway." Brad rose from the table. "I'm headed over to Bella's, but I can show you the station on the way."

In his hoody and jeans, Brian looked like one of the boys. "I don't want to leave you alone."

Jana replied, "I'll be in the bedroom reading my research. Gary's in the next room."

"Doesn't he want breakfast?" Brian asked.

"Gary talks to Tate!" B.J. said.

"He must be on the phone. I was so happy to see Tate at the benefit last night." She squeezed her husband's hand. "I'll be fine here with Gary."

Brian squeezed back. "I'll only go if you promise not to let Gary leave the suite."

"I promise." Jana raised her hand as if under oath.

He kissed the top of her head. "We'll be back in a few hours."

"Enjoy," she said.

"Going to the zoo!" B.J. proclaimed, as the three men left the hotel suite.

Taking advantage of the alone time, Jana rushed into the bedroom, took the library papers from the closet, sat on the chaise, and began reading. She scanned various newspaper and magazine articles, then she read the last two articles word for word. *That's it! I know who murdered Stanley, Katrina, and Tony. And I know why!*

She looked up with a gasp as Gary walked into her bedroom. "Where's B.J.?" he asked, buttoning the top button of his white shirt.

Try to remain calm. "He's out with his father. They should be back soon."

"Is Brad with Bella?" He pushed his glasses up the bridge of his nose.

"I think so."

"So it's just us."

Keep talking. "How's Tate?"

"He's doing better. Great benefit last night." He came closer. "What are you reading?"

"An article." *Here goes.* "About *you*."

"Me?" He came even closer.

"Yes. This newspaper article from thirty-eight years ago mentions you."

He chuckled. "I would have been only three years old."

"That's right." *Stay strong, girl.* "How did you find out about Katrina's play? My guess is you read in the newspaper that a new mystery was coming to Broadway, featuring a three-year old boy, my son. You saw the agency's notice for a nanny. You weren't interested. After all, you were making more money in your current job than I was offering. But then you read that the play was written by Katrina Wright. Though you had tried for many years to suppress the memories of what happened to you when you were three years old, the old nightmares once again haunted you. And you were determined to find out if Katrina was indeed telling *your* story. Now I know why you were so vocal and passionate about B.J.'s role in the play." She rose and stood face to face with him. "Katrina didn't make up the story of the play. It really happened. To *you*."

He grinned. "So you think art imitated life?"

"Not completely. And you wanted to make sure the story was told accurately. So you pushed and prodded until Katrina rewrote B.J.'s scene to reflect what really happened to you, how Bella's and Savannah's characters bullied and threatened you into submission and secrecy." *Just like when the chicken bandit bullied little Timmy not to tell on him in The Littlest Farmer.*

"Jana, there must be lots of guys named Gary Royale."

She waved the newspaper article in his face. "Gary, it's here in black and white. There's no point in denying it. Tell me why you did it."

Gary's shoulders slumped. He sat on the chaise with his head in his hands. "I was only three years old, but I still remember the worst parts of it. How that woman and her mother threatened to tell my parents that I was eavesdropping at their door." Tears welled up in his eyes. "When they called me a 'bad boy' who was going to Hell for spying on other people. The way they cornered me in that living room, and threatened to tell on me, even push me out the window if I told on *them*. And then the next minute they offered me candy to try to buy my silence."

"That must have been rough for you."

"Rough?" He looked up at her. "I was too afraid to tell anyone what happened. My parents knew something was wrong, and they brought me to a psychiatrist, but it didn't help. I couldn't forget what those women did to me. I was scared all the time. I woke up in the middle of the night crying. I didn't trust anybody. And I was afraid of anyone who came near me." He wiped his cheeks with his sleeve.

"That's why you didn't like Katrina, because Katrina's play isn't only your story, it's also *her* story. Katrina is *my* character in the play. The woman who babysat you thirty-eight years ago, and discovered her neighbor murdered her husband and his first wife for money and revenge. In the play, my character brings Bella's character to justice. But that's not what really happened. Is it, Gary? In actuality, Katrina, her neighbor, and the detective who Katrina seduced, split the money. And Katrina gave her share to Stanley to produce her first play on Broadway, *Sweet Nothings*." Jana paced around the room deep in thought. "I remember a time during rehearsals when you were talking to Katrina, and she spotted Tony and Sally kissing in the wings. Katrina grew pale. But not because of Tony and Sally. She already knew about them. Katrina had just figured out who you were, and she was terrified that her past would be exposed. That's why Katrina agreed to rewrite B.J.'s scene—to silence you. But she couldn't give in to your demand to rewrite the final scene."

"I asked her. I asked all of them. And nobody would listen to me!"

"Because Katrina couldn't risk the truth getting out. To protect her own reputation, she had to keep the false ending, where my character blows the whistle on Bella's character."

"That last scene was all a lie!"

"And that made you angry. You had taken this job to meet Katrina face to face. To tell her what damage had been done to you back then. Hoping to finally come to terms with your past. To finally find closure by seeing what happened to you played out on stage like a psychodrama."

"Yes! But Katrina changed the ending!"

"And when she refused to rewrite it to your specifications, you became enraged."

"But I didn't kill her or Stanley or Tony. After all these years, Tate is the first person who helped me to realize that the past is the past. And what happened long ago doesn't have to control my life now. When I told Tate about my past, he helped me see that anger and resentment just breed more anger and resentment. As hard as it was, I forgave all of them. Tate also showed me that I can love someone, and accept love without being afraid. And now all I want is to have a life with Tate." His face drained of color. "For as long as Tate lives."

The phone rang. Jana picked it up on the first ring. "Yes?"

The voice on the other end said, "Mrs. Otley, I have a message for you."

"What is it?"

"A Detective Douglas just phoned the switchboard. He was in a hurry and asked us to give you a message."

"What did he say?"

"He asked you to meet him right away at the theatre."

"Thank you." Jana hung up the phone.

"What's going on?"

Jana took the copy of the other newspaper article and put it inside her purse. "I got a message to meet Dwayne at the theatre."

"Do you want me to come with you?"

She shook her head. "I'll take a taxi."

"Be careful."

"When Brian and B.J. get back, please tell them where I went."

He nodded.

Jana made a quick phone call then raced out of the suite.

The elevator ride down to the lobby seemed interminably slow. When Jana finally got to the lobby, she hailed a taxi, handed the driver a twenty-dollar bill, and asked him to drive as fast as possible to the theatre.

Upon arrival, she entered the theatre's empty outer lobby. Not seeing anyone in the inner lobby, she continued into the theatre house. It was dark and quiet. "Dwayne?" Receiving no answer, she called out again. "Hello?" Still no answer. With the help of the faint ghost light on stage, Jana slowly made her way up the stairs and onto the stage.

Suddenly, she heard breathing. A light crashed to the stage floor.

Jana walked quickly across the stage, passing shadows of stage furniture. Hard footsteps followed her. She walked faster, and the footsteps grew louder and seemed more determined. Beads of sweat soaked her back, and her heart pounded in her ears. As in her nightmare, Jana sprinted across the dark stage with her assailant at her heels.

When she bumped into the sofa, reminiscent of her cactus move in *The Cowgirl and the Bandit*, Jana jumped over it. Then she pushed the sofa straight into her attacker, who toppled over it and landed on the floor at her feet. Jana reached for the pole supporting the tiny ghost light and shined the light in Peter Stevens' face.

"I didn't want to hurt you," Peter said. "I was trying to scare you." He sat up. "I asked you to stop investigating. I knew if you continued, you'd find out the truth."

"And the truth would put your mother in danger."

"She's such a good woman, Jana. She gave up so much to raise me and take care of me. And she still does. As I told you, I can't say no to Mom."

"Including when she asked you to kill Stanley, Katrina, and Tony."

He rested his elbows on his knees. "She begged them to rewrite the script, and they wouldn't."

Jana put down the light pole.

"Do you know the whole story?"

Jana replied, "I think so. After nineteen plays, the last two being flops, Katrina was desperate for a good storyline. As they said, Katrina, Stanley, and Savannah were friends and neighbors in the old days. And Katrina went back on her promise to Savannah not to write a play about what happened thirty-eight years ago." Jana sat next to him. "With her career in limbo, Savannah jumped at the chance to return to Broadway. Since Katrina wouldn't let any of us see the script before the first rehearsal, Savannah was devastated at the first read-through when she heard her life story in the context of the play—with Bella playing Savannah, and Savannah playing her own mother. Savannah pleaded with Stanley and Katrina, and later Tony, to rewrite the play to make the characters based on her and her mother more likable, so nobody would trace back the murders from thirty-eight years ago to her. But the three of them wouldn't do it."

Tears fell down Peter's cheeks. "When Mom told me what happened back then, it broke my heart. She was only twenty-two. A pregnant, unemployed actress. The man she desperately loved talked her into getting an abortion, then he seduced and married a young heiress with a heart condition for her money."

"Played by Tate and Sally in our play."

Peter nodded. "Mom was devastated. She thought about suicide. In a fit of hysterics, she told her mother the whole story, and the two of them came up with the plan. Mom would befriend the heiress, and hide her digitalis. After the heiress died, Mom would console, marry, then kill the man who'd wronged her. Since Mom is a terrific actress, their plan went off without a hitch. Mom convinced the police and the press that the heiress died of a heart attack, and her husband accidentally fell off the balcony after one too many drinks. But a little boy who Katrina babysat overheard Mom and her mother talking about what they had done. Despite their efforts to silence him, he told Katrina, Mom's neighbor, what he had overheard."

"But unlike in the end of *China Doll*, where I as Katrina blow the whistle on Bella as Savannah, in reality Katrina seduced and paid off the police detective. Then Katrina and Savannah split the rest of the money—taking an oath of silence about what really happened. Savannah married her young neighbor, played by Brad in the show. He was her second husband. The man you grew up believing was your father. But of course, he wasn't. And Katrina gave her share of the money to Stanley to produce Katrina's first play, *Sweet Nothings*. The play in which Savannah made her Broadway debut, and she had an affair with our father."

Peter wiped his cheeks with his shoulders. "You don't know what my mother went through. The abortion messed up her insides. The doctor told her she would never be able to have another child. That's why she was so excited during *Sweet Nothings* when she conceived a child with Scott Lane. I think that's why she loved me so much. Though she married again briefly, I was always the top man in her life, and I still am. She's devoted her life to me."

"But Katrina changed the ending of the play. Why was Savannah worried that someone would figure out the truth?"

"*You* did. With reporters like Roll around the theatre, how long do you think it would have taken for one of them to dig back into Mom's and Katrina's past, and figure it out? There's no statute of limitation on murder, Jana. Mom couldn't risk the possibility of getting carted off to prison." He took her hand. "Jana, all Mom wanted was for Stanley, Katrina, and Tony to change Bella's and her roles enough so that nobody would link what happened thirty-eight years ago to *China Doll*."

"But they all refused, so Savannah asked you to kill them."

"At first I told her I wouldn't do it, but she kept at me. Finally, I gave in, realizing I had to protect the true victim, my mother."

"So while all of us were milling around the stage, you tipped the bookcase that fell on Stanley. During rehearsal, you put xylene in Katrina's fountain pen. And you loosened the floodlight hanging over the section of the stage where Tony always stood during rehearsals, knowing it would eventually fall on him."

"I thought each one would be the last. But Mom continued to need me."

She unclasped their hands. "And then you came after *me*."

He held her shoulders. "The third murder finally got Dwayne to close down the show. It also gave Mom time to try to convince Bella and Sally to rewrite the play. When I heard Bella, Sally, and Brad discussing their performance from *China Doll* tonight, I talked them into doing scenes that wouldn't let out the real story. Nobody had to know the truth. But you wouldn't listen to me when I asked you to stop investigating the murders."

"So you stole Sally's lipstick and wrote that note on my dressing room mirror. And with everyone hovering backstage after the benefit, you pulled the rope that released the sandbag, then you pushed me out of the way as it fell to the floor. And this morning, after Dwayne and his officers unlocked the theatre to search for clues about the murder, you snuck in and hid somewhere inside. Once they had locked up and gone, you used the pay phone to call the hotel switchboard—pretending to be Dwayne, and you left a message for me to meet him here. Then you unlocked the theatre from the inside."

He put his arm around her. "Not to hurt you, but to make you promise to stop sleuthing."

She pushed him away. "Your mother has you under her spell, Peter. She's been controlling you your whole life. I thought she was just guiding your career. That you were being a good son. But she's a master puppeteer, and you're her spineless puppet. You have to cut the toxic strings, Peter, before anyone else gets hurt." She put a hand on his shoulder. "I'm your sister. Let me help you do that."

"You can help me by not telling anyone what you found out about Mom and me."

"I can't do that."

He screeched like a wounded animal.

"Peter, let me stand by you when you tell Dwayne the truth."

His face turned to stone. "That's not going to happen."

"It *has* to happen, Peter."

"Jana, don't make me choose between my mother and my sister."

"Peter, you murdered three people. You can't hide forever. If not me, someone else will figure it out."

He rose. "Nobody's going to figure it out. And you won't tell anyone."

She stood next to him. "Peter, don't make things worse. Admit to what you did. I'll hire a good lawyer. You can plead temporary insanity."

"The one who is insane is *you* if you think I'm going to prison—or let them take my mother away from me." Peter took her hand. "I don't want to hurt you or B.J., but believe me I'll do whatever is necessary to keep Mom safe."

"What does B.J. have to do with this?"

Peter said as if an after-thought, "He's in his dressing room."

"No, he isn't. He's with Brian."

"The night I met Brian, he mentioned his Las Vegas firm had a New York City Office. Before I left the hotel this morning, I listened at your door to see if you had uncovered anything. When I heard you tell Brian you'd be spending the day going through your research clippings, I knew you would eventually piece things together. I needed some leverage over you. So I charmed the desk clerk, an easy task, into giving Brian a message before Brian left the hotel. When Brian, Brad, and B.J. got to the lobby, the clerk gave Brian the message, which stated Brian was needed at an emergency meeting at the New York City office of his client from Las Vegas. When Brian told B.J. they couldn't go to the zoo today, B.J. started to cry. Lucky thing Uncle Peter just *happened* to walk through the lobby, and offered to take B.J. to the zoo himself. But B.J. and I made a little detour."

"I don't believe you."

"Follow me."

Peter walked Jana to the backstage hallway then called out, "B.J., are you all right?"

B.J. shouted from his dressing room down the hall, "B.J. tied up!"

Jana ran toward B.J.'s dressing room, but Peter grabbed her arm. "I'm a lot stronger than you, sis."

She called out, "I'll be there in a minute, B.J.!"

Grabbing her by the throat, Peter pinned her against the wall. His face was hard and angry. "So here's the deal, Jana. You swear to keep quiet about what you know about Mom and me, and B.J. and you go free. You don't, and as hard as it will be for me to lose my newfound family, I will stage another theatre *accident*—today! So what's it going to be, sis?"

As she struggled in Peter's grip with her son calling for his mother, Jana remembered a move she learned from the stunt coordinator in *Girl Detective*. She extended the knuckle of her middle finger and rammed it with all her might into Peter's solar plexus. He gasped in pain and shock. Jana ran into B.J.'s dressing room, locked the door from the inside, and untied her son from the chair.

"Uncle Peter play a game!"

"That's right, B.J. Uncle Peter is playing a game." *And he's not going to win.*

Jana heard from the other side of the door, "Don't make me break down this door, Jana."

"Don't bother, Peter, Dwayne will be here any second."

Peter laughed. "Good fake, Jana."

"No fake. I didn't believe your phony phone message, so before I left the hotel, I called Dwayne and left a message with the whole story. He'll be here any minute."

"You're bluffing, sis."

"Don't move, Stevens. Cuff him."

Upon hearing Dwayne's voice, Jana opened the dressing room door and shielded B.J. from the action.

"Peter Stevens, you are under arrest for the murder of Stanley Rothman, Katrina Wright Cuccioli, and Tony Cuccioli, as well as the assault on Jana Lane Otley and B.J. Lane Otley. You have the right to remain silent. Anything you say can and will be held…"

As Dwayne gave Peter his rights, Peter looked at Jana with sad eyes. "I'm sorry I disappointed you, sis."

Like father, like son.

Epilogue

One month later, Jana Lane stood in the wings of the theatre at the end of her performance in *China Doll*. The opening night performance had gone perfectly. The audience members sat at the edge of their seats, fully engrossed in Katrina Wright's story and Manuel Martinez' direction. The three-unit set, eerie lighting, and stunning costumes added to the thrilling mood of the evening. Jose, as stage manager, called every set rotation, lighting cue, sound effect, and entrance perfectly. *Katrina Wright got her wish.*

The viewers were tantalized by the early scenes, where Tate talked Bella into getting an abortion, then married ill Sally for her family wealth. They gasped in horror when Bella befriended Sally then hid her medication, sending Sally falling to the floor, clutching at her chest. The scene where Jana, as Bella's friend and neighbor, introduced Bella to Brad revealed the incredible magnetism between the two young actors. When Bella, married to Tate's character, threw him off their balcony, some theatre patrons screamed in horror. B.J. was the audience's favorite in his scene with Bella and Savannah's replacement. *I hope watching that scene was cathartic for you, Gary.* As the two women bullied, blackmailed, and coaxed B.J. in an unsuccessful effort to silence him about the murders, the audience "ooohed" and "aaahed" at the three-year-old's solid performance. *That's my boy.* Though Jana didn't feel the same chemistry with Peter's replacement that she had with Peter, their love scene caused many audience members to smile in delight. *I hope Brian wasn't too jealous.* There wasn't a sound in the theatre during Jana's final confrontation scene with Bella, as the theatregoers barely breathed in anticipation of the show's climax, where Jana turns the tables on Bella.

The audience members cheered at the curtain call when B.J. came out first. His soldier-like bow and wave to the audience caused them to laugh in delight. *He's definitely a Lane.* Sally rode the applause with her bow and kiss to the audience. *Sally seems to be getting on well with Peter's replacement.* Tate was next with a grateful and sincere bow. *Gary must be out there in tears. I'll miss him as a nanny, but I'm thrilled he is moving in with Tate.* Brad was next with a 'thumbs up' to the audience. *He finally made it to Broadway—a week before his wedding.* Wearing a low cut scarlet satin dress, Bella, Brad's fiancée and business partner in Brad and Bella Productions, offered the audience a deep curtsy. *Thank goodness there was no costume malfunction.* Peter's replacement then Savannah's replacement bowed next. *Peter and Savannah wanted to be together. They got their wish—in prison. I'll be visiting next week as usual, brother.*

Finally, it was time for Jana's bow. Wearing a coral chiffon dress with white pearls, Jana entered the stage to thunderous applause. Her bow garnered a standing ovation and shouts of, "Bravo!" started by Simon and Cornelius sitting in the front row with Roll next to them—smiling and nodding as he wrote his review. On the other side of Simon and Cornelius, Gary applauded wildly then blew a kiss to Tate. Dwayne winked at Jana. *He saw a non-musical.* Reverend Heather and Reverend Thomas smiled at her. Devon and Ed waved at their mother, brother, and cousin. Jana's best friend, Jackson, and his partner, Adam, beamed with pride. Brian reached up and handed Jana a bouquet of red roses. Tears clouded her eyes as Jana Lane Otley gratefully held the flowers to her chest. *I'm finally home.*

A word about the author...

Bestselling author Joe Cosentino wrote four Jana Lane mysteries and is currently writing the fifth. The Divine Magazine Award winning author has also written numerous other novels and novellas. As an actor Joe has appeared in principal roles in film, television, and theatre, opposite stars such as Bruce Willis, Rosie O'Donnell, Nathan Lane, Holland Taylor, Charles Keating, and Jason Robards. His one-act plays were performed in New York City, and he wrote an educational film. Joe is currently Head of the Department/Professor at a college in upstate New York, and is happily married.

http://www.JoeCosentino.weebly.com

~*~

Other Joe Cosentino titles
available from The Wild Rose Press, Inc.:
PORCELAIN DOLL
SATIN DOLL

Thank you for purchasing
this publication of The Wild Rose Press, Inc.

If you enjoyed the story, we would appreciate your
letting others know by leaving a review.

For other wonderful stories,
please visit our on-line bookstore at
www.thewildrosepress.com.

For questions or more information
contact us at
info@thewildrosepress.com.

The Wild Rose Press, Inc.
www.thewildrosepress.com

Stay current with The Wild Rose Press, Inc.

Like us on Facebook

https://www.facebook.com/TheWildRosePress

And Follow us on Twitter
https://twitter.com/WildRosePress